Robert Lewis is from the Black Mountains, in the Brecon Beacons. He has been a silver service waiter, painter, barman, secretary, bookkeeper, salesman, banker, shop assistant, web editor, yardcat, helpdesk staffer, storesman, high-voltage cabler, data-entry clerk, housing officer, mailboy, audit junior, welder's assistant, betting shop counterman, and unemployed. Now twenty-six, he is studying as a mature student at the University of Wales, Aberystwyth. *The Last Llanelli Train*, his first novel, was also published by Serpents Tail.

Swansea
Terminal

Robert Lewis

A complete catalogue record for this book can be
obtained from the British Library on request

The right of Robert Lewis to be identified as the author
of this work has been asserted by him in accordance
with the Copyright, Designs and Patents Act 1988

First published in 2007 by Serpent's Tail,
an imprint of Profile Books Ltd
3A Exmouth House
Pine Street
London EC1R OJH
website: www.serpentstail.com

Designed and typeset at Neuadd Bwll, Llanwrtyd Wells

Printed and bound in Great Britain by Bookmarque Ltd,
Croydon, Surrey, CRO 4TD
10 9 8 7 6 5 4 3 2 1

And the words that he spoke seemed like the wisest of philosophies: there was nothing to be gained by a wet thing called a tear. When the world is too dark, and I need the light inside of me, I walk into a bar and drink fifteen pints of beer. Because I am going, I am going, any which way the wind may be blowing.

Streams of Whiskey, The Pogues

He would be like that for the rest of his life and that was what his life was. You would never know how he got that way because even if he told you it would not be the truth. At the very best a distorted memory of the truth. There is a sad man like that in every quiet bar in the world.

The Long Goodbye, Raymond Chandler

ONE

DIAGNOSIS

I

Scotty and I had got up early to go to the beach, and the weather was so good you could stand on the beach and actually see the sea. We had walked through the middle of town, crossed the Kingsway and breached the Quadrant, passed the prison and the Vetch, and were sitting on the sand at the bottom of the big concrete steps on the other side of County Hall. I think it was about half nine. Already you could tell it was going to be a stunning day, and we had the place more or less to ourselves. It was a Monday morning, and the university had finished for the summer, so there weren't going to be any locals and there weren't going to be any students. I watched a gull hover effortlessly in the wind. He had the cloudless sky to himself too. Then he went for something I couldn't see and I lost sight of him.

'It's not enough,' I said.

Scotty looked at me.

'What do you mean it's not enough?'

He unzipped the cheap nylon sports bag and held it wide open.

'We've got one bottle Commissar vodka, one bottle Highland Spirit scotch, if you can call that fucking shite scotch, eight cans of Special and four cans of 'Bow. And we have smokes. We're all set, man.'

Scotty was a twenty-four-year-old heroin addict from Glasgow. There are other types of people from Glasgow, I know, but that was what he was. And he looked my age. All that stuff they say about heroin is true. A year ago I wouldn't have given him the time of day, and now he was the only person I really spent any time with. I looked for the gull but I still couldn't find him.

'No,' I said. 'I need more than that. I like to have a bit in reserve. I need it if I want to feel settled.'

'I'm going to score this afternoon anyway. You can drink some of my half.'

I usually did: there was a kind of synergy at work between me and Scott.

'No. You might not. Anyway, it's yours.'

'So what are you going to do about it, big man? You don't have any fucking money.'

'I can get some.'

'Where?'

About a hundred yards away up the prom I could see a small man in a polo shirt and pleated trousers carrying a metal detector. Scotty caught my gaze and followed it.

'Chester,' he said. 'For fuck's sake.'

Charlie Chester, Child Molester. Mind you, I don't think that was his real name. It was what all the leaflets and posters said, though, when they appeared on the lampposts and phone boxes: his shifty-looking face and a stark warning about your children and a lot of exclamation marks. It was perfectly plausible, I suppose. He was at least as boring as most deviants, and had arrived in town not long before either of us; a state-assisted relocation, was what they said, after he'd been released for some dark and terrible sexual offence. He spent most of his free time down here, talking to the bums, the drop-outs, garnering some feeling of social acceptance. I expect in his head he liked to think we were all dentists and engineers.

He had been a petrochemicals analyst, I think he said.

'Yeah,' I said. 'I'm definitely going. Look, stay here. I'll be back in a couple of hours tops. With more booze. Alright?'

'Suit yourself, big man.'

I went off in the direction of the High Street; all the way to the Neath Road without so much as a bus fare. Ten steps in I heard the defiant crack of a can being opened, and its sibilant hiss, but I kept going. There was a woman that wanted to see me.

She lived in one of the houses in Tom Williams Court, up past the train station, a little terraced block built out of that dark brick that they seemed to like in the eighties. It backed onto the Matthew Street flats, both blocks of them. She had an electric doorbell that played the opening bar of God Save The Queen.

'I'm Robin Llywelyn,' I said.

'You got my message then?'

'Oh yes,' I said. He had told me all about her, some shrivelled pensioner, some walking raisin, come down from the home opposite with pockets full of gambling slips to tell me the mad fat woman wanted to see me.

'How'd you know who I am?' I'd asked.

'Everybody knows who you are, Magnum.'

She led me down a pale green hallway into an immaculate kitchen. The whole house smelled of Shake n' Vak. The tap was dripping, but everything else in there was spotless perfection. It looked like something out of an Argos catalogue circa 1984, all beige and barley. The kettle matches the toaster matches the bread bin matches the coffee jar matches the drawn down blinds, at half eleven on a sunny Swansea morning. Ooh, she's a subtle one. But you could have taken the house and its contents and reconstructed it at St Fagan's brick by brick, called it 'Domestic Wales in The Eighties' or something, and no one would have batted an eyelid.

'This here is his photo,' she says. I can barely look at it. I did not think I would be doing this again.

'Do you have to smoke that in here?' she says, this woman. She must weigh thirty fucking stone. Christ, the strain on that heart. It will blink out one day not ten years hence, you can be sure of it, and leave her stranded in some bingo hall or shopping centre like a beached whale. The work you must have to put into being that fat, Jesus. I hold my cigarette up to the light like a glass of fine wine: I don't know where the tobacco comes from, I don't know where it's made, I can't remember where I bought my pack. I couldn't have told you what brand it was without looking. I used to be fussy about brands once, but they all taste the same now. They taste of transcendence. It surprised me, that.

'Put it out,' says the woman, and passes me a saucer to stub it out in. I use it. It's her house. I don't have an office anymore. I don't have a home anymore. 'I'll give you two hundred quid.'

'Fuck off,' I said. The woman pretended to do some sums in her head. It was funny to watch. It was clear that she was both very bad at pretending and very bad at doing sums.

'Four hundred,' she said. 'No, three hundred and fifty.'

I had to smile.

'That should do it,' I said. 'I'll take the two hundred now.'

'Fuck off,' she said.

'Two hundred and I'll fix that fucking tap.'

And I did. It was only a washer. Then I walked blinking out into the sunlight, quick as I could, into the Matthew Street estate in mid-June, with two hundred quid cash in one jacket pocket and a photo of this fuck-knows-who bloke in the other. I gave it a glance. It could have been anybody. Then I put it in the nearest bin.

She was well known, this woman, this female Forrest Gump. She should have been in the nearest institution, but her family liked to pretend there was nothing wrong with her. But oh boy. One thing she did, she had obsessions about men. Complete strangers, half the time. Sell her a bunch of bananas and she would turn up at your house at two in the morning screaming. Now this may seem strange to you, but I believe that there is love in the world for everyone, although we may not find it, or if we do, we might very well lose it or not know what to do with it. It might pass us by in an instant and leave us incomplete and broken for the rest of our lives, but it was there. Well, not for this woman. Nobody is going to share a bed with her twice, or possibly even once. There could be no love in this world for Rebecca Blethyn of 11 Tom Williams Court, of that I am sure. She doesn't have the right parts of her brain working. And she looks like a bus. But that is hardly my fault. If she wants me to see if her pretend fiancé is having an 'affair,' then I will play along. Delusion is all some people will ever have, and that goes for a lot of the bigshots in this world as well as the Becca Blethyns.

That's what I do, that sort of thing. It's what I used to do. People paid me to observe husbands and wives who may or may not have been having affairs. That progressed pretty quickly to surreptitiously helping the odd unwitting husband have an observed affair, thanks to a certain rapport I had with a particular type of woman, and the next step was blackmailing, and at that point the customers stopped telling me their real names or even if they were married. Which, in turn, led to me leaving town very quickly in the middle of the night, and to bad old Swansea and the Heathfield. That and a few other things. Being a private detective, I understand it's called. A lot of people do okay out of it, but don't look at me. People gossiped about me just like they gossiped about the huge woman at Tom Williams Court. The only thing worse than being talked about is not being talked about at all: Oscar Wilde said that, and he was wrong. He also said that the only thing a rich man cannot buy is his past. I used to like that one too except I don't have any money and I can't get my past back either.

I had thought about changing my name, but this is home territory for me and Wales is a small place. There are people here who knew me from before, and it would be hard to convince them casually that I was now Gary Roberts or Wayne Jones or anybody else at all, for that matter. The last thing I need at this juncture is for people to think I'm mad on top of my other troubles. They already thought I was half-way mad as it was, coming home after twenty-five years penniless and claiming to have been Humphrey Bogart or something. And you cannot believe how gossip spreads around these parts: everybody knew within days, and lots of people I don't know. There are corporations that would pay millions for that kind of access. With all that going on I thought they were bound to track me down, but nobody seems to give a fuck about Robin Llywelyn. Nobody wants to come to Swansea and get me. I reckon they think this is bad enough. To be fair, it was also the gossip that got me into that stupid fat bitch's house, mind, and got me out with two hundred quid in my jacket. And if you wanted further proof of her devastatingly low intelligence and pitiable grasp on reality, I would invite you to read that sentence again. But please do not mistake these traits for innocence.

Just over the road from those houses there's a pub called the White Swan. I hadn't had a drink in a pub for a while. Money was scarce and it went a lot further drinking on the street, and at that time of the year hanging about outdoors was no bother at all, Swansea in summer is full of dossers doing just that, but there was another thing. The thing was, when you've been living rough for a while you get to feeling a bit awkward about yourself. There's no reason for it, but it happens. Drinking constantly like a fish every day and not washing can't help, I suppose.

'Brains, please,' I said, after a little trouble. I tell you, I had never ever stuttered before in my life. Now I did it all the time.

The man pulled the pump and put it on the counter and I paid him one seventy and watched it settle. There are things you miss about pubs that you aren't even aware of until you stop going to them. The sound of them, even when they're empty, and the smell of them, of all that stale beer and smoke, that probably takes decades to truly mature, and that lower level of light, those horse brasses, that mock-Tudor woodwork, a mirror with a brand of whisky emblazoned on it maybe, and most of all the people, the presence of other people, all quietly working towards a common goal.

I picked up my pint, the Imperial Pint, five hundred and eighty six millilitres, twenty fluid ounces, the mysterious magic unit by which entire lives can be measured out. I wanted to hold it up to the light, because you don't get to actually see it when it comes in a tin, and I wanted to see that precious amber sparkling, but I thought it would look phoney. So I held it in my hand, and nobody threw me out, nobody insulted me or started a fight, nobody stared at me, or paid me any mind, and I drank it.

I put it down and watched a bubble drift lazily down the inside of the glass until it hit the bottom, and then I walked out. A quick pint. These things are possible. Then I went a little further along the High Street to Tariq's and picked up a four-pack of Extra and headed back to the beach. There are a lot of pubs on that street, though. I had a quick Guinness in the Shoulder of Mutton, just because I liked the look of the toucan, and after that I went back out. And I had a quick pint of Brains in the Adam and Eve. And I had a quick pint of something in the King's Arms Tavern, which it turned out is a gay pub, but all they had to do was look at me to know why I was in there. Nice hanging baskets, though.

By that point I was nearly at the castle, and I thought to myself, as I often did those days, whenever I was on my own and I'd had a few drinks, fuck Scotty, and fuck Rebecca Blethyn, you have a case of your own you're supposed to be working on. This personal interest job I was doing for myself. And I took a detour down Caer Street and went past all the shops and came out the other side heading for Uplands. I'd been down that way a couple of times since coming back, but I guess I was still finding my way around, because I turned up down by the cricket ground, and had to walk up through Brynmill, and I was already knackered. I wasn't up to much physically even then. But I had a few breathers and I made it: 4 Glanmor Road.

It was a good house in a good part of town. Right by the neighbourhood shops but private too, set back from the street with a low wall and a neatly trimmed privet hedge. The front garden was pretty small but there was a nice-looking tree in it, maybe a little cherry tree or something. All original features too, the front door was beautiful. I don't mean to sound like an estate agent, but it was a really nice house, and all I had was a room at the Heathfield. It had three bedrooms and two living rooms and a decent-sized kitchen. How did I know that? Because I had been in there. About twenty-five years ago. I used to go with the sister of the woman who lives there now. They were from a good family. Still, so was I.

I went over the road and sat down in my usual spot under an elm outside a hairdresser's, Headquarters or Hair Force One or some such bollocks, and opened the first can, and watched, and waited, none of which is new to me at all. I got moved on about an hour after that, probably that hairdresser ringing the station and asking for a bobby to come down, what with some alkie sat outside her place of business. It's a line of work that places a lot of importance on image, after all, not that you could tell from the fucking awful names they give their shops. The officer that came down was a different one to the one that had moved me on the other day, though. I gave it ten minutes and came back and sat a little way off, outside the photo shop. You could still see the front of the house.

I was on my last can when a white Ford Transit pulled up with Merlin Auto Parts written on the side. A man came out of it, about six two with dark, almost black hair and blue eyes. A young man. He went around the back of the van and opened the doors and then let himself inside the house, with his own key, and reappeared with an old bookcase which he loaded onto the Transit. Then he locked the van and went inside for about the time it takes to make and put away a cup of tea. And then he left. That was it. That was my lucky day. I watched his van nudge off into the distance through the traffic and stood in the same place staring a time afterwards, although it had long gone. Then I finished my can and put it in the carrier with all the other empties and left it on the doorstep of The Hair Necessities or whatever it was called, and followed it, down Walter Road, back into the middle of the city. Christ, I was doing a lot of walking.

I stopped in the Spar and bought another four pack, seeing how I didn't want to turn up at the beach after all this time without the extra booze I said I was going to get. I got a four-pack and a two-litre bottle of White Strike, one of those strong ciders that comes in a blue plastic bottle. Like detergents. But I didn't want to go back to the beach. I had money and I was in the middle of town and I had done a day's work, plus I'd had a result: my mark, as they sometimes say in my line of work, had turned up. When you get a result you have to treat yourself. And I really couldn't walk back in one go.

I thought it would take a bit of looking to find somewhere viable, being Uplands, which is supposed to be well-to-do. I expected all the pubs to be full of affluent men with cufflinks or their green-haired nineteen-year-old progeny, but it was late afternoon and the Uplands Tavern was free of both, of anybody, in fact. Nineteen-year-olds round here probably thought green hair was a bit passé now, and it had never really been a cufflinks kind of town, not even in Uplands. I got a pint and took it to a quiet corner and thought there's really nothing to this, is there, and then the same person who'd served it to me came up and said I had to leave. I finished it stood in the doorway with him looking at me.

Then there wasn't anything for ages until the George, which at first glance looked like your average British boozer, until you heeded the tubular aluminium furniture on the pavement, and the fact that the staff were all in black. Of course I was halfway to the bar by the time I'd clocked all that.

'Well he can have that one, and then he's out the door,' said the landlord when he came back from the pisser, just about loud enough for the passers-by outside to hear. I didn't dawdle over that one either.

Next door was the Royal Welch Fusiliers Club, for which I felt I lacked the obvious credentials, not having ever been a fusilier, but the drought was over by that point and I already could see a couple of bars on the horizon. A place called Reef I sailed straight by, the name alone was enough, and then picked my way through a couple of Kawasaki's to get into the Tenby, a rock/biker effort that met my demands for a scotch and water without raising a pierced eyebrow, but then some mohawk started pumping pound coins into the jukebox. And as much as I understand the need to roll back the borders of silence, as much as I appreciate the horrors that lurk within it, listening to some middle-aged yank bloke in tights screaming about the Anti-Christ never really seemed like much of an alternative to me.

A little further on I watched a man drunker than I was climb the front steps of Bunnies Health Massage, where he would undoubtedly do no more than pay his fifty and pass out, and not long after that I could see the huge concrete monolith that was Jumpin' Jaks over the rooftops, and I knew I would soon be back in the thick of it, soon I would be back in the middle of town and I could take my pick from dozens of bars and pubs. But it had been a hard afternoon, so I sort of gave up, and went in the Singleton, which is the pub equivalent of the Heathfield. In fact a lot of people in the Heathfield have stayed in the Singleton Hotel, either on the way up or on the down; it wasn't much of a stretch.

'Not you, pal, out,' said John the barman.

'I'm alright,' I said. 'I'm fine. Here, put this behind the bar.' And I gave him a twenty.

'You're sure you're alright, are you?'

'I'm alright enough to drink in here for fuck's sake.'

'Hey, no more of that. I'll be watching you.'

He did this every time I came in. I'd had some bad news a couple of months ago and I'd made a bit of a fool out of myself, and although I'd calmed down now John still liked to go through the motions. It was just a display, really, the way a dog might bark at cars, just to show whose neighbourhood it was: there was about as much chance of that dog catching his car as there was of anybody being permanently barred from the Singleton. John had seen plenty of bad news, and lots of people make fools of themselves, and nobody had been turned away once their nerves had settled. You couldn't turn people away from the Singleton. That wasn't what the Singleton was for.

John put a pint of something like Carling down on the bar towel and it must have been one third foam but I took it and gave him a smile which cut no ice, and then went and sat in the restaurant, behind a pillar, so no one could see me. No one ever went in there, the Singleton not being the sort of place you would go for an evening meal even if you were blind, starving and Japanese, so it was empty, and unlit. They do a breakfast, I'm told, but it doesn't have a good reputation. It was pretty miserable sat in there but it was better than sitting out front with the punters, I can tell you. Sitting out there was like being inside a country and western song. Several of them, actually, at the same time, in Welsh accents.

Of course, it doesn't make for an enjoyable evening, but then nobody expected that. It kept you drunk, and if you had the money, it got you drunker, and that was that. It's all any pub does at base, but no one wants to see the base. Trust me. You have to approach it from a pretty low angle. So I've developed a strategy for the Singleton, if you can call it that, the essentials of which are as follows: leave it as often as you can. Between pints, or even halfway-through, if it's not a busy night or you're desperate, take a walk up and down the street. Stand by the side of the road for two minutes. Actually, you'll find yourself doing this anyway, coming up for air like that, if the Singleton is where you have to drink. Drive past on a night when people are in there and you'll likely see somebody lurching down Western Street or leaning against the traffic lights: that's what they're doing. It's like those Indian divers who can stay under for minutes, except instead of a shiny new pearl you get a flat lager that tastes like fuzzy-felt, and when you surface you're standing under a lamppost in downtown Swansea on your own, shaking.

There are people who can stay in there all night, of course, without ever seeming to notice how bad it is, or caring. Given time I suspected I would become one of them myself, which was a knowledge that made nothing easier. It was one of the reasons you have to step out periodically, one of the key ingredients in its aura of misery. John stands it the same way most sober people who can stand it do, I guess, by making money out of it. Not much, something pitifully small, but enough to keep him sane and separate.

I think I tried a few other places around there during my jaunts outside, nothing too far away. I don't remember anyone letting me in, although they might have done. Actually I must have got in somewhere, because I met someone. The Garibaldi, in all likelihood, which was just over the road. They were closing down for good and they didn't care, I suppose. In there I met a man I hadn't seen since I'd left Wales, twenty-five years ago, a man I had known reasonably well, and I drank a little with him, but I can't remember who he was or what we said. Occupational hazard. Then they closed the bar in the Singleton.

I move my way across town, still with an eye out for the main chance, but the doormen had come out and I didn't look my best, I have to admit. I did try, once, in some place along the Kingsway, but he just looked at me and he didn't have to say a word. I'm in fancy dress, I was going to say, but I thought the better of it. I don't like being out at that time anyway, with all those people out drinking for fun. I don't like them at all, because they can, or because they think they can, I'm not sure which. Anyway, I felt it was time at last to hit the beach. I gave Wind Street the widest berth I possibly could, because it was always insane, and walked down to the end of Kingsway and

— 15 —

went left at the roundabout and then cut through the terraces around the Singleton, and what did I see down there, on Bath Street or maybe Paxton, but Merlin Auto Parts. It was all locked up for the night, or course, but it looked like a perfectly decent concern. It was about the same size as a Kwik-Fit but it was a far older building, part of that final, brash push of British industry that came after the war, before everyone just gave up and let other people do it. It looked incredibly quaint now, the thought of building an industrial unit entirely out of brick and then painting your company logo on the side, you don't see that anymore. The paint was faded, of course, and it was advertising some firm that must have gone bust donkey's years ago, but all in Merlin Auto Parts looked like a tidy concern. Maybe he owned it. Well I hope so, I thought to myself, as I crossed the four lanes of Oystermouth Road, and finally returned to the sands.

Scotty wasn't at the beach. I looked, but I couldn't find him. The sun had gone too. It was past midnight, I suppose.

There were a few small clumps of people huddled down under that concrete wall they have lining the prom after you get to the Marriott, but none of them contained Scotty, although I wouldn't be surprised if they boasted other young Glaswegian heroin addicts. Up and down the long stretch of coast you could see the odd little bonfire, with a small circle of dim shapes huddled around them. Like the bush fires of the Tuaregs. Funnily enough, Chester was there, standing on his own with his metal detector, off by the steps. His silhouette was fairly distinctive. I didn't bother saying hello, though. Then I sat down by a vacant stretch of wall and went through that extra bit of booze I had been lugging around all night, and fell into a deep, sound sleep. Well, I passed out.

II

First thing I did, of course, I checked my money, what was left of it, but it was still there. I had been rolled before, and it was one of the more palpable injustices I had suffered in recent times. Stealing from me, of all people, who had nothing, or something parked right next to it, just because I didn't have a locked door to sleep behind. And it happened to people who slept rough all the time, providing they could get any sleep at all. Money moves around fast down here, these are the rapids, shallow and fast, with dribs and drabs coming and going all the time. There is nowhere for it to pool, nowhere for it to collect. You have to go elsewhere for the depths of wealth. In fact, you probably have to leave town.

I got up, saw where I had slept. Everyone else had fucked off, whoever they were. I brushed the dirt off my suit, which was a dark navy, and it came up rumpled but okay. It was always rumpled. I like to think it represented a kind of casual chic, a formal insouciance, like Bryan Ferry or somebody. That's a danger sign right there, isn't it? Still, every night out of the Heathfield was a kind of victory. I blinked and rubbed my eyes. It was going to be a sunny bastard of a day. But I had been lucky. I had a hundred and sixty odd quid left, and I could afford to stay out of it, and out of it was where I wanted to be. Being alone, too, was something of a plus. A hundred and sixty could disappear like a smoked cigarette if you got other people involved. Sure, it would just be Scotty to start with, but then somebody else would come along who Scotty knew, and the next thing I might as well start handing it out.

I stood there staring at the sea for a minute, I don't know why. I had the money, and there were viable pubs all over town, plenty of places where they might have me if I was quiet, seeing it was early and a weekday. A few pints of bitter over in the Queens by what was left of the docks, or up and down the High Street again, or doing the neighbourhood pubs in the terraces around the Vetch. I had money, and it was early in the day, and the town was mine, those bits that would let me in. But I was tired, I guess. Then I saw Chester, walking stiffly down the prom, and I knew I was going to be better off somewhere else.

The Wetherspoons in Swansea was called the Potter's Wheel. Fuck knows why. They have to call them something, I suppose, and Wetherspoon number nine hundred and six probably doesn't appeal to marketing. As you might imagine, it's an absolute aircraft hanger of a place, but that has its pluses. There's plenty of room for people like me, and you will see plenty of people like me in there, sat at our tables of one. They need some people in there just to give the place a sense of scale, like little human figures in a landscape painting. If you avoid the main thoroughfares (street-bar-toilets-kitchen-fruit machines) then people aren't going to notice anything about you other than you're there. Later, when it gets busy, when you've had a few, that can be a different story, but for now it was a safe bet. Getting thrown out of here would be like getting thrown out of a bus station: it was possible, but you'd need to put a lot of work into it and the police would probably have to be involved. The nineteen-year-old manager that was supposed to be in charge probably felt no more proprietorial about this place than the four-fifty an hour Somali contract cleaners on Garden Street did towards their pavements.

I certainly had a good view of the street, everywhere did: the whole front wall was glass, seeing how the Potter's Wheel had been a car dealership before it was a pub. It was the only thing that made me uneasy, because when you have a good view of the street then chances are the street has a good view of you, but who did I know, in this town, to bother me? Exactly. So I put up with it. Then I went up to the bar, but they wouldn't serve me any booze, and I was beginning to wonder what the world was coming to, and then I realised they weren't serving anybody. It was half nine in the morning. Why open, then, I felt? It was basically false advertising, having a pub open and not serving booze.

I was going to have breakfast in the market and then I had a look at the breakfast menu in the middle of my table, which looked pretty reasonable, and very well photographed, and then I thought I'm not really hungry, I'll just have a cup of coffee, that's only seventy pee, and then I realised slowly that dotted about this cavernous room there were a few other customers and they had nothing on their tables at all, they were just sat there, waiting. So I just sat there too. Then it really did feel like a departure lounge or something.

Time passed. We waited for the morning flight into oblivion, for our daily one-way commute. A few old timers shuffled in with their pension money, fresh from the post office no doubt, and one of them stood right at the bar, not sat, stood, and looked at the girl with as much dignity as he could muster. From the back I couldn't see if he had any war medals on, but that would have been perfect. At something like five to eleven the girl took pity on him and served up a pint of a bitter, and then the rest of us were up there with him, like wolves around a carcass. I got a double vodka, neatly and effortlessly upsold from my request for a single, and a pint of lager plonked on the bar. I bent down to drink some from the glass, so I didn't spill any on the way back, seeing my hands were probably a spot shaky. Then I necked the vodka, one for the road, so to speak, and went back to my seat.

I was working on my breakfast pint, and taking my time about it, when my eye caught something outside, up on the street, and being fairly at ease by now I looked up without thinking about it, and there she was. Becca Blethyn, stood there on the pavement with her face almost pressed up against the glass. She was wearing a plastic red mackintosh and wheeling a little tartan shopping trolley beside her. I don't know if you've seen that film *Don't Look Now*, but she looked just like the little girl in that, except she was past thirty and obese. There wasn't a cloud in the sky, of course. She was just standing there staring at me with her gob open. Out of some misplaced first-drink-of-the-day bonhomie, I raised my glass to her and smiled, as if I was toasting her. But she just stood there and stared. Next to her that shopping trolley looked tiny. What would keep some old dear and her cat in groceries for a week looked like something she'd put her sandwiches in. The next time I looked up she was dragging it up towards the Kingsway, and I felt a strange sense of relief, and got on with business.

She came by again a bit later, took me totally by surprise, dressed exactly the same, standing there staring. Still had her little trolley with her. I raised my glass again and smiled. I had a feeling it was asking for trouble but I didn't know what else to do. I left it a while but she was still there so I did it again, but she didn't move, so I thought I'd best ignore her, which wasn't easy, and then I must have gone up to the bar or the jacks and when I came back she'd gone again. I didn't think that bode well at all, that. Never mind, I said to myself, when you have things to do, you have things to do. And I got on with them.

Must have been mid-afternoon when her brother came in. I was fairly self-absorbed by then, and I got these two hard fingers poking right in the shoulder blade, hard as iron.

'You're Robin Llywelyn,' said a deep voice, and I turned around to see this man with jet black hair, slightly curly, mid-thirties, built like a prop forward gone to seed.

'No I'm not,' I said. It was a reflex. But he ignored me anyway.

'I'm Tomos Blethyn,' he said.

Ah, I thought. Ah. I could see the resemblance, now he'd mentioned it. Both of them were huge and both of them looked unbalanced. This one gave off a certain smell though, and I caught it perfectly. Violence.

'You're supposed to be working for my sister. I don't like seeing my sister upset. You better not rip her off. You better not be a cowboy.'

He spoke in short sentences, with every full stop punctuated by another knife-like jab in my shoulder, and he had a lot to say for himself.

'She told me about you. You've been sat in here all day. You're supposed to be working for her.'

He didn't seem any brighter than Rebecca, it has to be said. But some stupid people will grow up meek and quiet and others will grow up loud and compensating, it all depends on your capacity to do people in, I suppose.

'I have a meeting,' I said, or was going to say, but he cut me short. He wasn't in the mood for listening. I don't suppose it would have cut much mustard anyway, someone like me sat in here around a table with half a dozen empty glasses on it.

'You'd better do your job, Magnum. You'd better keep your

promises. I'll be seeing her tonight. And I want to hear a good report. There better be a good fucking report. Understand?'

And he walked away. My arm felt like it was going to fall off. I looked around, but nobody in there had paid our little scene any attention. I think they would have needed binoculars to see it at all, in there. Then I finished my drink and got up. God, there's always something.

Having a few drinks inside me didn't make Tom Williams Court any nearer, and the sun was high in the sky. I was sodden with sweat by the time I got there, but you have to catch this kind of dissent at the source, to nip it in the bud. I pressed the button and heard God Save The Queen bleeping somewhere not too far away, on some old electronic bell. It was probably somebody's pride and joy when they fitted it, back in seventy-seven, or something.

She wasn't wearing the red mac anymore, which was some comfort.

'Hello,' I said. 'It's Robin Llywelyn.'

But she didn't let me in. She was on the defensive this time, wary, expecting trouble. It was inevitable really: she had to talk to somebody about me at some point, and there was only one thing that somebody could say, and it wasn't going to be good. It wasn't going to be a glowing appraisal of my services.

'I saw you earlier,' I said, trying to draw a response, but none came. She stood there in the doorway as if she expected me to make a dash for the front room and run off with the soft furnishings, but there was no way you could have got past her. There was no room left in the hall.

'Things have been going very well. I have been finding some things out about your... your man,' I said, failing to remember his name. Had she told me? I wasn't sure. I was beginning to feel like a bit of a heel at this point, I confess.

'Very well indeed. He's a very handsome man, isn't he?'

Rebecca looked at me fearfully for a moment, and then nodded. The ice had been broken.

'You must be very impatient for me to finish this assignment.'

Another careful nod.

'It must be worrying, having a handsome fiancé like this. I bet there are lots of women waiting to snap him up. But they've got their work cut out, hey? They've got to deal with you first, haven't they?'

I wondered if this guy even knew she existed. I hoped not. It would spare him the worry.

'And you've got me on the case now, looking out for him. If there's anything untoward going on I'll be able to tell you all about it. But I'm a very busy man, Miss Blethyn. I have lots of people I'm looking out for. Lots of cases I'm working on.'

Like a case of Commissar vodka, I reflected. Eighty quid a box, the card in the window had read. A week's holiday without having to leave your room. I looked her in the eye. She had stopped nodding, but I could tell she was still with me.

'So you see,' I said, 'I can't just work on your case all the time.'

'Why not?'

There was no good answer to this that immediately sprang to mind. Instead, some darker instinct kicked in.

'You'd like me to work for you exclusively, is that it?'

Nod.

'Well, that'll be an extra fifty quid a week, starting now.'

It was like taking candy from a baby, as they say, that was pretty much the sum of it. But what was money to her? What was anything? The council kept her clothed, housed and fed, in a nice house, all on her own, and she had family nearby that looked after her, lots of them, even if they were a bit odd.

I had nothing, and when I say that I don't mean I had a poky flat or a shit car, or that my job was going nowhere: I mean I had nothing. None of it. Yes, I felt bad about it, but I hadn't gone out looking for deranged clients, she had come looking for me. And in essence, this was really what I had been doing all along, when I was a pro, feeding false hope. The notion that there was nothing wrong, or that they could handle it if there was, that either way they were better off finding out about it. The delusion that knowledge would be a kind of catharsis. But love doesn't work like that. Love comes and goes and takes whatever it wants, but it always promises the world, and it never delivers, although it comes close enough for some people for that not to matter. In my old line of work you could see that every day, if you liked. As you can see, it's a discovery that's really paid off big for me.

But love is not a word you could use to describe any of the numerous problems of Becca Blethyn.

I took the fifty quid off the mentally ill woman and smiled a bit and gave her a few verbal pats on the head to keep her sweet and got out of there as quickly as I could, which is not quick at all these days, not quick enough by half. I'd already done all the pubs on that street yesterday, and I was mulling over my choices when I got another tap on the shoulder, although it was a lot softer this time.

'Hello,' said a man.

'Hello,' I said back.

'How are you today?'

'I'm fine.'

I was expecting to get asked to a bible reading at this point. It was the only plausible outcome I could think of.

'I was just heading into town. Got to go into the post office and do a few things.'

It was my turn to nod now.

'It can wait, though.'

'It's a nice day,' I offered.

'Scorcher. Bloody scorcher of a summer. No fun at all, hey?'

'No,' I said. 'No fun.'

'How you keeping, anyway?'

'Fine,' I said, like everybody does. 'Fine.'

'Fancy one in the Queens? Hair of the dog?'

'The Queens?' I said. I couldn't help myself. 'Is that still there?'

The Queens Hotel was part of the old Swansea, the town that I knew, and it would have been over on the other side of the dual carriageway in the old docks. There were all new flats there now, of course. I hadn't expected there to be anything left that I recognised, and being on the other side of the dual carriageway I had more or less forgotten about that part of town entirely. But it was still there, alright, in all its high-ceilinged Edwardian glory. The man showed me so.

It hadn't changed that much, I suppose, although it was on a street corner, and if you looked down the end of either one, you could see that things had changed unrecognisably all around it. Somehow they'd missed this patch. The first thing you saw when you went in was the big stuffed bear, and somebody had put a ladies' hat on it. Somebody was always putting something on it. The walls were still covered in old photos and paintings of ships that had come by this way, or maybe nowhere near it, and it was still busy, although maybe not as busy as it once was, and people were still talking, although the voices were older, and quieter. It had a couple of wooden tables outside.

'We'll sit here, hey?' I said. I was concerned they wouldn't serve me.

'Naah, go in, mun, it'll be fine. What are you having?'

I was having a pint of Buckley's Best, and so was he, and

we sat around a low, square chipboard table covered in wood-effect vinyl, off in a corner, and supped them. I stared out the big windows at the warehouses that had been converted into offices. It was a bit like looking out of your kitchen window one morning and seeing tropical rainforest or something, it just really wasn't there before. There were cars parked up and down the street now as well, and some of them were quite smart. Then eventually I had to stop looking outside and start looking inside, and soon after that I had to start looking at him. I think the awkwardness was mutual.

'Different, hey?' he said. 'Round here.'

'Yeah.'

'You seem surprised. You've been away, what, twenty-five years?'

'Yeah,' I said, perhaps a little taken aback by his accuracy. 'Twenty-five years.'

'So what did you expect?'

'Well, this is Swansea, isn't it. Nothing's supposed to change here. That's supposed to be part of the deal.'

One of the old regulars at a neighbouring table was looking at me as if he wanted to say something. I looked at him back.

'You should have seen this place sixty years ago, before the Luftwaffe worked it over,' he said, before extricating his aged body from its seat and wandering off into the back of the pub, as if he'd embarrassed himself. My drinking buddy waited for him to walk out of earshot.

'That's just it, Robin. Places change all the time, even Swansea. Even the people in it. Just because you're not around to watch them, it doesn't mean they don't get old, it doesn't mean they don't get ill, it doesn't mean they don't die.'

And he gave me one of those meaningful looks that could mean anything, although I had a feeling he was talking about someone I used to know, in a different century. She's dead now, although she wasn't supposed to be. She was supposed to live a nice long happy life and die in her sleep at a hundred, but she didn't, and there was something in the breeze some days that said it was my fault. I can understand why some people might want to blame me. I'm generally a very handy person to blame. Sometimes that's how I like to spend the day, blaming myself. We were silent then for what felt like about four hours, and then all of a sudden he just blew his cheeks up and sort of gave up, I guess.

'Do you remember Jimmy the Rat?' he asked, leaning back in his seat.

Jimmy the Rat! I had forgotten all about Jimmy the Rat. Middle-aged, black hair going rapidly grey, dead-straight centre parting, brylcreem, regimental blazer from somebody else's regiment, upturned moustache. It was as if he'd seen the Ealing comedies not as comedies but as serious studies in crime, and had made a career decision to plump for the caddish major type. I suppose he might have seemed classy from thirty feet away, as long as he wasn't talking. Or eating.

'Was he ever in the Army?' I asked.

'Not a day in his life,' the man said.

Jimmy the Rat was dead. He'd been dead for years. So was the Shadow. If you're a burglar who looks at all hard, eighteen-year-olds will call you that, if you like, the Shadow. Jimmy The One had passed over too. So had Togo Bevan. We ran through a whole host of eccentrics and petty criminals that had made cameo appearances in our youth, bit part players in the history of our town, losers all, to the very end.

'And now you,' the man said. 'People will talk about you like that. Won't be long now, will it?'

I didn't say anything to that. I didn't nod either.

'Do you know who I am?'

'I met you in the Garibaldi last night,' I said.

'I'm Mark Griffiths.'

In the dark pit of my stomach nausea bloomed.

'You're Carol's brother,' I said. 'You're Owain's uncle. I've been meaning to… I have been thinking, you know, about…'

I trailed off. There was was never any point in talking about it. There was too much to explain, and too much to ask about. It would have been like asking how sunlight smells or what air feels like; it was just the life you didn't live, and never would. Mark waited for all my unfinished little sentences to peter out.

'I felt like a bit of a loser staying, to be honest,' said Mark. 'All the smart ones, all the hungry ones, they left years ago too. I thought the people that left could look down at me. But look at you. You're the fucking lowest of the low. And you left, and you got lower.'

My mouth was suddenly dry.

'It's my round,' I said. 'What are you having?'

But Mark Griffiths just shook his head and leered at me, and I went up to the bar, just out of defiance, to get myself another, but instead of serving me the barman looked back over my shoulder at Mark and I turned to follow his gaze and when I got there I saw Mark slowly shaking his head, and when I looked back at the barman he was doing the same thing.

'Get wrecked somewhere else,' he said. So I did. I went straight back to my old seat in the Wetherspoons to pretend nothing had happened. It was a manoeuvre I had some experience in.

As far as Wetherspoons was concerned, I was working on a sort of sleeper strategy; to sit there in my remote corner and let the place fill up around me. Had I walked in at half nine in the evening, say, they might have turned me away, but if I went in there early, and stayed there, and managed to keep my mouth shut, then maybe I could ride it out till closing. I nearly made it, too. I don't know what time it was but night had fallen when I got that sharp stabbing pain in my shoulder again.

'Have you been in here drinking all day?' he said.

My eyes narrowed. Was there a smart way to play this?

'I said, have you been drinking in here all day, you fucking twat?'

'No,' I said. 'I had a quick one in the Queens.'

And he pulled me up by my lapels, and dragged me out the double doors at the front and down the alleyway at the side to the little municipal car park at the back. He had to drag me, really, once he'd got me upright, because I wasn't able to walk. I had in fact been sat there behind the dog end of a pint for some time before he'd arrived, wondering what my next move was going to be, seeing how I couldn't make it to the bar and I couldn't make it to the exit. But Tom Blethyn turned up and deposited me in a corner of the car park and saved me the bother. I knew what was going to happen next. It had happened to me before, and it had happened plenty since coming back, but it had never got any easier.

'You fucking cuntox,' he said. 'You fucking state.'

I slumped down against a wall. I could feel broken glass under my arse. I looked for witnesses but saw no one. There wasn't even a single parked car.

'I'm going to break your fucking legs,' he said.

The fear rose inside me, but that was all it did. It rose to a point and stayed there.

'I'm going to put you in the fucking hospital. You don't fuck around with this family.'

I didn't say anything. I wasn't even thinking of something to say. I was just watching the way Tom Blethyn's thick black eyebrows met in the middle whenever he swore. And the size of his nostrils. You could have kept golf balls in them.

'Got nothing to say for yourself?' he said, and his piglet

eyes darted around until he stomped off into the shadows and came back with a plank that had been torn off some palette. 'I'll batter you into the fucking ground. I'll send you straight up into the air.'

That made no sense to me. How could he batter me into the ground and then send me up into the air? If he was going to do both, wouldn't he want to do it the other way around?

'I know how to fucking kill a man,' he said. 'You wouldn't be the first. Stop smiling.'

Had he killed a man, I wondered? Death was a funny old thing. Apart from the pain, and maybe the uncertainty, we worry all the time about how we're going to get it, and why, and those things are the least of it. The least.

'Stop laughing!' he said. 'Do you want to fucking die? What's the matter with you?'

'I have lung cancer,' I said. 'I have terminal melanoma of the left lung.'

And I laughed. I laughed and laughed and laughed.

III

The Heathfield was off Mount Pleasant. It's one of the places you go to when you can't go anywhere else. Of course a person can always go somewhere else, if he isn't disabled or tied down, but that's not what I mean. I mean a person has to have somewhere to go, somewhere that isn't anywhere else, even if that distinction is purely in the eye of the beholder. Home, though I shudder to use the word: whatever it might be, it takes a rare soul to truly get by without one, although they are around. They get a reputation for themselves very easily. Swansea maybe had two of these noble savages, these ancient Britons: Teabag Pete and the Killay Woodsman, nomads standing still. For the rest of us there were places like the Heathfield, and they have saved lives, no doubt, but they have seen many more destroyed. After time they became worse, if anything, than being outside, but being on the right side of a locked door is ninety nine per cent of what civilisation is all about. The Heathfield was like being trapped in an abusive marriage: you know it's bad for you, but you think you need it, and it's all you've got.

'You,' said Graham, answering the buzzer. 'Your room's gone.'

But he left the door open, and I followed him further into Bedlam.

'You didn't come back last night. I had to let it go.'

'Don't put me in the hall, Graham,' I said. 'Please don't put me in the hall. I'll sleep on the stairs.'

God, the hall. It was a lower ground floor room, as the estate agents would call it, about twelve feet by thirty, with a bare wooden floor. The windows were slits, right up by the ceiling. You took your bedding from the cupboard at one end, which was usually a couple of blankets, and if you were early you might get a camp bed, but you were never early. You didn't want to come back early to the Heathfield. If you'd turned up looking for somewhere to sleep ten or twenty or fifty years ago I doubt you'd have found anything much different, although maybe they'd have expected you to sing a few hymns or something, to show willing. It would probably have been quieter, though. The last time I'd been down there I hadn't slept a wink. Some girl had gone with a bloke in the bedding cupboard for ten quid, although they'd argued about it for at least an hour beforehand, and afterwards. And there would normally be a sleepwalker or two, or at least that was what they said they were doing, when you woke up and they were going through your things. If it was full you'd get stepped on a couple of times. That was on top of all the other things you were bound to get anyway, like the fights and slanging matches and snoring, the people who made strange noises in their sleep, the occasional vomiting, pissing in the corners, all that.

Graham looked at me, as much as he ever looked at anybody, his face downturned, his eyes aimed somewhere around my chest.

'What do you want me to do?' he said.

Poor Graham. You felt sorry for him, you really did. In a big house full of hard-luck cases (and fools, I admit, and people that were a bit of both) he stood out as having the look of tragedy about him, and I would not be surprised to hear about a wife or child dead before their time, about bankruptcy or some bad civil litigation. This is not to say he was pathetic. He was just a good man. There are a few of them about, and they aren't too difficult to spot. They look like they are drowning.

Graham walked into his little office, just off the main door, and took down a lever arch file from one of his shelves.

'I'll just have a look in the day book but I can't promise anything. You shouldn't go off like that.'

Graham was paid by the government but even if he wasn't he'd probably still be here at least some of the time, volunteering or do-gooding or just finding something to do and somewhere to be, like the rest of us. Like I said, you felt sorry for him.

He opened the day book to today's date and traced a finger up and down the entries.

'Why'd you go off that like that anyway? We gave you a regular room. You know the rules.'

My regular room was below the hall. Being built on Mount Pleasant, which is a fairly steep hill, there was a lower ground floor and a smaller basement below that, to make up for the gradient. That was divided into tiny box rooms with their own door and a bar lock on the door. If it was at the front of the house you got a window and if not you got a sixty watt bulb. It was near enough the hall to hear everything that went on, and the walls were thin enough to hear your neighbour break wind, but it was as good as the Heathfield got.

Graham's face shifted into an expression that looked even more uncomfortable than usual.

'I shouldn't really do this,' he said, 'but you are one of the more mature residents and you don't generally cause any trouble. Apart from that one bad spell, but that's over, right?'

I promised nothing. He took a key fob out of his trouser pocket that was attached to his belt on a length of blue curly plastic and used it to unlock a green metal box on the wall. Inside there were rows of pegs with room keys on them and he took one off and gave it to me.

'You're in one of the penthouses,' he smiled, lamely.

'What?'

'Top floor,' he said, and held out the key.

'I can't be arsed going up and down those stairs all the time,' I said. 'We're up a hill as it is.'

'They're good rooms,' he said. 'They're supposed to be for designated vulnerables and other volunteers, but one of them's empty. Take it or leave it.'

There were moments, although I concede that it was physically impossible, when it seemed that all of Swansea was uphill. It never mattered where it was you wanted to go.

'I'll have to take it back if it's needed,' he added, once I was up the first flight of stairs.

'Good night, Graham,' I said.

I took my time with the stairs. The Heathfield was a detached Victorian house built on five floors, and I knew too that when I got to the top one it was going to be pretty hot. It was. The little landing up in the attic was like a sauna. There were six doors leading off it and my key was for number two so I opened it, my clothes sagging with sweat.

Inside there was a double bed, which was unusual, an armchair, a chest of drawers and a wardrobe. All the furniture looked pre-war, or maybe just after it, when they had to knock out a lot of cheap stuff in a hurry. It also had a huge dormer window looking out onto east Swansea and the Bristol Channel, and I watched the orange streetlights like little amber threads snaking off over the hills up past Briton Ferry to Afan Forest and the Brecon Beacons, which were over that way somewhere. I could see the flames from the steelworks' blast furnace in Port Talbot billowing into the night sky, eight miles down the coast. If I stood right by the pane I could see the centre of town, all the neon and tat, from where I had just come, and above it all I'm sure there were stars too, if I'd thought to look for them. It was a good view.

I didn't bother turning the light on. If you kept the curtains open, the lights of the city were bright enough to show you where things were. I took all my clothes off and laid them on the armchair. They stank. I stank too. I would have to do something about that tomorrow. I opened the window a little and lay down on the bed, on top of the covers, and listened to the city, to the growl of the distant traffic, the chorus of sirens, police cars, fire engines and ambulances, to car alarms and house alarms, to the singing and fighting, now that pubs were chucking out, and to the calling of the gulls. From the room next door I could hear a man moaning softly in what sounded like Arabic; was he in a better place now, I wondered, than where he was before? And from below me I could hear all the usual sounds of the Heathfield, but softer now, its creaks and shrieks, its shouts and whispers, its calls and notes. I do not remember ever closing my eyes, but somehow morning came around.

I woke up with sun, which came up over Kilvey Hill and beamed through the open curtains full force. That had me out of bed alright. It was better than a mess hall full of drill sergeants. I got up and pulled the curtains shut and went back to bed, with my face turned to the wall, but the curtains were cheap and thin and about as much good as a sheet of newspaper. I listened to the city, and the Heathfield, and both of them were pretty quiet for once. It must have been about six in the morning.

I admitted defeat, got out of bed, and put my fetid

clothes back on. I didn't want to, but I had nothing else to wear. Then I went downstairs and knocked on the door of Graham's little office. There was a little notice on it that said: 'You have talked so often of going to the dogs – and well, here are the dogs, and you have reached them, and you can stand it. George Orwell.'

Next to Orwell somebody had added the words 'is a twat.'

I knocked again and tried the door, which was unlocked, so I stepped inside and watched him jerk awake in his swivel chair.

'I need to get tidied up,' I said. 'I need to clean my clothes and stuff.'

'What do you expect me to do about it?'

'Well, could I borrow some soap and a towel and some change for the washing machine and stuff?'

'No. Use your own money,' he said, rubbing some sleep from his eye.

'I haven't got any. Somebody took it off me last night.'

'Took if off you?'

'Yeah.'

'Have you reported it? Have you got a crime reference number?'

The idea of reporting Tom Blethyn to the police was alarming and amusing in equal parts.

'No,' I said. 'Come on, Graham.'

But that was it. The office door shut and I heard his chair creak as he put his weight back down on it. I opened the door to the hall and had a look for Scotty but I couldn't find him, and he was unlikely to be in a room. Scotty didn't have those kinds of privileges. I had a look in the TV lounge, where a few people crashed out on the easy chairs, if none of the staff noticed, but he wasn't there either.

It could get packed out during the day, the TV lounge.

Programmes about doing your house up were probably the most popular, for obvious, vicarious reasons. It made sense, in here; out in the real world the popularity of these programmes worried me a little. The phenomenon of property development as portrayed in daytime television: that it was not a matter of gazumping buyers, or of taking an impossibly transient approach towards location, or of managing construction labour, or of bargain-basement material, or dodgy connections on the planning committee, or of cut-corners or cheap capital or quick sales, but simply a matter of personal taste. That making money comes down to having the right sort of cushions, or curtains, to being, in short, the right sort of person. That you are entitled to property, and more property, simply because of who you are, curtains and cushions being in this day and age an incontrovertible manifestation of the inner being. They were right, in a sense, of course. The rich get richer and the poor get poorer, and even a freehold on a two-bedroom terrace puts you on the way up, up like a rocket, compared to the low arcs we will etch across the evening of life.

My little search for Scotty proved fruitless so I took my stinking self down to the benches by the train station, under a sky that was already spotlessly blue, and waited, wondering who would show. For a while, I saw nobody, except a few postmen and the milk. The first London train left the station, and it must have had about three people on it. Then town woke up. The morning traffic started, and the buses got more frequent, and had more people on them, folks started filing into offices, and the shopping crowd came out. A little after that, about half nine, say, the regulars started to turn up, in ones and twos. There have always been a lot of homeless around in this town, especially in summer, all drawn by some secret migratory instinct to the beach, perhaps, to illusions of a Welsh Riviera, who knows. If we knew, we wouldn't have come. A few of them stayed separate, like me, for no discernable reason a person might figure out, except maybe to beg. I hadn't begged yet, or if I had, I didn't remember it. The rest, like me, I suppose, picked a spot and stood there, and just sort of looked around without knowing what they were looking for; just sort of hoped, without telling themselves they were hoping. The rest congregated in a loose group over the road, on a low wall, with their cider and lager and sherry and talk, and began the day. Local people called them the Wild Bunch, although they were tamer than pit ponies most of the time, and they looked just about as lost and redundant. Their faces changed all the time. I watched on, unabashed and unblinking, at the four-packs and the plastic bottles in their carrier bags, at the half-litre flagons of spirits sticking out of coat pockets, at the green glass bottles of cheap sherry. Nobody asked me over. Nobody offered me any. Some people in my situation would have gone over and said where they were from and made some small talk and sat down and they would have got a can or something, I expect. I'd seen it happen. But I didn't care for them and I didn't mind if they knew it, and if you think that kind of integrity is rewarded down here, you are mistaken.

I was sitting there watching them and wondering how long it would be before I went over to them and stayed there, a couple of hours or a couple of weeks, when I yawned and looked over a shoulder and saw Scotty a little way up the road, on the same side as the Wild Bunch. He was sitting on a little grass embankment outside a small block of flats with his head in his hands and he looked like a bad February afternoon.

'Waiting for your man?' I said, when I got near.

'Well, I'm not waiting for a fucking taxi,' he said, through clenched teeth, and he sounded like he was in pain. 'Where the fuck did you get to?'

I remembered about how I was supposed to meet him back at the beach.

'Oh, I had some work to do. And things got complicated. Sorry.'

'Work? Well, did you get any money?'

'Yeah, but I had it taken off me. There was this guy who didn't think I was really serious about the job. He was right, too.'

Scotty took his head out of his hands so he could look me up and down.

'It doesn't look like he worked you over much,' he said.

'I think he felt sorry for me.'

Scotty gave me a look of plain disbelief, which I could well understand, and then put his head back.

'Aye, well, that makes a change, hey?'

'I thought you were going to score the other afternoon?'

'Well I fucking didn't.'

Scotty's dealer hadn't turned up, for whatever reason. I gather it's something that happens a lot. And being a relative newcomer to Swansea, he had decided to go and find some likely-looking crowds and hang around them, like drinkers did with the Wild Bunch. He had talked to a couple of small groups, both for quite a long time, and got nothing but a couple of street names, and then he had gone to find a couple of squats, but they were empty or no good. He had stayed out both nights in parties on the beach and in a boarded-up house on Craddock Street, but neither of them had been able to offer his particular poison. Whenever he had gone back to the Heathfield there had been no one there he could ask. Scotty was still a young man, I guess, and maybe he hadn't been around enough yet. And although he looked like he was suffering, maybe he just hadn't suffered enough yet either. Both of us still had a little further to fall, a little more time to go, before our respective needs would call the shots entirely. I stood there on the pavement and watched young mothers pushing prams and went back to thinking about a drink, until I heard Scotty's teeth chattering in the noonday sun, and just to get my mind off it I said:

'I can probably get you some heroin.'

He looked up at me, with great effort, and was probably finding the energy to say something derogatory, and then he looked past me and his eyes grew until you could see all round his pupils.

'You won't have to,' he said.

I followed his gaze and saw a man walking out of Tŷ Nant, a government office block near the station. He was probably about mid-thirties and he was wearing jeans, Caterpillar boots and a tucked-in shirt. He had a day's worth of stubble and ragged-looking mousy blonde hair. He projected a kind of rugged image, but if you looked at him for long enough, as I did, while he waited to cross the road and come over, you could see that under it all he was far, far too thin to be anything like rugged.

He looked at me and nodded once at Scotty.

'Alright, man,' said Scotty, beaming. 'How are you? Did it go alright?'

'It'll go through,' said the man. 'They used illegal evidence.'

Dimly, I remembered the Appeals Service was in Tŷ Nant somewhere. The man stood there and did an impression of someone for whom time was money, and not a prison sentence. Scotty smiled and looked like he'd just been asked on a free holiday.

'So could I have some gear, then?' he said.

I watched the man shake his head, and waited until Scotty stopped smiling, until he realised what the man meant. It took a while.

'Why not? The money's right here.'

I saw the man's tongue touch his upper lip on the word money, but he kept his hands in his pockets, kept his stern rugged look on his thin drawn face.

'You're Magnum's mate, aren't you?' he said to Scotty, nodding in my direction.

'What?'

'You know, Magnum, PI. Him.'

'So fucking what?'

'No gear for Magnum's young Scottish chum. Orders.'

'But I'm a paying customer!'

'Oh sure. I'm really going to miss your trade. One skaghead out of hundreds.'

And with that, he walked off, at a brisk manly pace. Scotty got up and followed him. Actually, so did I. I wanted to find out who the orders were from, and why, but Scotty got loud and pleady and the man pulled a little leather cosh out of his jeans and tapped Scotty on the knee with it. By the time I caught up with him he was lying on his back on the street and the man had walked out the other end of the alley.

'What the fuck am I going to do now?' he said, when he could talk.

'I said I could probably get you some heroin.'

'You better fucking had, you prick. What have you done now?'

'Could be anything,' I said. 'Are there any places you haven't tried to score yet?'

Of course I got another twenty minutes of abuse and general moaning before I got anywhere with him, seeing how he was in withdrawal and freshly disappointed and he'd just been twatted on the knee. When the blame was over, or had simmered down to manageable levels, he said something about the tower blocks on Griffith John Street.

'I don't know where though.'

It was a start. There were only three of them, and from the right place I figured you could probably see everybody who came in or went out of the estate. Which was correct, as it turned out, although it involved standing in the middle of a long pedestrian walkway over the Neath junction. We must have looked a bit ominous to car drivers, two rough-looking down-and-outs standing perfectly still in the middle of the Greenhill footbridge, gazing out like sentinels. Or possibly just like twats.

'Does he sell anything else, this dealer?' I asked, after quarter of an hour.

'Charlie, maybe. Bit of crack.'

'Alright,' I said. The crack had sort of narrowed things down for me. 'Let's try a closer look at that block at the back, that looks the roughest. We look like a couple of pillocks stood here.'

The block at the back was the roughest by a long chalk. Considering it was a twelve-storey building, there were only four cars parked out front, and none of them looked like they had MOTs. The concrete outside was badly potholed and littered with the ashes of impromptu bonfires. I walked around it once and saw a flat about halfway up that had tin foil stuck to the lower half of all the windows. No good reason for that as far as I could see. Inside a row of fairy lights twinkled on and off.

'If we go up there,' I said to Scotty, 'what are the odds that flat's got a steel door?'

It had. Lots of them had, actually. I pressed the buzzer anyway, and then the letterbox opened and Scotty knelt down to talk into it.

'Merle Evans said you did a bit of trade,' Scotty said. And the door opened. It was that easy.

The man who let us in was barefoot, wearing torn black jeans and a purple shirt that had the first three buttons undone. He had some sort of white man's afro going on, and he clicked his fingers a lot. We walked down a narrow hallway and when we got to the end of it you could just about see every corner of the flat: the bedroom door was open, showing an unmade double bed, the bathroom door was ajar, showing some fusty-looking green tiling, and the rest of the place was just one room, an open plan kitchen and living room. It wasn't a big place at all. There was a coffee table with the usual drug paraphernalia on it and a chocolate brown three piece-suite, and on the settee a heavy-set black guy with a shaved head seemed to have passed out. I went over to the window and looked out onto the houses of Cwmbwrla and pretended I wasn't there. The carpet was deep shag pile, and it had been light blue, once; it had probably come into fashion and then gone out of it twice since it had been laid, and there were things in it. I wouldn't have wanted to walk on it barefoot.

Scotty and this guy went into some small talk about why he hadn't come round here before, and how he really should have, 'cause the guy had a totally sound reputation, all the Neath boys did, they were good lads, and Scotty said, sure, it was unbelievable, but he was from out of town, and he didn't know any of the Neath boys at all, and they lied to each other like that for about twenty minutes. Then Scotty put some folding down on the table and the guy nudged past me to get into his own kitchen, and took some stuff out of the sideboard and put it on a tray and brought it over like it was tea and cake.

'Do you want anything?' he asked me. 'A few toots?'

I shook my head and he left it at that. It wasn't really a business that required salesmanship, really.

I tried to keep looking out of the window but I could see Scotty rolling up the sleeve of his German army jacket and going through the rest of the motions. There was a little curved dish that had been cut off from the bottom of a can of pop, and Scotty took an alcohol swab from a multipack and cleaned it off. Then he picked up the little clingfilm parcel, about the size of your thumbnail, and unwrapped it, and put the black tar heroin inside onto the bottom of the can. At this point the guy's mobile starts ringing and he asks us to excuse him and he goes into his bedroom and closes the door. Scotty nods his assent and then takes a syringe from the needle clinic out of its packaging and fills it about half full with water from a glass on the tray, which he squirts into the can, and the heroin starts to dissolve. He pulls the plunger out of the syringe and uses it to stir his dose, making sure it's all liquid. Then he takes a thumbful of cotton wool from the little see-through Boots bag, and rolls it down until it's as big as the tip of your little finger, and he dips it into the heroin and it fills up like a sponge. I have seen him do all this half a dozen times at least, and it still seems like an incredibly personal act. Certainly nothing like drinking a pint, or even seven pints.

'You ever injected yourself?' he asks me, while he's doing this. He's all talk now he knows he's getting a bang.

'Nope,' I say, awkwardly. He knows I don't do drugs. 'I tell you what though, I was going up the side of a house once, pissed, you know, and I started to fall so I reached out to grab something and this was about two in the morning so I grabbed the nearest thing I could find and it was this climbing rose bush. Thorns an inch long. Tore the fuck off my forearm. So I landed on the ground, and so did my bottle, both of us in one piece, and my arm looked terrible so the first thing I did was pour a load of whisky into the wound. To sterilise it. I reckon I must have taken four shot's worth straight into the bloodstream, because I had an instant blackout, for the next four or five hours. In fact the next couple of days were a bit weird.'

Scotty met my ramblings with a business-like nod. I don't think he was even listening.

'You don't like dealers, do you?' he said.

'No. I don't.'

'There's no difference, you know. Between dealers and users.'

'Not from where I'm standing.'

'You take what you can get, you do what you can. I'd deal if I could.'

'Yeah, but you can't,' I said. 'You'd be shit at it.'

'It's the law that's fucked up, you know. It's the law you don't like.'

'No,' I said, 'it's the dealers.'

We'd had that argument enough times before for us to run through it without thinking. I suppose we just wanted to fill in the silence, to feel a little bit more at home in this strange flat seven floors up in the Griffith John estate.

Scotty took up the length of orange surgical tubing that lay coiled on the tray and wrapped it around his upper bicep. Then he took another swab and started wiping a patch on his arm and then the bedroom door opened quite violently and the guy practically ran out, looking worried but firm.

'Sorry, guys, you can't fucking have any,' he said.

I think it took Scotty a minute to process this. It wasn't a message the neural network wanted to deliver.

'What?' he said. 'What the fuck?'

The guy went around him and into the kitchen sideboard.

'You can't fucking have any. You're off the list,' he said, opening a drawer.

'The stuff's in the fucking needle!'

'It'll keep. I want you out, now.'

And he turned around and he had a machete in his hand. But he was talking to Scotty and he had his back to me, and down on the floor by the armchair I could see a big purple porcelain bong, and ever so slowly, so slowly my muscles ached, I bent down to pick it up.

'I'll pay you more,' said Scotty, his eyes darting between the needle, resting against the tin, and the guy. 'I'll pay you extra. How's that?'

'Yeah,' said the guy, 'how much more?'

That was when I got him around the head with the bong. The thick porcelain smashed into a hundred little pieces and the guy slumped to the sticky shag pile like he'd been shot. I looked at the guy on the settee but he hadn't moved, hadn't even flinched.

'What the fuck are you doing?' said Scotty, with anguish in his voice. Maybe he said it with more of an exclamation mark than a question mark.

I reached down and picked up the machete, and looked at the blade. There was a little brown rust on it, and it rubbed off on my thumb. Blood. Not much, though. It had been used before. I looked down again, stared at that white man's afro, and waited to see some more of it, fresh, seeping out.

'What the fuck are you doing!'

I couldn't see any. For some reason this seemed unnatural. As an afterthought, I knelt down and put my hand to his neck, but his pulse was good and steady, thank Christ.

'What the fuck are you doing! You can't do that. You cannot do that to a dealer. What the fuck are you doing!'

'He had a machete,' I said.

'He was scared. I could have haggled with him.'

'Shoot up, mate. Fucking shoot up and let's go.'

— 46 —

I went into the bedroom, to make sure there wasn't another sleeping beauty in there, but there was nothing. Just an unmade bed and some clothes on the floor and some more in the wardrobe, thrown haphazardly onto the hangers. In the corner of the room there was an All Sports carrier bag and a white shoe box half-out of it, with the lid off. New trainers, or whatever they called them these days. There was a little bamboo bedside table with nothing on it but an ashtray, and a couple of squares of tin foil with dark brown burn marks in the middle of them.

When I came back out Scotty had jabbed himself, as I knew he would. I stood there and watched the rest of the pantomime. They were all the same. Shooting up was only the half of it, every time they did it they had to sit there like they had found what they had really wanted, like they had found the only thing that was worth pursuing. It was all a sham. Walk into any cheap pub in the country and you'd find drinkers just as dedicated, but with none of the delusion. People who know they can't get what they want, that know that the wanting is all they'll have, vague and empty but there and wanting all the same. The drinking was just something to do in the meantime, and nobody called it a kick, nobody thought it a secret. It made junkies look somehow adolescent. I watched Scotty smile and beam and roll his head and sigh and sink back into the armchair and all the rest of it. I had a feeling I wouldn't like him much for the next couple of hours.

'You know,' he said, sounding very cool and smug, 'now I come to think of it, that was a brilliant idea.'

I went over to the window and then down to the front door, and stuck my head out of it. I was worried we might have visitors.

'About hitting him with the bong,' Scotty said. I took a seat perched on the arm of the settee and looked down at the guy

on it. He looked like he worked out a lot. I was glad he was
still under.

'Yeah,' I said. 'Genius. Let's go.'

'You know what we should do?'

'Leave. Now.'

'No, we should clean him out. We should clean the fucker
out, yeah!'

'Hold on,' I said. 'This guy was taking the piss. You give
him the money, he gives you your drugs, all the kit you need
to take them with, you practically have the thing hanging out
of your arm and then he comes out and starts haggling. With
a big knife. He was asking for it. You want to clean the guy out,
you're going to have him and God knows who else looking for
you. You clean this guy out you're talking about another level
entirely. Neither of us are cut out for it.'

I talked and kept talking and felt my voice grow cracked
and hoarse. I kept talking because it was all I could do, because
my eyes had already fallen on Scotty's crumpled banknotes,
sitting there on the coffee table looking naked and vulnerable
and lonely.

'I could just take a bit more off him,' he said. I wondered if
he'd heard a word I'd said. He wouldn't have to, as long as he'd
heard the tapering tone of my voice.

'I'll just take enough to see me through the week,' he said.

'I'll take the money,' I said. 'You shouldn't have to pay for it.'

'That's my money.'

'I'm the one that hit him, remember.'

So we took a little of what we wanted, neither of us really
taking the piss, or at least not openly raiding the place. Scotty's
money only came to forty quid, so I pulled the guy's wallet out
of his tight black jeans and there must have been four or five
hundred quid in it. I don't know how he managed to sit down.
I took another twenty out of it, and then, as an afterthought,

or maybe more of a reflex, something unthinking, anyway, I pulled out another twenty, then clipped it shut and put it back in his trousers, which turned out to be a lot harder than getting it out. Then I did my best to forget it was there. Scotty showed me a handful of little brown clingfilm packages before he put them in his jacket pocket, maybe half a dozen of them, maybe a little more. It didn't seem too much, all in all. Maybe he wouldn't even notice. I put the remains of the broken bong in the hands of the comatose guy on the sofa, so it might look like he had attacked him, if the dealer woke up first. You never know. Then we fucked off.

Outside the flat, on the way down the hall, just as we got to the long stairway and the pissy lifts, some guy about thirty years of age came up, wearing fashionable clothes and listening to an iPod. His hair had been cut into one of those spiky fins that were probably very popular in London last year, and on the wrist of his right hand he had a couple of those brightly coloured plastic charity bands. As we stepped into the lift, just out of curiosity, I kept my finger pressed on the doors open button until I saw him knock on the steel door of the dealer's flat.

Funny how an educated middle-class person might avoid eating meat, say, and buy fair trade coffee, and worry about global warming and third world debt and then go and buy cocaine a couple of times a month. Cocaine, heroin, stuff like that: they are the most socially destructive commodities in the world, except maybe for oil, and oil is at least useful. The guy with the iPod gave the door another knock and waited. He would be waiting a long time. I let go of the button and the door hissed shut and sealed us into our dark, stinking little box, and I felt our shuddering descent in my knees.

Outside the sun was still doing business, still plying a roaring trade. It was as if the world was melting. I started sweating again instantly, felt it collecting above an eyebrow, saw it appearing on my shirt, like I was sponge, and some part of me was being squeezed that I could not feel. We walked past the other blocks and through the trees and climbed another one of those long, arcing footbridges, and came down at the top of Dyfatty Street. We were heading back into town, I supposed.

'I've never had to haggle with a barman,' I said.

'Ever seen one with a machete?'

'Actually, yes.'

We passed the medical centre and then the community centre, a small brick building that couldn't have been more than twenty years old, but it had a high wall of brambles around almost all of it, and the pathway that led to its door was cracked with weeds.

'Seriously, though,' I said, two words that are always a warning sign, always a preface to tediousness. 'I'm not being funny.'

That's another one, right there. I'm not being funny: no, no fear there.

'Drugs are for fucking wankers.'

'Oh yeah?' said Scotty. We had been here so many times. 'Have you seen Wind Street on a Saturday night?'

'Wind Street on Saturday night is pretty rough, but, I mean, it's not downtown Medellin, is it? You don't need to shoot anybody to manufacture, distribute, sell or purchase alcohol.'

'It's the law!'

'I'm not sure I care about the law.'

'You're just a fucking bigot,' he said.

'Yup. All us alcoholics are, you know. We're just insufficiently progressive. But it you want to change the world, buying coke and heroin seems a strange way of going about it.'

I don't know why I have to have this argument, over and over again. Or rather I do. Probably, I would prefer it if Scotty didn't take drugs, but Scotty is a heroin addict, and that is that, and a part of me enjoys the rare opportunity to feel self-righteous about it. It's unfair, really, to pick on somebody like Scotty, but there you go. He's the only person I can pick on.

'You're so fucking naive,' he said. He, too, has all his responses down pat. He has had this argument with plenty of other people, he has heard it made for him by his peers, as I have by mine. But he is fighting an uphill battle, is Scotty, and I feel a twinge of guilt, a little spasm of shame.

'People are people and drugs are drugs, whatever they are and wherever they come from, and you are a little small-minded superior conformist who just likes to pick the winning side. The side of the fuckin' herd.'

'I didn't think I rated particularly high on naivety,' I said, eventually. We were at the castle already.

'So long,' I said.

'Cheers,' he said.

And we went our separate ways, off to our own unspoken assignations. Every time we said goodbye it was like that. If you are on the down and out and you have a friend down there with you, you hoped to see them again, but you also hoped you didn't, because there were better places for them to be. So you just said so long, and knew that you would see them again soon enough, whatever you or they or anybody else wanted.

I stood by the lights and watched him stroll leisurely off to the beach, a man enjoying his bloodstream.

'So long,' I said again, to his back, as I watched him turn the corner by Princess Way. He was happy now. Never mind that no one in town would sell to him, and that neither of us knew why, and that he had just ripped off a dealer: in his jacket pocket, amongst his little bags of black tar, were the next four or five days of his life, and they were all good.

IV

It didn't take more than twenty-four hours for it all to kick off. I was doing my own thing, of course, back on my own little case, my work, or perhaps I would have picked up on it sooner. But I had things to look into. I had questions I wanted answered that I was unable to ask; I was for once a client to myself.

After leaving Scotty I went back to Bath Street and Merlin Auto Parts and stood there until I could remember the phone number they had on the company sign, which took a lot longer than it would have done twelve months ago, I'm sure. My short-term memory is shot. Then, when I felt I had it down, I went off to find the nearest phone box.

I had no change, of course, and security wouldn't let me in Tesco's, so I went over to the newsagents on Wind Street, where security was a small unscrupulous wooden bat under the counter, and bought a four-pack. Just normal lager, this time, not the old purple tin. Then I had to carry it back over to the phone box without drinking any of it, which I did, but then I forgot the phone number so it was back to the company sign on Bath Street and I was so pissed off by then that I cracked one open without thinking about it.

It was my voice that I was worried about. If you've drunk heavily for a long time, it will leave its mark on you. You will sound like a drunk even if you haven't had anything to drink that day, or even that week, or month, or year, depending on how seriously you went into it before. The parts of the brain that keep you eloquent and enunciated get rubbed off, somehow, and you get the slow, mumbling monotone of the drunk. I was pretty sure I had it, and I knew it would sound worse over the phone. But one lager, I think, was a good idea. One lager got me positive and on the upshot, and smoothed me down a bit.

They answered the phone after seven rings.

'Hello,' I said. 'It's Swansea Council here. Could I speak to the owner, please?'

'What's it in connection with?'

'Rates exemption,' I said. I was pleased with that one. He was on in about a second.

'Hello, it's Swansea Council Enterprise Department here,' I said, more or less spontaneously. 'In connection with the Welsh Assembly Government and dedicated European funding we are testing a pilot scheme to give full exemption rates to certain small businesses in the area for the next five financial years. Are you interested?'

I had them all in there: Swansea council, the Welsh Assembly Government, and Europe, three public bodies whose spending patterns could never be predicted by anybody, that lay outside the realm of chaos theory, even. If I'd said we want to make a compulsory purchase of the site so we can erect a twenty-foot bronze banana I think he would have been half-convinced.

'Well, I don't think you have to do very much,' I said. 'I don't know a huge amount about it myself, but if you're interested we can arrange a time for somebody to come around and talk to you about it. It's still very experimental but I know it's going to go ahead. Can I just check your business details? Our records look like they might be a bit out of date.'

He would have happily given me a detailed description of his last stool by that point, I think. I got the business address and the nature of the business and all the rest of it, and I left appropriate pauses after each item, as if I was writing it down. Long pauses, in fact, seeing how I probably didn't sound too bright. Then I asked for the name of the owner.

'David Mitchell,' he said. But David Mitchell was no good to me.

'Is there another owner?' I said.

'Well, there's Owain Griffiths, but he's on the way out,' David Mitchell said.

Bingo. But I didn't like the sound of that last bit.

'The way out?'

'Yeah, I bought him out. He only comes in maybe one or two days a week now. We had a gentleman's disagreement, I think you'd call it. And he needed the money.'

'Oh yeah?' I said, aiming to sound sympathetic and amused, but he didn't expand on it. Couldn't figure out how I could get him too, either.

'Well, I'll just be needing your residential addresses,' I said. I knew I'd have to ask for these. If I went through Companies House it would cost thirty quid, take two weeks, and I'd get a form back saying they both lived in the workshop. Business directors are cagey like that. It makes them feel shrewd. But wave some money at them and they make a different set of noises entirely.

Mitchell gave me his, told me all about it, some little pile up in Pontardawe, a new-build courtesy of his mate the builder. I could imagine it. I could see him in the back garden, barbecuing.

'And Mr Griffiths?' I said. I watched my credit shrinking in the phone's LCD display. If I had to put in any more change he might hear, and then he'd rumble that I was in a call box.

'You don't have to know about him, do you? He's pretty much gone.'

I guess, all things considered, I didn't have to. Like I didn't have to drink.

'I think I better had. There's a space here on the form for him, and that's what I'm supposed to be doing, filling in these forms.'

'Hold on then.'

I looked in my pockets for more coins but they were all copper. I only had two pence' worth of call left when he came back.

'Little Hill House, Rhossili.'

'That's it?'

'It's not a big place, you know, Rhossili.'

'No. I remember.'

And I thanked him and hung up. Bloody Hell. Rhossili. I'd need a car to get down there, and that sent my mind spinning, because I hadn't even been inside a car for seven months. I drank another can and went down to the bus station anyway, just to see. When I was a lad if there was a bus going out that way at all it probably only went on Saturdays, or bank holidays. But you never know. I walked up and down the bays, reading the panels above the doors, and they told me nothing I didn't already know. Then I got to the third one from the end and it said there were buses out there pretty much every hour. I couldn't believe it. Rhossili.

If you had money in Swansea you lived in the west. I don't know why. What with Cardiff and England on the other side you'd think the des res's would be that side, considering the commuting and what have you. It's the same in lots of other places, for some reason: look at London, look at Bristol, even. But you couldn't get more west than Rhossili. That was right at the tip of the Gower peninsula, down by Worm's Head.

After that it was the sea, and Wimpey haven't figured out how to build on that yet.

I finished my can and waited for the 118, which was daft. I should have gone into town and got some more, because it wasn't going to be a short journey, out there and back, but I was excited. I was going to see the house, the family even, maybe, from a distance anyway, and it was a nice spot, Rhossili, beautiful. I hadn't been there since I was a kid. The bus came more or less on time and it was packed. It left the station with three spare seats, and by the time we got to Sketty people were standing. This on a weekday, too.

It took about an hour, through the Killay woods, through Parc Le Breos, up over the scrub of Cefn Bryn common and down again at Penrice Castle; passing a few little places with campsites and caravan parks and one-room potteries where you could have a go at throwing yourself a vase. We passed a few pubs but they barely registered. They looked nothing like the pubs back in town. They looked like they sold sherbet and lemonade and the worst it ever got was when somebody lost a domino. When we got to the top of the penisula the bus turned round, somehow, in a triangle of concrete you couldn't have parked two cars on, and everybody got off. I stood there a moment to get my bearings and by the time I did they had all disappeared, off to Worm's Head and the visitor centre or down to the wide sweep of Rhossili beach.

Right, I thought. Little Hill House. There can't have been more than two dozen buildings in the place, so I started looking. Most of them looked fairly old, pre-war, anyway, except for the bungalow some councillor had probably put up. Near the bus stop were a couple of cafés, although they'd probably prefer to be called tea rooms, and the Worm's Head Hotel. Obviously none of them were contenders so I went back up past St Mary's Church and started looking around there, and I found it in about thirty seconds, in a little lane that led up to the Rhossili downs.

It must have been a farm building or something once. Long and low, made of dark stone and brick, with a five-bar gate leading into a courtyard I couldn't see and six or seven windows facing the sea. We were so far west you couldn't see England any more from here. It was just the sea and the sky, and way off up to the north-west the long arm of the Pembrokeshire coast, sitting there like a bank of distant cloud. The people down on the beach looked like dots now. You couldn't hear them and you could hardly see them. There was something strange in the middle of the sands, something that looked like a dead tree on its side, and I couldn't figure out what it was.

I walked up and down the lane a couple of times, staring into the windows. It looked like a nice place on the inside, as far as I could see: it backed out onto the hillside, so some of the rooms were pretty dark. Then I caught a flash of movement and my heart was in my mouth, and I could feel my pulse in the tips of my fingers. I stood in the middle of the lane and stared, and saw a woman in her late twenties holding a baby in one arm and another little kid, a girl by the looks of things, running about around her ankles. A wife and kids. I couldn't believe it. She opened the fridge door and when the soft electric light hit her face I got a half-decent look at her, standing in the kitchen, raven-black hair and hazel eyes, five and a half foot, maybe, wide-hipped, small mouth. Well, I thought, we shared a similar taste in women, if nothing else. Then she caught me looking at her and startled a bit, and I went off down the end of the lane, give her time to forget about me and get on with whatever it was she was doing.

The next time I passed by it was ten minutes later and they were in the room next door. There was a load of cardboard boxes on the floor and she was putting books into them, lots of books, and not Jackie Collins either. Big, solid, clever-looking ones. Why's she doing that I wondered, and then I looked up and saw a big For Sale sign hanging off the upper part of the house. That's not good, I thought. You can't move anywhere nicer than here, surely? Not unless you were clearing out entirely. Then when I looked down, when I looked back into the room again, she was staring at me, openly, and not happily, and I cleared off for good.

The next bus wasn't due for another forty minutes so I sat on the wall around the church and tried to get my breath back. But my breath would never come back again.

The little graveyard was almost full now, if it wasn't already; I couldn't see anywhere you could squeeze another one in. It was a nice spot for it. The sea, the wide sands of Rhossili beach below you, the downs, high up above, green fern with a band of purple heather at the top, Burry Holms sticking out into the sea to the north, and Worm's Head to the south, two long, empty stretches of headland framing it all in. If you had a relative already buried here they could put you in the same grave: one Morris who died in the nineties had his name on the same stone as a Morris who died in 1905. And there was another stone, Christ, which had the mother and father and eight children. The most recent grave was around the back, right up against the wall, in black marble. It had three lines on it, and that was all: the name, then his job (engineer) and then the year of his death. I liked that. I thought that was a classy stone. I wouldn't have minded a stone like that. What to put for the middle line, though? Drunk? Failure? Idiot? Private investigator? Private investigator was the worst. It seemed to say all the other things and a little bit more: deluded, deceitful, impressionable, cheap. I wouldn't have minded, though, if I could be buried here. Stuck in a coffin, six feet under, being eaten by worms: I would enjoy it, here. Not that I'd be likely to get in.

Will there be anyone there to watch my cardboard coffin rolling down the crem? Not bloody likely. And my ashes, what will become of them? The local tip? Or maybe the groundskeeper might rake them into the compost. They're good for compost, I believe, the ashes. It would be the pinnacle of a glorious career, alright, the perfect full-stop to twenty-five years in the gutter keeping my mouth shut. The most useful thing I might ever do, and I'd be dead.

The bus came after what felt like a lifetime, and when I moved off my seat on the low stone wall I had a throat like sandpaper. I hadn't had a drink for hours, and it would be at least an hour before we got back. I joined the end of the queue, and went on staring out to sea while the people filed on. I could still see that strange skeletal thing in the middle of the Rhossili beach. I remembered what it was, then: the wreck of the Helvetia, some cargo ship full of timber from Norway, beached in eighteen-eighty something. The first mate fell in love with one of the girls in the village, but she refused to marry him and he fucked off, leaving her to die a spinster sixty years later: a true story, but not a new one. The shores of Swansea and the Gower are full of wrecks. All kinds of wrecks.

The bus laboured on, swollen with passengers, back down the same lanes, and some new ones too, seeing it had to stop in Oxwich and a few other seaside places. There was a lot more traffic now, all coming the other way, out of Swansea, and it was a squeeze in places. Perhaps it was something to do with our driver, who was a local boy alright, some guy in his fifties with the usual tattoos and sideburns. He had a line on everything and everybody.

'Ooh, there's drivers down there,' he would say, when

somebody didn't pull over, or reverse eighty yards to let him through. Later this would get abbreviated to just:

'Drivers!' which he sort of hissed. There was a constant stream of it.

'Wait there!'

'You're going too fast!'

'Turn your wheels in!'

'There's a wall there, love!'

'Three women, in a row, I ask you!'

People thought he was very funny for the first five minutes. Outside Oxwich he harassed a geriatric in a Peugeot estate until he drove into a hedge and they applauded. But they were all very quiet by the time we got into town. As a matter of fact the guy opposite me called him a fucking idiot: we'd had five near-shunts by the time we'd got to Uplands. He spent half his driving time reading from a laminated sheet of route stops, and the other half on his hands free, moaning to some sympathetic or hapless woman about how he'd really had enough today. He made driving a bus look like something the equivalent of running a hospital single-handed. A living rebuttal of the maxim that if you want something done, you should ask a busy person, he could have looked busy standing alone in a darkened room. A one-man trade union, was what he was, membership and executive all rolled into one, making up the constitution as he went along, feeding off the traditional unity between yourself and whatever it is you think you want at the time. It's the only kind of solidarity you see these days.

Whoever our driver was, I had surrendered to a boundless loathing for him by the time we pulled back into bay number three, but maybe that was partly the thirst. Even those little sherbet and lemonade saloons had got me salivating on the way back, and I did think about getting off, but they wouldn't have served me and then I would have been stuck seven or eight miles out of town. It would have been like drinking saltwater when you're lost at sea. After I'd disembarked, though, he did something that knocked me flat. I only stuck around because I was too dumbstruck to move.

After everybody had got off, there was a bag on the bus. A briefcase, to be precise. It had been there when we got on. If I had to guess, I'd say one of the morning commuters had brought it on and then forgot about it. I saw the guy go up to it, try to open it, which he couldn't, because it had a combination lock, and then call a colleague over. And not ten foot from me I heard him pronounce, with utter seriousness, that a bomb scare was underway. Lost property, they used to call it.

Within ten minutes a patrol car appeared at the top of the street with the sirens on. One of the coppers inside tried to open it too, but like I said, it was a combination lock, and I guess he didn't want to force it so he called in and then started clearing the area. Everyone's shift was over now. The bus driver who'd had enough got to go home early, along with everyone else, and thirty or forty coppers turned up, a car or a van at a time, including a couple of sergeants and (for some reason) two armed response officers, and a big white van from the Ordnance part of the Royal Logistics, carrying one of those green robots on caterpillar tracks and a couple of NCOs. They cleared the bus station and then they cleared the car park and then they cleared the street I was standing on. I asked the cop who was shooing me away about it.

He didn't look at me for more than a second, something very fleeting, a glance, really.

'Fuck off,' he said. 'Or I'll lock you up.'

I found out later that all this had already happened three

times in the last fortnight. The war on terror rages on. If there really was a war, and somebody was fighting us, then here in Swansea, they have already won. We were just looking for an excuse to finally lie down, and blame somebody else.

When I turned my back on it and came to my senses I remembered where I was, and why, and where I'd been earlier. I remembered Little Hill House and the woman with the two little kids, and more or less at the same time I remembered I was thirsty, with the sort of thirst that makes you shake, and up the road by the lights I could see the Singleton Hotel, sort of crouched there, some sort of invisible smile of apology locked in its mortar. And I really have made tremendous progress today, I thought to myself, I've done a lot of good work. You deserve a few tonight. Today you've really had enough: he'd had enough, we've all had enough.

'Oh, fucking hell,' said John the barman. 'Not you.'

It was the smell, apparently. I didn't know whether they were taking the piss or not. If they weren't, I felt sorry for the people on the bus. I couldn't go into the public conveniences because of the bomb scare, so I went round the corner to the Spar and bought a can of Lynx, and I must have used half of it right there on the pavement.

'Alright, but you'll have to sit in the breakfast room,' said John.

'Well, I'm not going to sit out here with you cocksuckers,' I said, and John told me to watch my manners and gave me a pint. I don't know what of. He gave me a lot of them. I sat there in the dark of the breakfast room pouring the stuff down me, spirits and all, watching the strange reflected glow up on the artex of all those distant blue lights. They were still getting worked up about it, about the fuss over the way, maybe a hundred trained professionals, acting like utter twats. It was a chance for some summer overtime, I suppose. In the distance you could hear a whole chorus of sirens kick up, like a very bad orchestra getting into tune. I thought about Little Hill House. I don't remember much after that.

Maybe about three or four in the morning, sometime before sunrise, I was on my knees in the dirt, somewhere near the marina, throwing up. I didn't make it back to the Heathfield, was the first thing I remember thinking. Some voice from along the way told me to fuck off and throw up somewhere else, some other rough sleeper, and when I could move I sidled down the sea wall until I got to the observatory, and laid me down there. My guts were shot. I couldn't work out when I'd last had something to eat: three or four days, maybe. You just don't get round to thinking about it.

I didn't really sleep after that. The sun was up by six, and maybe if I found somewhere shady I could have a siesta in the afternoon, but that seemed like ten or twenty years away. It was a pretty rough morning, one of the worst. It was so bad I went off in search of some fresh water, to clean myself up a bit. I wasn't going to drink any of it. A glass of water the next day and sometimes you're on the floor again. I don't know why that is. One of the ground floor flats in the Harbour Lights block had a standing pipe outside it, so I crept into the garden and used that. I have no doubt that if anyone had seen me the police would have been around sharpish, but it was still not far off six. I ran my head under it and saw half the beach fall out of it, then rinsed my mouth out, and then swallowed a couple of tentative mouthfuls. I didn't feel drunk again. I didn't feel anything but bad.

I went and sat on the steps of the observatory, on the other side, away from the sun, and stared at my shoes, and wondered if I had stopped throwing up. My fucking shoes. I was losing a sole. I was turning into something from a Charlie Chaplin film. In a while I saw a few people come onto the beach, joggers and people with dogs, all going about their lives, enjoying themselves.

'Fucking cunts,' I said. But I didn't shout it.

Then I got up, somehow, somehow proved capable of standing, and after doing the standing thing moved off in the direction of town, like a man who had been recently concussed. My joints weren't working, my belly was full of bile and my mouth was full of cold ashes. I kept going, though. Maybe it was something to do. I knew exactly what I must have looked like. You have seen dozens of men walking that way through the middle of British cities, alone, at strange times.

I found a little stretch of shade under the prison, near Bath Street, and sat down again there, with my back against its high stone wall. The rush hour came on, with its traffic and fumes and pedestrian throng, but it didn't make things much worse. Nothing could have done. I lay there in the foetal position like one of those people you see all the time. When things had calmed down I went and had a look at Merlin Auto Parts, from as far away as I was able, to see if my mark was working today. He wasn't. He would have to come in soon: he'd hardly been there at all this week. Then I went back to my spot under the prison wall, which was still free, and sat there like a Mexican without a sombrero, until I felt well enough to walk more or less normally. They were good ideas, I reckon, those sombreros.

'Fuck off,' said John the barman. 'Absolutely fuck off.'

'I only want a cup of tea,' I said.

I couldn't remember ever going into pub and asking for a cup of tea. I think this was the first time.

'I'll have a pint if I makes you feel any better.'

'No, have a cup of tea, mun.'

It was a cup and all, not a mug, a cup and saucer and a little bourbon biscuit in a plastic wrapper, and I took it all, feeling a little ridiculous, but not displeased, over to a little round table by the window, and sat down. I didn't go into the breakfast room. Anybody that had to go into the Singleton straight after opening wasn't going to mind me.

I don't remember ever picking the actual cup up, don't remember ever lifting it to my lips. Very likely it was still full of tea when I heard a nervous tapping on the window next to me, and looked out to see Scotty, who in direct contrast to me, seemed absolutely unable to stay still.

'It's all kicked off,' he said, when I went out.

'What do you mean?'

'They've sent Teen to the fucking hospital.'

'Who's Teen?'

'Kind of a mate. They sent him to the hospital. Did his ribs and one of his arms and probably ruptured his spleen, they say, the hospital says.'

Scotty was more or less hopping on the spot.

'Who?' I said. 'Why?'

'It's that dealer, isn't it? And his mates.'

'Oh dear,' I said. It was all I could think of. It wasn't particularly sympathetic, but then I wasn't in the mood.

'They're looking for us. They came to the Heathfield in the middle of the night and caused a right fucking barney.'

'Ohhh,' I said. ' I see. Right. Shit.'

I understood now. I remembered. I wasn't surprised.

'What are we going to do?'

'Have you reported it to the police?' I said.

He managed a laugh. It was forced, but I admired the effort.

'Stop fucking about,' he said.

'No, seriously, you should. The police in Swansea are very keen to make inroads into the local homeless heroin community. They need to know your needs and fears. You need to help them to help you. We all need to work together for a more just society.'

'You're not funny.'

'Alright,' I said. 'I need to talk to some people about it. Get the lowdown on a few things. It shouldn't take long.'

I pushed open the door of the Singleton.

'Don't go back into the pub!' sang Scotty, plaintively. 'I told you to stop fucking about.'

'I'm not. I'm on it. This,' I said, pointing inside, 'is my wavelength. My frequency. I don't hear things anywhere else. You work your side of the street and I'll work mine.'

Scotty's eyes glazed over momentarily.

'Steve McQueen,' he said. 'Bullitt.'

'Probably,' I said. 'I'll be out in ten minutes.'

And I had that pint after all.

'What do you know about the Blethyn family, John?' I said, leaning against the bar. John gave me that look of displeasure he always gave people when they were so forward as to call him by his Christian name, especially if they came in just after opening and slept on the beach.

'What about them?'

'They're one of the families, aren't they?'

Every town has them, even the little market ones. John nodded and said he supposed so, and showed how reluctant he was to talk to me by wiping the bar down, which wasn't something you saw him do very often.

'How many of them are there? Or were there?'

'Five,' he said, eventually. 'Four brothers and a sister.'

'What are they like?'

John went on rubbing the far end of the bar. I waved a fiver at him and he took it without a word of thanks and poured himself a pint.

'The two eldest are both locked up. I heard they tried to do over a cash and carry in Liverpool. They've been in a couple of years now, I don't know when they're getting out. The next one is Tomos, I think, a big fat thick fuck, although I wouldn't say it to his face, mind. He's been inside too, but only for little stretches. Assault and things like that. He's another nutter. The only reason he's not in now is probably because he's too dull to get into anything serious. Strong, mind, Christ. Then Rebecca, who I'm sure you know about, the mad one with the ninety-inch waist, then James.'

'James Blethyn?'

'Yeah.'

'From Llanelli?'

'Dunno. Maybe. He's a half-brother, 'cause their dad went off. I think they lived out there for a while then, yeah. Anyway, that's the five of them. James Blethyn is the youngest. He's still around.'

'Fucking hell,' I said. 'I thought he went to London.'

'Yeah. Well he came back.'

I finished my drink and reached into my pocket for another note. When John saw me he necked his and put his empty glass purposefully down onto the bar next to mine.

'Same again?' he asked.

'Yeah.'

He poured us each another pint, and took for both out of my tenner. Again, not a murmur of gratitude.

'Cheers,' I said, when he served me mine, just to add a bit of irony to it. 'What's he doing these days, then, James Blethyn?'

'Runs James Blethyn Enforcements, doesn't he. On Mansel Street?'

'He has an office? An actual office?'

'Well, yeah.'

'What does he do in it?'

'Dunno. Debt collecting, stuff like that.'

'I used to be in that, years ago. Exact same game. That's strictly for cunts, that is.'

'You don't say,' said John the barman, slowly, but I let it pass.

'Do you think he has much clout with the dealers in town? The drug dealers?'

'How the fuck would I know?'

I looked at him, a man that sat in the Singleton most of the days and nights of his life, not even able to get properly drunk, for something like thirteen or fourteen grand a year. No, I thought, how would he know something like that? How would he know anything? He has his beat and he sticks to it.

'Does he do security?' I asked. 'Does he run bouncers?'

'A bit, I think.'

Then he wouldn't be a stranger to them, I thought. If you ran a security firm then there was a good chance you had some truck with the drugs trade. Even if you weren't into it at all, you came into contact with it, because bouncers like to work out, like to be big, so bouncers take steroids. And the guys that sell steroids probably sell a few other things as well, and know plenty of other people who do too. That was one connection. But if a security firm was into drugs, and some of them are, then you were talking about another whole level. If they ran security for a big nightclub, say, then they'd get to choose who dealt in there and who didn't, and when you have to make choices like that you do it solely on violence and intimidation. And when a security firm runs on violence and intimidation you were practically a whisker away from racketeering. You'd be there doing it without thinking about it. That's what some of these firms are like. I wondered if James Blethyn Enforcements was one of them. It would tie in very well with the debt collecting.

'Why do you want to know, anyway?' asked John, half a pint later.

'I think I've pissed him off.'

'How'd you manage that? I wouldn't have thought James Blethyn'd give a toss about someone like you.'

'Well, Rebecca Blethyn…' I began.

'You fucking cuntox,' he said.

'It wasn't anything sexual! It wasn't anything romantic! She just wanted me to do some work for her.'

'Dun't matter. It's all the same, to her.'

I finished my drink and thanked him for his company and kind words. Scotty was smoking a cigarette on the other side of the street, and he didn't look appreciably calmer in any way. I crossed the street with an open hand held up to him, and said I had some news to tell him, and he told me I was a twat who had been in the pub for almost half an hour, and then I brought him up to date about the Blethyns, leaving out the little upset with Becca. I had this inkling that Scotty's supply problem had more to do with me than he realised.

'So what?' he said.

'We're going to have to talk to them. Well, I am.'

Scotty said he didn't see what good that would do, although not in as many words.

'I went to school with the youngest brother. Bryngwyn Comprehensive, Llanelli. We were friends. Well, we weren't friends, exactly. We weren't friends at all. But we knew each other. That should count for something, I reckon, if you've gone to school with someone and not got on their tits.'

'We'll have to get you sobered up,' he said, after he'd lit another cigarette.

'I am sober.'

'More sober. We'll have to get you some coffee and a cold shower or something.'

'Nah, that's a myth, all that stuff. Don't worry, I'll start sobering up when I get in there.'

Scotty looked at me briefly, from head to foot.

'You're going to need a haircut, a shave, a good wash and a complete change of clothes. And coffee. Coffee and a hot meal. How much money have you got?'

Perhaps he had a point.

'Maybe another thirty or forty quid,' I said. 'Why?'

'Tesco's.'

'They won't let me in,' I said.

'Good.'

Scotty spent seventeen pounds of my money in the supermarket on a pair of black, rust-finish jeans and a pale green long-sleeved t-shirt. He got me a three-pack of black cotton socks as well, but he slipped those into his jacket. I could have got them all cheaper in Asda's, I know, but it was further away. Still.

'No shoes,' he said, when I saw him coming back with his carrier bags. I was sitting on a perforated metal bench not far from the sliding doors, or I had been, until security moved me on. When Scotty found me I was sitting on the concrete slabs around the multi-storey over the road, with my back against the brick. 'We'll have to go to TK Maxx for the shoes.'

'Fine. But we need to cut through Bath Street.'

'Bath Street? Where the fuck is that? How can we cut through somewhere that's nowhere near our fucking way?'

We couldn't, was the short and unspoken answer, but we went anyway. I told Scotty that I needed to keep an eye on a place down there as part of this case I was working on, this little case of my own, and he was curious enough, in a contemptuous sort of way, to tag along. Anyway, I was insistent, and it wasn't, in truth, that far away from where we were.

The first thing I noticed; there was a four-year-old BMW

parked in the tiny staff parking area that I hadn't seen before. It wasn't a bad car. It's probably his, I thought to myself. The building had two big bay doors and it being the middle of summer both of them were wide open. I could see the building had been used as a garage once, and the doors were big enough to drive a small truck through, and behind them I could see a couple of inspection pits covered over with steel plates, as I walked by on the other side of the road, as casually as I could muster. The sun was in the wrong place to see into the office windows upstairs.

'Well?' said Scotty. I had slowed down until I was barely moving at all, and then this dark-haired man comes down the stairs at the back, dark-haired, mid-twenties, talking in a relaxed, confident way with an older guy in a brown storesman's coat. The younger man was wearing a pair of khaki trousers with a brown belt and a blue shirt. He looked pretty smart.

'That's my son,' I said.

We had both stopped walking now. I don't remember what Scotty said. He said something like what the fuck, or maybe, you have a fucking son? Something like that, I'm sure. I can only remember what I said. That's my son. It was not a sentence I had ever expected to say. I must have started walking then, I was fairly terrified he would start to take some notice of us, to wonder what we were doing, and if he did that I had pretty much blown my cover, and I wasn't sure that it was such a good idea for that to ever happen. We reached the end of the street and sort of stopped there, and I felt some sort of expectancy in Scotty, some waiting for an answer, but it's more likely I was just projecting. We stood there in the shadow of the traffic lights, waiting for the change. It's complicated, I wanted to say, but it wasn't. Like so many things in life, it was excruciatingly simple when you boiled it down.

'I buggered off,' I said. 'I don't really talk about it.'

The shoes in TK Maxx were fake leather trainers and they cost twelve quid.

Then we went up Mount Pleasant to the Heathfield, and I signed in for the night, even though it was mid-afternoon, because I didn't want to lose my nice new room. I showered, twice, and I shaved. I had to look in the mirror. It took a long time.

When I was dry and clean-faced, with some mouldy towel wrapped around my waist, Scotty came in and handed me the carrier bags, and I yanked a few labels off and put them on. They fitted pretty well, I suppose, as well as modern clothes are supposed to fit anybody. The jeans were the size I'd asked for, but they seemed a tad baggy, and I wondered if that was the idea or if it was just me: they say you start to lose weight, when you're in the final stages. Then again, I couldn't remember the last time I'd had anything to eat. Not for days, I was sure of it. I'd had that biscuit in the Singleton.

I must have been standing there thinking like that for a while.

'Come on,' said Scotty. 'Let's go.'

'Give us a minute, we only just got here. I'm knackered. I feel like a stroke victim.'

'You're knackered? I'm the one that's done all the shopping. And you still need a haircut. We'll miss him if we're not careful. Let's go.'

I went to a barber's on Mansel Street where they did not trim me so much as shear me, like a sheep, but then they only charged four fifty and they slapped a load of gel on it afterwards. There wasn't much black left up there now, just a lot of grey and some white at the sides. It was fighting a losing battle up there, on two fronts, because my hairline was receding too. It was way back from the temples already. By the looks of things, though, it would win out. Something told me it would last the course.

When I stepped outside it was a quarter to five.

'Smart,' said Scotty. 'You ready?'

'I don't have a jacket.'

'What?'

'I like to wear a jacket. It makes me comfortable. There's still the one from my suit.'

'Forget it,' he said. 'Your suit days are over. You looked like Rab C. Nesbitt, anyway.'

I wasn't happy about not having a jacket. I was prepared to make changes, you know, but one step at a time. In the end Scotty gave me his, some massive pseudo-military job with half dozen belts and buckles hanging off it. It wasn't in my line, but it made me feel better, made me feel less frail. I looked bigger. I looked... I saw myself in a shop window.

'I look like an e-victim,' I said. 'One of those guys that took too much ecstasy back in the early nineties.'

I was a middle-aged homeless alcoholic dressed like a music promoter. We moved along the street a little.

'No,' said Scotty. 'Not with that face.'

I wasn't sure just what he meant by that. Then we were there: James Blethyn Enforcements was three doors down from the barber. I didn't want it to be there, but it was, and so was I. Suddenly I felt very nervous, I felt that useless hollow energy billowing in my stomach. I looked at Scotty and found myself wondering, what did he really hope would come out of all this? His faith distressed me. Anyone's did, if it was in me.

'Don't worry, mate,' he said, 'you look fine. You know those Benetton adverts where they get old people to dress up in really nice clothes? That's what you look like.'

'I have no idea what you're talking about,' I said.

And I went inside. Alone. I figured if it all went pear-shaped then the fewer people who knew what Scotty looked like, the better.

In terms of front the office didn't have a lot. I don't suppose it was the sort of business that needed a lobby and a leather suite and complimentary magazines on the coffee table. It had a front of an entirely different kind. I could feel it, and all I could see was a small empty room with a windowed counter at the other end, like you used to see in old banks. There was nobody behind it, but I knew what it was for: it was for taking money. Taking was a speciality of the house. I breathed in, as much as I could, and smelt the air. I was on familiar territory after all.

There was no sign of life anywhere. It was almost as if they had shut up shop and left without remembering to lock the front door, but that would never happen. They knew all about security in here. There was a little white buzzer screwed down to the narrow counter-top and I pressed it, I held it down and made myself count to three. I didn't want to sound timid. A man appeared in one of the windows, but he made it clear he was in no hurry.

'Robin Llywelyn to see James Blethyn,' I said, like I had an appointment.

'Got an appointment?' said the man. I don't suppose I was in any state to pull the wool over anyone's eyes, not unless you were Rebecca Blethyn.

'No,' I said. 'But he'll see me.'

'How'd you know?'

I felt in my pocket for a business card, but it wasn't my pocket, wasn't my jacket. My jacket was in a bin somewhere, and I had run out of business cards seven months ago. I had given my last one to a nurse in north Bristol, I remembered. And I wasn't a private detective any more.

'Just ask him, will you. Then we can find out.'

'What's it concerning?'

'Whatever he likes,' I said. The man grunted and shifted out of view. Minutes later a door opened to the left of the counter and he gestured me through it impatiently, and then walked me down a short corridor and gave the door at the end three quick knocks. On the other side of it I could hear the racing channel on a very quiet television, and then I heard nothing.

'Enter,' said a voice. The man held the door open for me and then more or less pushed me through it. Inside was an office which was a little bigger than the first room I'd been in, with a series of windows along the rear wall which probably looked out onto some back street, and although the blinds were drawn on them they still let through a lot of the powerful July sun. The rays sneaked through here and there, and if the room was at all dusty you would have seen it floating in the air, but it was spotless. To my right the wall was covered in a shelving unit that held neatly arranged box files and whisky bottles and a large flatscreen television, and to my left the wall was bare except for a framed centrepage from the *Welsh Mirror*, showing the team that beat England in Twickenham in 1999. In front of the blinds was a large desk with not a lot on it and James Blethyn, I guessed, sat behind it.

'Thank you,' he said, looking over my shoulder, and I heard the door close behind me. A little silence hung in the air. James's face was unreadable, although I was pretty sure mine wasn't.

'There's the small matter of my sister and some money,' he said.

'Yeah, I'm sorry about that,' I said, in a friendly sort of voice that I hoped suggested I recognised him in some way.

'How much did she give you?'

'A hundred and fifty,' I lied. I didn't mean to, it just popped out.

The fat woman's brother smiled coldly.

'We know how much she gave you. She's our sister. God, you're a lying bastard. And you're in no position to be a lying bastard, are you?'

'Why's that?' I asked.

James Blethyn got up and went over to the unit and poured himself a couple of fingers of what looked like Laphroig, and then added a couple of ice cubes from the ice bucket. He took his drink back over to his desk and then motioned to me to sit down.

I sat.

'Don't believe me?' he said. 'Ask me what you came here to ask me, then. We'll see how it plays out.'

'Leave Scotty alone,' I said. 'He's done fuck all.'

Blethyn laughed.

'Who's Scotty?'

'You know who he is. When your brother Tomos wanted to do a number on me he... he didn't. He didn't think I cared. So you went after Scotty instead. Somehow, you made him persona non grata with the dealers in town. He couldn't buy.'

James Blethyn took another sip from his glass and leant back leisurely in his chair.

'Some friends would think that was a good thing, you know.'

I shrugged.

'He's an addict,' I said.

'Yes. Getting a bit worked up about now, is he?' he chortled. 'You see,' he said, 'you still have to behave yourself, Magnum. Whether you're dying or not.'

'I'm not dying,' I said reflexively. 'That was just a lie. To get him off me.'

Blethyn studied me with mild curiosity.

'Well we'll see,' he said, 'won't we?'

I looked at the whisky in the glass. It was good whisky, that. You'd feel it on the back of your tongue and all the way down your throat and in the pit of your belly, and it would sit there like a gentle fire, and warm you, in a way that sunshine couldn't, in a place where I felt very cold. It looked like liquid copper. I looked at it there on the desk and swallowed.

'I was drunk,' I said. I tried to shrug but there was some tightness between my shoulderblades.

'Maybe if you reimbursed her the money you'd already pissed against the wall, and added something for our troubles. I know you don't have a lot of money, let's say five. Not much, is it? Five hundred, a sincere apology, and we could put it behind us. Consider it a favour.'

'It's more complicated than that,' I said, still looking at the glass.

'Not if I say it isn't.'

'We had some problems with a dealer in the John Griffith Street flats. He pulled a knife on us, pretty much. We had to knock him out. They're after us now.'

'Aw,' he said. 'You held your little friend's hand on one of his shopping trips, did you? I'm sure he's glad you came along now.'

He finished his whisky.

'You're both fucked,' he said.

'That's my point. If we're fucked then I can't pay you back, can I?'

'So?'

'Wouldn't you rather have the money? I mean who am I, in the grand scheme of things? I'm a nobody. You don't need to make a big show of sorting me out, right? Let me get you your five hundred quid. I'll work it off. I'll do whatever you want, within reason. Just, you know, fair play, this doesn't have anything to do with Scotty.'

'You'll work it off,' he laughed. 'What sort of guarantee can you give me on that?'

'I'll tell you about why I had to leave Bristol,' I said. And I did. I filled him in about the last time I ever amounted to anything. Christ, if you'd told me then I had further to fall, I wouldn't have believed you.

'Stands to reason there should be somebody after you. Why else turn up down here? To go sunbathing at the beach? I don't think so. Ah well. The police,' he nodded. 'Oldest firm in the world. I'll check it out, of course.'

'You do that, as long as you don't tread on any sleeping dogs. Do you remember Richard Jenkins? He's a police surgeon out there. Ask him.'

'I will,' he said.

James Blethyn more or less owned me completely now, and I wondered if he knew it yet, because if he traded that information lightly I was a dead man. Or, at least, my death would take some other form than that I had been long expecting. It didn't make that much of a difference now, I guessed.

'So will you help me out, here?' I said. 'Will you speak to this dealer?'

'Yeah. He's not one of my boys, though. He's one of the Neath lot. Could require a bit of diplomacy. Did you take anything off him?'

'Only what Scotty paid for,' I lied. If you lied all the time then some of them had to get through. 'How'd you get him off the list, if he wasn't one of your boys?'

'I put word out he was a snitch.'

'Is he?'

'Only a little one. Grasses out other dealers he doesn't like and stuff like that, otherwise someone would have taken him on the long drive by now.'

'Well, I'm willing to work things out.'

'Willing? Christ. Willing doesn't come into it. I know what your problem is. Take a guess.'

I could think of a few things.

'You have no conception of duty. Yeah, we all know about you, Magnum. You're a little too fond of the disappearing act, aren't you?'

'So we can work this out?' I asked, again, helplessly.

'Yeah,' he said. 'You can work it out, maybe. You work for me now.'

And that was it: clang. Somewhere far off in the distance, I heard a steel door close. I would hear it again later, but I heard it here first.

TWO

DUTY

I

It worked out like this:

James Blethyn told me to get my stuff and come back in an hour. I didn't have any stuff to get, except maybe two pairs of black socks, which Scotty had lifted for me that afternoon, so I didn't bother going back to the Heathfield. I just crossed over the road to where my Glaswegian friend was waiting with minimal subtlety outside Studio 95. That's the biggest brothel in town, by the way, great location, slap bang in the centre. Used to be the offices for the General and Municipal Workers' Union, back in the day. Before we all moved on.

I told Scotty if he lay low for a couple of days everything would be okay. The Blethyns were on team. If he was still pissed off about me, he didn't seem it, didn't seem bothered about anything except the score, now he knew it was being sorted. Me, I was flattered that somebody in this world thought that somebody else mattered to me, mattered enough to be fucked about with, and I wanted to enjoy that slender aura of humanity for as long as I could, without diluting it with the old familiar flavour of failure and betrayal. It was kind of touching. Then I went to get some chips.

Except, there were no chip shops in town. I hadn't noticed that before. You could get yourself a kebab or a curry or a Chinese, there were plenty of hard-working men from

Pakistan, India, Turkey and the Middle Kingdom who'd be willing to knock something up for you in that line, sure. There were some young black and Asian kids in McDonalds and Burger King who for the minimum legal wage would sell you a burger that probably had no phlegm in it at all. But there wasn't anybody in town anymore who would sell you a bag of fish and chips. It sort of depressed me. So I went into Wetherspoons and had two Guinnesses, which is as good as food, practically.

I was back in front of the Enforcements office more or less on time. There was a sleek purple people carrier there waiting for me with tinted windows, and the big side door slid all the way back. James Blethyn was sat in the back and the man I'd met in his office was sat in the driver's seat. James shut the door after I'd got in, because I didn't have a clue how to do it, and we headed off east, towards the river. It was a pretty nice way to travel, sailing through town staring out at people that couldn't stare back, encased in leather upholstery, in a car where the loudest noise was the hum of the air conditioning. It must have been eighty degrees outside, and in here it felt like a cold Bass. We passed the big gun monument and crossed the Tawe bridge.

'What have you got lined up for me, then?' I said, as casually as I could muster, as I saw the sanctuary of town disappear in the driver's rear view. Fuck knows where we were going, but it didn't look like anywhere where there'd be a lot of witnesses. James Blethyn sat next to me and smiled and said nothing. He was probably enjoying it. Then we parked up next to a fifties pub called the Cape Horner.

I suppose Swansea was known for something once. Rounding the Cape was the most dangerous thing a sailor could do, treacherous straits, fierce wind against you, the fastest current on earth, and flowing the wrong way too, poor visibility, uncharted waters, sub-zero temperatures, all of that. They had been rounding the Cape for centuries before they discovered Antarctica, a whole new continent, just waiting for them below the horizon: no one wanted to take the risk of going any further south than they had to. Below forty degrees, there is no law, below fifty, there is no God. That's what they used to say. Swansea had more Cape Horners than any other port in the country, and that includes London, taking coal from the valleys round to Chile and bringing back copper, coming back in barques loaded to the gunwales with metal, a couple of years each trip. Huge, stately things covered in masts and sails. Famous, they were. Good old Catherine Jones got her middle name from one. It all stopped when the Panama Canal opened, which was decades before the pub was even built, but I suppose it was just possible that one or two of the old Cape Horners had actually been in it, when it was new. A couple of Cape Horners and nobody else since, by the looks of things. Inside I could just about make out the feeble glimmer of a fruit machine features board, the only visible trace of life.

'Look after the car,' said James Blethyn, and they went in. There was a clock on the dashboard that said six ten. When they came out it was nine forty-nine. I was convinced that they had done it as part of my punishment, that those three hours and thirty-nine minutes were part of an elaborately worked-out programme of retribution. I'd had two pints at midday and two Guinnesses in the afternoon, and that was it. That had been my total alcohol consumption for the day, so I was thirsty when I'd got into the car, and by seven o'clock I thought my hair was falling out in clumps. It was all I could do to stop myself from shaking, and perhaps I even failed at that. When they got in the car the pub smell was so strong you could have got half a glass out of them if you picked them up and wrung them. I didn't think it was advisable.

Minutes later, maybe another half a mile down the A483, we pulled off by an old railway bridge, and passed part of the old steelworks at Crymlyn Burrows and drove through a pair of chainlink gates. In the dying light of day I recognised the flat, darkly reflective expanse of King's Dock down on our right. We took another right and drove a little way down that bit of man-made land that separated it from the Queen's Dock next door, two long rectangular bodies of motionless water, without a single boat on them. The five big jetties in Queen's Dock were all empty. They had been for years.

Halfway down we stopped at a small industrial unit that had clearly been thrown up on the foundations of something that was older and grander and not there anymore. You could tell from the ocean of vacant concrete around it, vacant save for the remains of some load-bearing walls and the weeds. James's man got out and unlocked the personal door to the side of the roller-shutter, and stepped inside. Seconds later I heard the hum of an electric motor. Then James got out and waved for me to follow him, and once the big shutter had rolled far enough up for us to walk under it without our heads bowed we went on in. I could see there was a decent amount of stuff inside, big square packages stacked up on wooden palettes to about ten foot high, but it was too dim for me to see exactly what it was. Most of it was bound tight in thick, blue plastic wrap.

'Well, this is it,' said James. It was too dark to see his face. A little way off I could see the other man, but he wasn't doing anything but standing where he was. 'Stay here and look after this place.'

'What?' I said.

'Security,' he said. 'This place doesn't have any at the moment. So you stay here and if you hear anyone snooping around outside make a racket and sound busy.'

'I think that's about the limit of my abilities, security wise,' I said.

'Yeah, well. That's what you're doing for me, for the time being. When are your benefits due?'

'What day is it?'

'Thursday.'

'Tomorrow.'

'Well, Gavin here will have to come and give you a lift into town. Are you claiming housing?'

'I don't think so. I was staying at the Heathfield.'

'The shelter? Oh for fuck's sake. Well, we'll sort you out with a few lines when you go in. You should be getting housing. Or rather, I should be getting your housing.'

The two of them made to leave. Gavin hit the down switch for the shutters and then went out through the personal door, locked that, and started the car.

'Don't touch the spirits,' James said, as a parting shot, craning his head under the descending steel. 'Remember, I'm counting on you to be cheaper than a dog.'

I didn't quite get that, seeing how I was being locked in a warehouse. Not touching the spirits seemed an inevitability. The muffled laughter from the other side of the metal suggested he knew what he was on about, anyway, and with a final clang, a sound I had foreseen on Mansel Street, the shutter finally dropped to the floor, and I was alone, in total darkness in an unknown building.

I was not surprised: when bad things happen to me I rarely am, these days. I told myself it couldn't be far off ten in the evening, and that Gavin was coming round tomorrow morning, so I couldn't have much more than twelve hours of it. And then I took a deep breath, which did not sound too good at all, all alone in there, amplified by the acoustics, what with my invaded lungs, my clotted chest, my breath of the dying, and the fear started to rise. Well, I have lived below forty degrees most of my life, I thought, and we will soon see what's south of fifty.

The first thing you need is a light switch, I thought to myself, stick to the walls until you find something, and I hobbled tentatively towards one in a fairly random direction, what with there being walls on all sides of the building. After about three or four steps waving my arms in front of me I suppose I got cocky, or impatient, and I stepped up my pace until I smacked into one of those square stacks of goods, wrapped in blue plastic, piled up on palettes. And I didn't even have time to swear, because the noise it made I recognised instantly: a dull, metallic boing. I can't think of another sound like it. Maybe the sound that a fuel can makes when you put it down on the tarmac. That stack was full of multipack boxes of canned drink. It could, I suppose, have been Coca Cola, but I didn't think so. It was already singing to me.

It must have taken me over half an hour to get the plastic wrap off. It was thick stuff, and all I had was my hands, and later, when things got the better of me, my teeth. Then, from the tear I had rent, from the sodden mass of plastic and cardboard, I extracted a single can, from the corner of its box. I felt the gentle tug as it came free from its plastic collar, and then held it aloft, feeling its familiar weight in my hand. And it actually glowed. It shone a light. And when it faded, I reached for another one.

I remember sitting on the bare concrete floor, surrounded by empties, realising where I had heard about this sort of thing before. The Discovery Channel. Ancient Egypt. This was what they did, with their top people, sealed them in their tomb with ample provisions for the afterlife and let them get on with it. That was just what it felt like. It wasn't unpleasant. Until the morning, when I awoke to the sound of creaking steel, and a shaft of widening light almost biblical in its intensity, to find myself curled up in the dust, stiff and unprepared, surrounded by hollow cans of Harp, booze that belonged to someone else, and a silhouette whose tone of voice suggested I wasn't with the top people anywhere, not on any list. There was time left to serve, and an ending more inglorious.

'I see you made yourself at home,' said Gavin. 'Fucking tramp.'

'What time is it?' I asked, like I cared.

'Gone ten. Get yourself into gear, we have to be into town and back by half twelve.'

That didn't seem too difficult to me, as long as the queues in the job centre weren't horrific. The drive in didn't take more than minutes. I thought he'd head up the high street and park nearby, but he went onto the roundabout at the end of the Kingsway and went all the way around until Orchard Street, where he let me out.

'Go down to the lawyers' on the roundabout and introduce yourself,' he said. 'I'll be along in a minute.'

I couldn't find the lawyers' at first. It wasn't that I couldn't see it, in truth I saw it and walked past it four or five times, but it didn't really register. It looked nothing like the lawyers' firms I used to know, Jones Jones and Davies and all that lot, a brass plaque on a doorway and three names etched onto a front window. This lawyers' had big glass windows like a carpet showroom or something, and a bright plastic hoarding above it like you'd get on a shop front. Big blue plastic letters spelt the words 'The People's Champion.' It looked like a booking agency for superheroes.

I pushed my way in, and found that the doors opened automatically, and then stood there in front of reception like I'd fallen in.

'I'm Robin Llywelyn,' I said, when I caught the girl's eye.

She came back with a man who wasn't far into his thirties, some guy six and a half foot tall who looked like a regular and active member of one of the city's better rugby clubs.

'You're from James Blethyn?'

I nodded.

'So where's Gavin?'

'He's parking up.'

'Good. As soon as he gets here we're out the door. James has asked me to maximise your claim. You're staying on at the Heathfield, is that right?'

I filled him in on my personal details while we waited. I didn't think I was getting any housing because I was staying in a shelter, I wasn't getting jobseeker's allowance but I was on the long-term sick. Then he told me that when we got in the place I should shut up and agree with everything he said, and then Gavin arrived and we walked down the street.

As I went in I reached for a numbered ticket from the dispenser but the senior partner tore it roughly out of my hands.

'You won't be needing that,' he said. 'Sit down there.'

And he strode purposefully off between the kiosks, to the back desk, as if he managed the place. I cast my eye about me and saw all the sort of stuff you'd expect to see, the usual listlessness and melodrama and the odd spot of genuinely affronted dignity. A huge black guy in dreadlocks was pretending to sob, very badly, in front of three customer advisors, as I believe they're now called, who stood around fussing over him in that sincere but meaningless way that Welsh people have. It was hard to tell if the act was working for him. Reading backwards, through the paper, I saw an advert in the window for production line jobs somewhere outside Milan.

'We're done,' said the solicitor, appearing very quickly out of nowhere. 'Sign the book and let's go.'

There was another customer advisor standing next to him with my benefits book open in his hand, pointing with a biro to the relevant box. The biro had a small length of chain dangling from its top, from where it had been wrenched from its cradle. I wondered why they called them customer advisors. Presumably somebody in government hoped the whole thing would be privatised one day, and thought that pretending it was a business already might speed things up a bit. If it was a business customers would be the last thing they'd call us, I'm sure. Not on the golf course, anyway.

'What happened in there, then?' I asked, when we were outside.

'You're signed on for housing and long-term sick. Because you're a homeless alcoholic. Fuck knows what you were claiming before. I don't think they knew either.'

'Put on a show, did you? These things normally take a couple of weeks.'

The lawyer seemed to swallow something distasteful, narrowed his eyes, and looked off to the distance.

'All you need, to threaten somebody with legal action these days, is for something bad to happen. Pretty much anything at all. And you look like the sort of person to whom bad things have certainly happened. Didn't you know, these days, that bad things are always somebody else's fault?'

Then his face glazed, and I imagine I got the same detachment that all the rest of his clients got.

'I have a lot of experience in these matters. Many organisations are prepared to go to tremendous lengths to stay out of court. We may press for extra money for personal care, although you'll be informed in advance. In any case, all monies will be received in an account you will share with Mr Blethyn, for which he will be a co-signatory. He will be adminstering your funds. I can't say I fully understand your relationship with the man, but I would appreciate it if you stayed out of my offices. Don't call us, as they say.'

And he turned to walk away.

'This a favour for him, is it?' I asked, over the traffic. 'For one of your clients?'

'Partly. I'll be putting a retrospective claim through on legal aid as well. You'll get the relevant documents.'

And he turned the corner and went back to his fiefdom, the People's Champion; defending the people, accusing the people, and billing the people, all at the same time.

'Well,' said Gavin, 'I have some business of my own to take care of. Do you think you can meet me back at the car in two hours, Magnum?'

Gavin pointed at the alley called King's Lane.

'It's in there,' he said.

'Fine.'

'Don't make me come looking for you.'

I stood and watched him walk off and into the Grosvenor Casino. It was gone opening time, I realised. I looked in my pockets: I had thirty-four pence. Considering I had scrubbed up a bit, with the haircut and the shave and the new clothes, I thought about trying to lift a little something from Spar, but it wasn't really in my line (not that I didn't drink stuff that other people had stolen). Anyway, if I got caught I'd be late for Gavin, and I didn't want to push my luck too far in that direction just yet. Thirty-four pence. Not even Wetherspoons could save me. Instead I set my jaw and walked as fast as I could in the direction of the beach, feeling something like a tight iron band around my chest, and perspiring heavily from the forehead.

I couldn't find Scotty, which was probably for the best, considering he was supposed to be lying low. I did find Chester, however, of course, keeping his lonely vigil on the prom, fighting his dark little battles with himself, the lines in his nylon trousers straight and firmly pressed. Some unwitting stranger was asking him for directions to the ferry terminal, and I could tell he was too shocked by the contact to make the most of the company.

'There's more than one way to get to Swansea docks,' he was saying, staring nervously into the middle distance.

'Amen,' I butted in. The stranger, a decently-dressed backpacker with a beard and a bourgeois accent, took one look at me and smiled inanely and backed off.

'Found anything interesting today?' I asked, after the stranger had made his excuses.

'...' said Chester, fiddling with the control panel on his metal detector. I don't think he was used to us acting as if we liked being near him. There was a grin on his face that sat halfway between awkwardness and terror.

'Seen Scotty?'

'There was a man in Hampshire who found three Spanish doubloons on Tuesday,' he said. 'No.'

'If you see him, tell him everything's okay, and I'm working for James Blethyn out at the docks. Hampshire's a long way from Swansea, Chester. Hampshire's somewhere on the other side of that lot.'

And I pointed off across the channel.

'I know that. I'm from Portsmouth. They had an estimated value of thirteen hundred pounds.'

'Yeah? Well he isn't going to get it, is he? If he found it on the beach and then reported it to the papers.'

'...' he said, examining the earpads on his headphones.

'Got any change?'

Chester looked at me ruefully.

'I need some money for the launderette,' I said. 'You and Scotty and me will go out for a drink sometime next week, and I'll buy you a pint, how's that?'

He gave me near on three pounds. Together with the thirty-four pence I now had enough for two pints. I left him talking mostly to himself about zinc alloy and magnetism and headed back into town, where I popped into the Potter's Wheel and drank two Strongbows. Two pints: it was all over so quick I was back by Gavin's Chrysler in King's Lane wondering if I had ever gone into a pub at all. But not really. When you're a drinking man, it only takes a thimble for your body to know you're on the right track. It's the difference between up and down.

Gavin came back with the grounded, self-assured step of a man who had spent two hours at the tables and managed to stay about even, and without saying a word to each other, we got in the car and drove back to the warehouse. When we got there the big shutter at the front was rolled all the way up, and a Mercedes Kompressor was parked outside. James Blethyn emerged from the depths with a black bin bag in one hand and a couple of my empties from last night in the other.

'What's all this then, hey? Thought you'd have a few on the house?'

I tried to gauge the expression on his face. There was something at odds in it, some contrast between the mouth and eyes, but nothing that spoke of anger or surprise, so I just gave him a big bashful grin (it hurt to do it, and I don't mean my pride, I mean my face: the corners of my mouth are not used to that sort of usage).

'You better watch yourself, Magnum. You're not here as a guest.'

That was all he said on the subject. He asked Gavin how everything was, and Gavin said fine, the Casino wasn't too bad, maybe a five per cent loss, and that was clearly as much as they wanted to say with me present, so James told me to stretch my legs and come back when I saw a lorry pull up.

There weren't an awful lot of sightseers in Swansea docks. In fact there were none, and I never saw any the whole time I was there, save for the odd cautious businessman, sat in his saloon, watching his modest shipment or convoy load onto one of the small trawlers that pulled in, and set sail for Ireland, which was where most of the shipping was destined. It was strictly short-haul, for the most part. Next to D-Block, one of the few warehouses that were still standing, albeit only just, with its impromptu buttresses and sagging brick and asbestos roof, there were about a hundred steel rolls from Corus, formerly British Steel, laid end-to-end, with 'destination Mumbai' chalked onto the side of each rusty one, but how long they had lain there was anybody's guess. There was a row of tugboats and a single fireship moored up along the north side of King's Dock, and outside the biggest tug a small group of men in the modest national dress of some Islamic country squatted around a little fire, cooking something in a battered pot; crewmen from the last big Asian freighter who had decided to stay behind, living off the gangway of these smaller ships. Funny kind of life. I doubt they never went far from the boat, and the tugboats certainly never went far from the dock. I saw huge heaps of old coal, almost as fine as dust now, sat in vast wooden pens like the dunes of a black desert, and over by the Queen's Dock a massive pile of timber rotting silently away. There was a depot of some sort a way off that might have seen some use, an empty yard edged by a wall of damaged containers, like a corral of wagons from the old American west, but I don't know what for. At my feet an old tabloid flapped limply in the summer air. And that was it, for a patch of land that was bigger than Swansea centre itself: the rest really was wasteland, strewn with debris and fragments of ancient machinery, lined with leaning posts and patchy chainlink. Square miles of it, criss-crossed with train tracks the moss had covered over, guarded over by cranes taller than buildings, jibs locked into a silent starward salute for the last load out. This is the architecture our empire gave us, this steel rusting out-of sight, this mossy iron, these acres of nothing, and the lapping of the oblivious waves, these ambivalent faces on the shoreline.

Movement was obvious to the naked eye, from whatever distance. I saw the lorry as soon as it arrived, but I didn't exactly hurry back. Heavy lifting was a job for somebody else, and that wasn't laziness talking, that was mortality. But I needn't have worried. All they wanted me to do was sign the docket: 6,912 cans of Stella Artois, 1,152 cans of Dry Blackthorn, 144 bottles of Smirnoff Red and 144 bottles of Famous Grouse, all safely received, or most of it, at least, anyway: I have to admit I didn't bother to count it. But as somebody who was able to write his own name unaided, I am happy to say I lived up to requirements. Then I signed the form for a small consignment of mobile phones, and everybody seemed happy. Gavin and James began to gather their things, their paperwork and tobacco, and head off.

Off by the road leading from the ferry terminal a couple of dirty white transits had stopped to unload a surprisingly large amount of human cargo, of stubbly, pasty-faced men in cheap track suits and club rugby tops.

'See them?' said James Blethyn, conversationally. 'Labourers. Spend the week on sites in Ireland. All from round here. We *export* navvies now.'

'Fucking hell,' I said, to be sociable.

'You went to the job centre this morning, right?' he asked. 'Did you see them advertising factory work in Italy?'

I nodded.

'This isn't a boom anymore, you know. This is a recession with credit cards. My advice to you,' he said, as he loaded his stuff into his car, as the shutters rolled down, 'liquidate your portfolio!'

And for the second time in as many days I was treated to the sound of his laughter muffled through steel, sat alone in the dark.

'Where are the lights?' I yelled, to the sound of two far-off engines revving up, and disappearing. I didn't mind. Everything I really needed was within arms' reach, can after can of it. Actually that isn't strictly true. I had first to feel my way around to the back of the warehouse to where I had already perforated one of the thickly packaged stacks, so I could skip all that old teeth-and-claws kerfuffle, but that wasn't too hard now I'd seen more of the place in daylight.

Lager was fine for me. I wasn't hungry, I could piss in a corner, and I had washed yesterday. Now a good real ale is probably the best pint a man can drink, but when you've lost the taste for lager you've lost the taste for booze. Nobody is above a bit of Stella or Kronenbourg and the rest, nobody that is a man and drinks alcohol, anyway, and I had something of a stockpile, of lager and more besides. I could hear it. The sunny amber hum of lager, the gentle auburn tenor of proper beer, the acidic crack of the nitrokeg ciders, the brash tinny treble of neat vodka, the sonorous bass of dark rum, the distant and earthy siren-like song that whisky makes when you take a bottle and throw away the cap. I stood there in the midst of it drunk already, like a lover of classical music amidst one of the world's best orchestras, frozen mid-note in the middle of his favourite symphony, awestruck before the power and the glory suspended.

There can be the richest of textures under the darkest of rocks; especially there.

II

I spent Friday night like that, cocooned in my crypt, and all of Saturday too, without a peep of light or crumb of food. I hardly missed either: fate had placed me in my own flotation tank, and I was off on one, as the young people say, rolling around on some strange static voyage of my own. It was how I had spent most of my weekends, back when I'd had money and clothes and a home of my own, when I was only hiding from myself, and cancer was nothing but a bad dream, sat stubbornly in some backstreet boozer in the nearest city over the bridge, a cigarette in one fist and a glass in the other. A hundred different pubs, in good neighbourhoods and bad (mostly bad), sat next to all sorts of people, and it turned out none if it mattered. Lock me in a dark room with enough booze and I could have the same sort of time; better, maybe. If, in moments, I missed the hubbub of human activity, or just the mindless beeping of a fruit machine, then I could remind myself what day of the week it was and be content. Friday and Saturday nights were not when you wanted to be about in Swansea if you were a serious drinker. The place was full of rank amateurs, flooding down from the estates and the university and the valleys in their minicabs and minibuses and their cheap American limos, in fancy dress, half of them, in groups of twelve or larger, determined to have 'a good time', and convinced they were having one, even when the tears came out, and the slaps and the shouts and the punches, the cacophony of bad songs, badly sung, at loud volume by the oblivious subjects of a bad night, staggering reluctantly back to the taxi rank, only dimly aware of some short-changed feeling, some suspicion there should have been more. Once or twice I pressed my ear up against the shutter and I heard it all, carried across the dead water on the shipless wind, like the sounds of a long battle, fought by weary combatants: the clubs and pubs of Wind Street, turning out their fodder, the giddy fools who thought that drink was some sort of lubrication you could rub on, instead of a lament that you could swallow; who thought it was a taking, instead of an offering.

The rumpus never stopped for long. I remembered what I had heard about the Cape Horners, lying at anchor off some desolate Chilean bay, specks in the wilderness, ears to the wind of an evening, listening for the music from the next barque down the coast, for the squeezebox and the piccolo and maybe a good Welsh tenor. What cape had I rounded, to spend my nights straining for this?

On Sunday I needed to defecate. It was probably mid-afternoon when the need seized me, somewhat by surprise, as I hadn't had anything solid to eat for a week easy. Still, there was fire in the bowels. I considered groping for a corner but some greater sense of self kicked in, and I realised I wasn't going to put up with it, squatting blindly over the dank concrete like a moron. Perhaps the basest test of man's humanity is that he does not freely stand in his own shit, a test many of your lesser mammals fail daily, as would I, if under drink I laid cable in the pitch dark of an unknown warehouse. Sooner or later it would get underfoot. Instead my fingertips reached out for the breezeblock, and I began the first of several bruising laps, looking for a light switch in so many blank feet of obstructed wall. Now that I knew I needed to I found it with surprising ease, within half an hour probably. A single fluorescent bar flickered with agonising slowness into pale blue life, hanging stock-still on chains dangling from the lofty ceiling. It was nowhere near enough light for working under, and it left swathes of darkness between the bundles, but it was enough for me to see that in a corner someone had built a breezeblock cubicle that came halfway up the wall, and as I drew near, I saw a small makeshift office, no more than some plywood bracketed to the wall for a desk and a red plastic chair on metal legs, and beyond that, a door ajar, and the familiar closeted damp of dirty porcelain and liquid soap.

After I'd finished I turned the light off again, without even thinking about it. And I shuffled blindly back to my spot, near the bundle with the magic hole and the limitless lager, and drank, and drank, and time passed, and its wake became small and soft.

I was woken by the hum of an electric motor, the clank of moving chain and steel plate, that widening shaft of bright summer light. Again. Like the world raising a stage curtain rising on a single, captive audience of one.

'Ho ho,' said James Blethyn, eyeing me curled up on the floor in Scotty's jacket, surrounded by scattered empties. 'Had a good weekend, did we?'

'Yes,' I said, sincerely. He eyed with distate some dark patches of concrete a little way behind me.

'Use the shitter next time,' he said. 'Fucking tramp.'

'I did,' I said. 'When I found it.'

'Not too late for the main event, I trust. Now fuck off and stretch your legs for a bit, will you? Oh, before I forget.'

He reached into the open passenger window of his car and brought out an aluminium vacuum flask.

'There's some coffee left in there. Come back in an hour.'

I was pretty stiff, I realised, as I stumbled blinking across the sunny yard. I'd need a night in a bed soon, maybe in a proper room. Shit, I thought to myself: they had just given me a good room in the Heathfield, and I was never going to get that back. That was somebody else's now, you could be sure of it, and if they were smart they would keep it for as long as they thought they might need it. It had a lovely view, that room. I had been sleeping on the bare floor of a draughty warehouse for three nights now, and while Saturday and Sunday morning had been okay I woke up on Monday feeling like I was never going to wake up again. God, and my chest, my chest. It was full. I needed a blanket at least, or was that, was that the other? Was that the disease? Sleeping like that couldn't help, anyway. God. Monday mornings. Even without a job to go to…

The coffee tasted good. It was nice to have a little bit of something that wouldn't get you drunk for a change. It was instant, but if you put enough instant in, a good two or three spoonfuls a cup, I found it came out on a rough par with the real thing, and James Blethyn obviously worked on the same principle. A fag would have been nice, just to complement the texture, that heavy taste. I hardly ever wanted a cigarette now, I was happy to smoke a few if they were around, but I rarely yearned for them. Why should I? They had done their job, after all. They had reached their culmination, their unseen blossoming inside me.

I walked a little down King's Dock until I came to the tugboats again, four or five of them, moored up one after the other. Up-close you could see they were decades old: next stop after Swansea was probably the reclamation yard. The skipper was down cleaning one of them out, and his car was parked up outside; a seven-year-old Ford Escort. They were pretty big tugs alright, taller than a house, but I suppose there wasn't much call for them anymore. Strange to think of being in charge of something like that, being the owner maybe, and having to drive an old Escort. I went a little further down and stood a way off from a group of Indian or Pakistani crewmen squatting around the remains of their old fire. I gave them a wave and two of them nodded back.

I thought about going and finding a nice bit of scrubland to lie down in, something sandy and soft and clean, to relax and take in some sun, some warmth, but it was hopeless. The ground around there had held heavy industry for a long time, and the earth was still damp with it. It would have been like rolling around in a diesel sump. Old industry never dies: it just fucking rots. And there was the traffic from the little concrete depot, the ready-mixed concrete lorries, not exactly frequent but loud as hell. I stood still for as long as I could bear it and then went back.

Gavin was sat in the big black Kompressor listening to the sports commentary for something on Radio Five, and James was sat in the driver's seat of his Chrysler, with the door wide open, reading a *Mirror*.

'Am I late?' I said.

James looked at his watch.

'Nope. Not at all. Don't worry about it, mun.'

And he got out of his car and stretched and then went over to the warehouse with its tiny office, and beckoned me to follow.

'Just the usual papers to sign. And another consignment of mobile phones.'

He nodded off to a corner and I saw another large cardboard box there, identical to the one I had signed for on Friday, about the size of a small fridge, except there was a bad dent in the top corner. Like before, it had the carrier's sheets stapled to the top in a see-through plastic envelope, the original and a couple of carbons, and I signed and dated the uppermost and James snatched off the one underneath. Then I went into the desk and signed off two more loads of booze, going out this time, not in.

'I must have missed them,' I said. 'The lorries.'

'Oh. Yeah. They came when you were out.'

'That it?'

'Yup,' he said, and waited. And then I waited. And to my surprise, I said it.

'Listen, James, how long is this going to go on? I can't live like this for much longer. Christ knows, I should have something to eat.'

'You want something to eat? I can get Gavin to nip down to Greggs.'

'Yeah, that'd be great. But James, tell me, I'll help you out here, but tell me, how long is this going to go on?'

'How long is what going to go on?'

'Me locked up in here. I don't mind working for you, and sorting things out and the rest of it, but for fuck's sake.'

James stroked his chin.

'Are you complaining?' he asked.

'No.'

'Good. 'Cause you've got no right to. You're the one that fucked things up, not me. We didn't need to see each other again, did we? But I take your point. You're in the dark.'

It took me a second to twig that he was using this as a metaphor. He had no idea I had been sitting there with the lights off all weekend.

'Well, listen to me here, now. You fucked off some people. That was a drug dealer you knocked out in that flat up in town. One of the Neath boys. And he wasn't hustling out by the train station, was he? He had his own pad. If you'd have searched it, you'd probably have found a shotgun or an old revolver around the place. It's not a situation that will solve itself overnight. Do you think I'm a drug dealer? You think I'm a drugs baron, do you? No. Of course I'm fucking not. But I know my way around and I'm respected. You let me sort your little problem out, like you asked me to, and then you can do a few other things for me. Get out a bit more. But until then, this is probably the best place for you to be. It's got all the amenities you need, hey?'

I nodded, and I think I even tried a sort of friendly smile. It still hurt to do it.

'See? But for now let's take it a step at a time, and the first step is: do what the fuck I tell you to do.'

And James Blethyn, who was maybe two years older than me, and the two of us being well into our forties, patted me on the head. On the way out he stuck a small key into an electrics box by the side of the entrance and flipped a switch, setting the shutters in motion, and Gavin darted in to pick up the mobile phones. I must have had a face like a horse.

'Don't worry, Gavin'll bring you some pasties in a bit,' he said.

How long was a bit? What time was it now? God, I could have cried. Maybe I did, while I went back to the open stack and tugged out another can. I think there must have been something wrong with me because I still had the same one in my hand when Gavin came back.

Without looking me in the eye he handed me a big warm paper bag that smelt of pastry.

'Can I have the door open?' I said.

'No fucking way. Not with all that in there.'

'Well, can you lock me out? I'll just kick around here for a couple of hours, out front. You can lock me in again later. How's that? Night-time's when you're going to get somebody coming round, isn't it, that's when you need me to look after the place? And it's not like I'll be going anywhere. I'll be stood here.'

Gavin paused for second, which was probably as awkward as you would ever see him look.

'I'll ring the boss.'

'Don't', I said, but he was already five feet away, with some little thing the size of a fag lighter stuck to the side of his head. Meanwhile, I ran into the back of the warehouse and filled the pockets of my jacket with cans.

'The boss says it's okay,' he said, when I came back out.

He flipped his phone shut and slipped it into his pocket. Phones were so small these days, that thing made his hands look like shovels. Actually, they were like shovels. He was a big bloke.

'The boss says it's okay but you better fucking stay here. I'll be back later.'

And as if to underscore his point, when he moved off in his car, he treated me to a bit of wheelspin as he went. I should imagine that's a tricky thing to do in a people-carrier, but he managed. Stay here? Fine. Staying in one place was something I had grown good at, over the years. Staying in one place had become something of a speciality. Just don't ask me to do it sober. I sat down on the earth, warm from the midday sun, high in the sky, and finished off my open can with my back against the shutters. There were six more in the pockets of Scotty's capacious jacket. In what felt like no time at all the steel shutters behind me grew as warm as a radiator, and I sat there perspiring like a man in a sauna. I kept the jacket on. It felt quite pleasant, that intense heat and the lager and just being outdoors, and I sat there and watched the world through half-closed lids.

There wasn't much going on, to be honest. Apart from the clouds and the birds nothing moved. I think I was on my third can when I saw a blue saloon, maybe an old Nissan Bluebird, moving towards the timber yard on the other side of the dock, bouncing along on that old, unused road, throwing up a cloud of brown-black dirt behind it. God, I thought, that'll be some pensioner turned up to catch the Cork ferry nine hours early, worried to hell about missing it, and driving all over the docks because he could only see about ten yards in front of his face. When it got to within ten feet of the edge, right up against the sea, the driver finally gave up and turned round. On his next leg he thought he'd come by me, and as it drew nearer it really did look like the sort of car a pensioner would drive: probably fifteen years old, spotless bodywork, and a box of tissues on the back shelf, on top of a travel blanket. Then it stopped right in front of the warehouse and Scotty got out.

'Where the fuck have you been?' he said.

'Whose fucking car is that?' I replied.

'I've been fucking looking for you all fucking day.'

Then Chester got out of the driver's side and gave a little cough.

'Language, gentlemen,' he said.

'Fuck off, Chester,' we said.

Scotty, it transpired, was not at all happy. From his perspective, nothing had changed: he was still persona non grata with most of the dealers, even if one or two of them were growing apologetic about it, but the threat of violence had not rescinded. His little hijacked supply was gone, and he wanted answers, he said, although I think he would have just preferred to get off his face. He didn't look his best, I have to say. But then we were never a very photogenic pair.

'Relax,' I told him. I was still sitting on the ground with a can in my hand at the time. 'The boss has told me he's on it. It's not the sort of thing that can be sorted out overnight, you know, but he's on it.'

Scotty's face crinkled into a familiar picture of disgust.

'That's easy for you to say,' he said. 'Where'd you get that?'

'This is from stock. He's got me looking after a load of it in there.'

Tenderly, I patted the steel shutters at my back. There was something of a pause then, the sort of pause you really wanted to remark on just to break the silence, but nobody did and time passed and Scotty's expression hadn't changed a bit.

'He's got you looking after a warehouse full of booze?' was what he said eventually.

'Yeah.'

'Do you think you're really the right man for the job there?'

'Relax,' I said. 'It'll be fine.'

Scotty managed to hold it in for a moment and then his knees buckled and his fists clenched and the eyes in his downcast face closed tightly shut and stayed there.

'Jesus Christ,' he sort of sang, in a drawn-out way, between gritted teeth. 'Relax, he says! It's alright for you! Look at you! If you think I'd gone in that office instead of you do you think he'd have asked me to look after a container from Karachi or something? No, he fucking wouldn't. It's okay for you, you jammy bastard. I'm dying here.'

I hadn't really thought about it, but he had a point. While I was thinking about it I noticed the lager in my can had gone a little flat, so I gave it a shake, and the gesture infuriated him for some reason.

'What have you fucking done!' he demanded. 'You've sold someone out, haven't you! Who've you crossed? Me?'

'How could I sell you out?' I said. 'What are you worth? Same as I am. Nothing, to anybody. As a matter of fact I get locked in here every night like a prisoner, and I sleep on the concrete floor. I'm pretty much held captive here, in case little Kelly or somebody tries to break in and run off with a box of Bacardi Breezers, and for that I get a few cans a day.'

I tried to remember how many cans I had on me without patting my pockets, and when Gavin was likely to come back. Another four, maybe five? And probably another four or five hours to go, at the outside. I wanted to offer Scotty a can but it was impossible: I was only just covered.

'Ooh, poor you,' said Scotty, and then I think Chester may have said something about alcopops and his niece's GCSE party.

'After that he said something about doing a few other things for him, maybe. The only person I've sold out is me, Scotty. I was a private investigator for nigh-on twelve years, you know. I don't exactly carry a clean sheet. I knew things. I've crossed some people. I had to tell him all about it.'

'So what about me?'

'Well, I'll help you. I really will. When I have a hand to play, I'll do it. If there is something I can do for you, it will be done. But right now I'm playing a waiting game, I'm getting the lay of the land. I can't think what else I could do. But for now let's see if this James Blethyn fella can sort it out. He told me would.'

'Did he now?'

'Yeah,' I shrugged. 'He did. You have to give a man time, Scotty, don't you know that?'

Scotty looked like a man who didn't know anything but pain and injustice. He looked like a middle-class actor trying to do working-class stoicism in a bad British movie. Scotty could be terrible when he was in withdrawal, but I always thought he was at his worst when he'd just come out of it.

'Look, I'll talk to him. I'll talk to him next time I see him.'

'Yeah, you have yourselves a lovely chat,' he said. 'And when that does fuck all?'

'Well, if that's the case, well. I'll make it up to you, man.'

Make up what? Looking back, Christ knows. Scotty spun

on his heels and went back to Chester's car. Chester said something about when were we going to go for a pint, and I told him I was working, me, sat on my own in a stretch of industrial wasteland with a can in my hand. But he accepted it and the two of them went to get back in the Bluebird. Almost too late I remembered something so important I flinched with agony at how close I had come to forgetting about it, and I got up and ran to the car's passenger window.

'Scotty, I've got a favour to ask you.'

'Fucking hell.'

'I'm serious, Scotty. You remember that young man I pointed out in that garage? Down by the prison?'

I swallowed.

'My son?'

'Yeah?'

'Just keep an eye out for him, will you? For me? Walk by there every other day, or something. Or if you see him about town let me know. I'm worried about him. I don't think he's doing too well financially, and he's got a young family. Will you do that? This is my son now we're talking about.'

'Alright,' said Scotty. 'If he's got financial problems I'll sure he'll want to talk to you.'

Money. It can do so much and it means nothing. Wealth couldn't even be considered the smallest of virtues, but it has proved to be as hard to come by as the biggest of them. Why is that, I wonder? What is missing in us that is for once not something good, that keeps it from us?

We both sort of silently acknowledged the joke, and then I watched Chester strap himself in, take off the handbrake, check the rearview (in six hundred empty acres), fucking indicate, and turn around and head off, at certainly no more than the regulation dockside twenty miles an hour. Even at that speed they kicked up a lot of dust. It was old land, and it was the middle of a dry summer. Then I went back to my spot by the shutters, in the full blare of the sun, and reached for another can. To my surprise I found I was carrying another six full cans, so I probably could have given Scotty one, the thing had so many pockets. It wasn't even my jacket, I remembered. It was his.

When Gavin pulled up I might have been asleep, or something like it, stupefied by a little bit of slow drinking and the heat. I didn't come to until he was standing over me, and even then I wasn't sure he hadn't called out or nudged me with his foot.

'Seen any suspicious characters, have you, Magnum?' he was saying, while he turned a key in the exterior box. 'While you were securing the perimeter?'

I felt the ribs of the steel links begin to move behind my back, and stood up.

'What time is it?' I asked.

'Half six?' he suggested, without bothering to look at the watch on his wrist. I don't suppose it mattered.

When the shutters had opened high enough for me to walk under I went in, although he didn't bother. He just stood outdoors with his key stuck in the switch.

'No more papers?' I said with my back to him, so he couldn't see my face, as cheerful as I could manage. 'Nothing for me to sign?'

'Not today,' was all he said, and then I was on my own in the dark, or near dark. It was still July, and outside the sun was not going to set another for another four hours, but that was another world. I grabbed a few more tinnies from the back and sat next to the shutters, watching the tiny dots of light in the gaps between the steel plate fade and disappear as night came on. Sometime after I should have faded out myself, but the pain in my chest had resurged, and crescendoed. I could only take shallow breaths without being stabbed in the side, and shallow breaths were not enough. My pulse raced and I got dizzy and when I got dizzy I found myself taking a deep breath without thinking of it, and then I would grimace and clutch my ribs and double over, and when my eyes opened the tiny dots of light would reappear and dance around, although it was the middle of the night. This is how I will die, I thought, alone, in pain, in the darkness, waiting to catch a breath that never comes. I did not sleep and took only sips from the can and was wide awake when morning rolled around and the shutters rolled back up, although the pain had lessened. It comes and goes, I thought, and one night it will come and stay and I will go instead.

It was Gavin. I came straight out with it.

'I need to see the doctor,' I said.

'What? Straight away?'

I daresay I looked pretty rough.

'Okay,' said Gavin. 'But make sure you get a sick note.'

And he got me to sign the papers for a couple of pick-ups and told me to get going. I would have to be back before five to sign for some more of those mobile phones.

'I was hoping for a lift,' I said.

'I'm not a fucking taxi service.'

'Can you lend me twenty quid?'

'I'll lend you fucking twenty quid,' he said, in a voice that sounded threatening and incredulous, but he did.

It was probably no more than two miles to the Health Surgery on Swansea High Street. Assuming Gavin had come round at half nine, which was as late as he ever did, then it took me an hour and three quarters. It was more fear than pain, I think, more wallowing than anything else. A man is entitled to indulge himself about his own death, and I frequently did, although looking back, Jesus Christ to God,

I wish I'd indulged myself with something else. As entitled as you are, it's a terrible habit, I can promise you. There is no vindication in the inevitable, none at all.

Of course, when I got there the morning surgery was closed. In fact, the morning surgery ran from nine to ten thirty, which I had definitely missed, and after that the afternoon surgery ran only from four to five. The fucking surgery was only open for two and a half hours a day. But I tried the door and it was unlocked, so I opened it, smelt the familiar scent of NHS waiting rooms, and went in and sat down and waited.

Despite the posted hours there were three other people in there, a young couple and a single man, none of them older than twenty one, all of them fairly obviously addicted to something harder than spirits. Over the next sixty minutes a few more of the condemned came in for their little reprieves, and around lunchtime a woman appeared behind reception and shuffled some papers for long enough to see I was there.

'Can I help you?' she said.

Inside I heard some distant laughter from the blackness at the back of my mind: of course she could, of course, but the tone of her voice...

'I need to see a doctor,' I said.

'We're closed. Have you got an appointment?'

Oh-ho, said that mournful, sonorous voice, there's another question she knew deep down she never really needed to ask. I remember some Guinness advert on the telly a while aback, about how only twelve per cent of human communication is verbal. It's a good fucking job, I tell you, a good fucking job. If you did nothing but listen you'd go mad, the shit, the poison that comes out of some people's mouths.

'No,' I said.

I am dying, though, I thought. I am in pain.

'Well, we aren't open again until four o'clock, and all the

doctors are fully booked. You can come back at four and wait to see if there's a cancellation,' she said, ending her voice in a raised pitch that suggested she was asking a question. People talked like that all the time now, even when they weren't asking a question at all, half the time anybody made a statement there was that patronising inflection of doubt: do you understand me? Have I made myself clear? Can you grasp the subtleties and complexities of this truth that only I have mastered? But there were questions that needed to be asked, oh yes. Don't ask me what they are; I don't know, but there are an awful lot of unclaimed question marks floating around the aether, and they must belong to something, and it must be something big.

'I'll wait,' I said. 'I really need to see a doctor. It's an emergency. I saw a doctor here before,' I said, 'but it was all such a blur.'

I had not taken it well, I suppose, looking back, Christ knows why. It was not, could not, have been a surprise. What was his name? What did he look like? He had a moustache, I thought, or maybe a beard, and he was white, and he was probably Welsh. It was useless.

'I can't remember who. It was a few months ago.'

'What's your name?'

'Robin Llywelyn.'

And she looked, and it was not there. Nothing. Not a single slip of paper to record the sound predictions of my own demise, the arrival of my cause of death.

'I'll wait,' I said.

'You'll have to wait outside.'

Fuck it, I thought. I almost said. Had I been able to, I would have taken a deep breath. Instead I looked at a spot on the wall and counted to five.

'Why do I have to wait outside? These other people that

have been coming and going out of here don't have to wait outside. They don't have to wait much at all, do they?'

'They're private patients at the clinic here,' she said.

'So this is a private clinic during the middle of the day and a doctor's surgery at either end, is it? Have you proportioned your funding from the health board, then? Seeing you're only NHS for two hours of the day? I'll tell you what. I reckon this waiting room must be NHS all week, money-wise, so I'll wait here. And before you ask me to leave you'd better check about that funding, love.'

She went off then. She reappeared with some other women a little later and they talked in hushed voices about me for ten minutes, but nobody did anything, and I sat there and waited. You're always hearing about the stress and hassle that NHS staff get off their patients, always frowning at what you read in the papers. I was one of the troublemakers now, I guess.

There was the usual pile of women's magazines on a low table between the seats, and I picked a copy of something off the top, without really thinking about it. Anything to take my mind off. It had all the stuff you'd expect. It explained how it might be possible for you to have a nice meal, if you had two hundred quid to spend in a restaurant, how you could dress well, if you had nine hundred quid to spend on a coat, and how you could probably have a reasonably enjoyable holiday if you didn't want any change out of three thousand pounds. It explained how you could look, eat and sound like celebrity. If you could afford all these things, and you did look, eat and sound like a celebrity, it slagged off your dress sense, showed photos of your cellulite, and paid your old friends to say terrible things about you. Journalism, I thought. Magazines. Apparently it was very competitive, to get into it.

I was doing one of those multiple-choice quizzes when my name was called. This was not the first one of these things I have seen. Apparently, they are for people who want to find something out about themselves. If you really believe that some halfwit in an office in Wapping or somewhere could take you and your life and at five hundred quid an article tell you something you did not already know are you:

a) Simply in a state of denial, knowing the truth about yourself all along, and, irony of ironies, needing only *Woman's Week* to push you into catharsis?

b) So desperate for something to vouchsafe to your own fragile sense of self that the simplicity of these worse-than-armchair-psychology questions does not occur to you, nor the effortless way in which all answers may be predicted?

c) Rebecca Blethyn?

If you answered mostly a's, oh, if you answered at all, it is too late, it is already too late.

'Yes?' I said.

'I'm Dr Hill,' said Dr Hill. 'I don't normally see patients at this time, but if you can accept that this is a one-off, I'm happy to see you now.'

He didn't look happy, but then doctors aren't supposed to, are they? They're not supposed to look anything but grave and concerned, and he could do that okay. He was your typical, average-looking doctor: he had a fleece jacket, a twill shirt, corduroys, a pair of dirt-free hiking boots and a look that said he had the weight of the world on his shoulders, which was fine by him, as long as you understood what he was about, and even if you didn't.

His room was as conventional as any other doctor's room you might imagine, which can hardly be an accident. In the profession it must be considered best practice to have as bland a room as possible, so as not to sully the noble art of medicine with any earthly individuality, like methodist chapels and God. Then again, maybe the doctors want to keep themselves out of it for their own sake, so they can keep themselves sane in a sea of pain and death and other bad news. He was of the right age to have some young kids, and sure enough there were two bright, cack-handed paintings of stick figures standing on green grass up on the wall behind him. They make an exception for that: the paintings of your children, as long as they are very young and artistically inept. You can put those up in your room, if you're a doctor. They stood out like balloons in a cemetery.

'What seems to be the problem?'

'I came in here about late March, I think,' I said, 'but they must have lost my records. I have lung cancer.'

'Right,' he said, with a mixture of gravitas and resignation and muted sympathy that worked very well. He asked me to pull up my top, and then I felt the cold steel of the stethoscope, and the impersonal touch of clinical fingertips along my ribs and sternum. The only people to have touched my body in twenty-six years are doctors, nurses, prostitutes, and men who are hitting me in the face. Not for twenty-six years. Not since I left Swansea in the first place. I am not homosexual, but the sensation of his touch was strange, and powerful, and sad.

'Yes,' he said. 'There's no doubt about it. You've got a large tumour in the left lung and it's almost certainly cancer. Is there blood in your phlegm? A lot? You've been feeling some pain?'

I nodded to all them.

'My lungs are causing me some discomfort,' I said.

'Well, actually there aren't many nerve endings in your lungs. The feelings of pain come from the parts of the body around the lungs, like maybe the intercostal muscles, between the ribs.'

That's interesting, I was about to say. I see. But it seemed somehow inappropriate, and insincere. So I let it hang.

'So were you given a prognosis? When you came in here last, what was the outcome?'

I laughed, just a little laugh, just the once, just for me. The outcome? I drank like a man with gills, as much as I could, whatever I could, wherever would have me. It was a rapidly diminishing circle that ended up in a fine point, in some unremembered location, of vague timing, when I could swim no more and rose to the surface like a dead fish, not healed, not resigned, but just stupefied enough to stay still. I would like to say that I had never drunk so much in my life, but the truth is I cannot remember how much I drunk at all, only that I was desperate. I did whatever I could to get booze or the money for booze, and I was in a city where there have always been a lot of other people trying to do the same thing. I was rumbled pretty quickly, and the bottom zoomed up towards me like a rocket. It didn't hurt when I hit it. I couldn't feel a thing.

'I can't remember,' I said. 'I know I'm on the way out.'

'Did you have an MMI scan? Or an x-ray?'

God, an x-ray. Now you mention it, I thought, there was some bus trip up to Singleton Hospital, early in the morning, a half hour sat in a room full of old people with broken bones, waiting to go in, and then two minutes behind the screen, and the young woman looking at the monitor around the corner: they could see the results instantly on those things, although they leave it to the GP to tell you. They're just technicians, I suppose, they're not paid to tell you your number's up. But her face did. Her face said it all. I went over and looked at the thing myself and then I walked out and over the road and straight into the pub. And I didn't stop for about six weeks. That, in the fullest sense, was the outcome of my last visit.

'I had an x-ray,' I said. I honestly hadn't thought about it since April. 'It wasn't good.'

'Okay. Did the doctor tell you? Because we would have records here if he did.'

'No. The woman did.'

'She's not supposed to…'

'No, I mean I could tell. From her face. And I looked myself.'

'Perhaps the records are still at the hospital. I can have them sent back if they are. Do you want an MMI scan? It's practically an essential if you want treatment.'

I wished he hadn't said that. It was what the last doctor had said, and I hadn't been able to quash the hope which came with it, and so in turn the hope had quashed me. Maybe someday things will be different, but as far as I know, you don't beat cancer, although if you fight it and you're lucky it will leave you alone for a few more years. I thought I might stand a chance, or I tried my hardest to believe it, and then I found out the average wait for an MMI was eighteen months, and they might put you at the front of the list if you were serious, but still. I would be dead in half that, probably. It was pointless.

I shook my head.

'I just want the pain to go away,' I said.

'Well there are some very strong painkillers I could prescribe to you. If you have become terminally ill I can prescribe something stronger, but we need to ascertain that you are actually terminally ill. If that is the case you should also be thinking about counselling. If there are emotional problems I can give you some anti-depressants. But can you come back in a couple of days? We should have found your records by then.'

As I left I turned around to close the door behind me, softly and reverently, like a schoolboy leaving the headmaster's study, and saw him taking a cheese sandwich out of his desk. Then I booked an appointment at reception and walked out, on legs that felt as hollow as reeds, and over the road was the White Lamb, and I walked in and drank eight pints of Stella Artois.

Gavin and James found me wandering the north side of Fabian Way, six or seven hours later, when the sun was disappearing over the Gower. I had overshot the docks and was passing the oil depot when they spotted me, over the boundary into Neath Port Talbot. God knows where I thought I was. I was of sound enough mind to expect some trouble, maybe a beating, maybe even the hospital, but they were all smiles. I couldn't understand it, but I was happy enough to accept it. I was grateful, grateful for the ride back to my tomb, where I could be safely locked in, in the quiet, away from everything and everybody, and lay myself down on the steady concrete. A room in pitch-black darkness cannot spin. But we did not stop at the docks. We kept going, went back over the Tawe, from where I had presumably come, and then went up the New Cut. We were going to a party at Tomos Blethyn's. Tomos Blethyn lived in Mayhill.

I knew it before I was told it, of course, the moment we turned off. I sensed it. Where else would Tomos Blethyn live? Through the narrow, parallel terraces off Carmarthen Road I spied the Jewish cemetery, with its high walls and barbed wire, forlorn and abandoned, and the Boys' Brigade, boarded up for donkey's years now. Then we were onto the estates, the same houses you see on estates all over Britain, late fifties, lots of wall, very little window, pebbledash grey some of them, others pale lime. If the difference signified anything I don't know what it was.

Then we went by the Junior School, a prison in primary colours, the benevolence of a distant state casting a very faint glow, and the view out to sea nearly knocked me sideways: all of Swansea was down there, the docks and all, the streetlights and neon, the headlights and brake lights, just starting to shine in the onset of night, and the Bristol Channel flowing out in there in the bay, a blue so dark now it seemed almost mineral, and beyond it still visible the shady undulations of the Exmoor headland, of western England, seemingly devoid of life, save the odd flicker of some unknown, solitary light. Looking out over all that lot, it was almost enough to make you forget what was behind you.

In some cities the rich people would live up here and the poor people would be down there, amongst the fumes, in the thick of it, looking out at some vista that ran thirty feet and then stopped at a wall. You could almost say they'd swapped places, except there were plenty of poor people down there too, and I was one of them, right down there on the bottom stratum these days, with hundreds alongside me, in the hostels and on the High Street, on the beach and by the station.

The people who had any money, if they didn't go out onto the Gower, got flats in the marina development. They liked to live right out there in some non-community on the edge of town, staring down at a car park full of mid-level saloons or a fathom of dirty water with other people's boats on it, or if they were exceptionally lucky, the bay, any one of those three, as long as they didn't have to look at or acknowledge the actual city any more than they had to. Of course, when I say they had money, these people, I mean they only had Swansea money. It wouldn't get them anywhere worth shouting about in most other places. It seems to me there is still something exotic, abnormal, even, about a Welshman with real money, and worse, far worse, there is something hauntingly familiar, something basically and disturbingly ordinary about places like Mayhill, streets and estates and sometimes entire towns that look like they should be cleaned out and condemned when they were just brutally accepted; a token nod of the head towards the passing of steel and King Coal and socialism and you were on your way, back to your balcony.

Tomos's place was just around the next corner, and was easy enough to spot. There were a few people milling around on the grass outside with tinnies in their hands, dance music being played at dance-floor volume from somewhere inside, and the house still had its Christmas lights on. It looked like the last place I wanted to be. I was still strung out from the doctor's, and tired, and what was more, pissed enough already, and all I wanted was peace and quiet. I would have preferred it if they'd let me sleep in a hedge.

From what I could gather, it was Tomos's birthday. Most of the guests were bouncers from his half-brother's security firm or people who were young enough or stupid enough to feel awe in their presence. As far as I could see it was all-male. The house was sparsely furnished and had not been decorated for a good ten or fifteen years, although someone had had a go with a paintbrush in the lounge. There were still drops of paint on the carpet. There was a three-piece suite with a palm tree motif patterned onto the fabric, a mute telly showing a Van Damme movie, and in front of it a crappy old black vinyl coffee table. Someone had probably fallen onto it once, and one of the legs had been stuck back on with a load of silver gaffer tape. On the coffee table was a pile of knives and martial arts weapons, which Tomos, ensconced in an armchair, was gesturing towards with nonchalant pride. There will be trouble here later, I thought.

When he saw me he gave me what he probably hoped was a lingering and menacing look, although it didn't halt his monologue on the efficacy of nunchucks, 'as long as you knew what you were fucking doing, like.' Then somebody pressed a plastic tupperware cup full of vodka into my hand and I sank into a corner and drank it. A little while later James sent Gavin out to the Chrysler for some paperwork he'd forgotten, and it occurred to me they were both half cut when they picked me up. I signed a sheaf of papers and then sloped off upstairs, which was entirely empty, and fell into the nearest bed. I must have come something close to sleep, although the dance music from downstairs was so loud I could feel the springs in the mattress moving. In other neighbourhoods you would have had police visits by now, and with other families, altercations in the street, but nobody in any of the houses nearby was going to do anything about what went on in here. The bass beat ran on furiously for what seemed like hours, with barely a change in tempo, and I realised after a while it ran no faster than my own mortal, racing heart, and then I must have gone under.

Very late at night, or very early in the morning, just as the night was changing hue, I saw two or three figures I did not know stood around the end of my bed. None of them said a word, and for a moment I thought I was having some sort of visitation, some end-of-life palpitations. Then one of them said:

'Nah, s'not worth it. Look at his trainers, they're from fuckin' TK Maxx, mun. He won't have a thing worth havin',' and they stumbled back out onto the landing, drunk and tired.

The next thing I remember the sun was just coming over the hill, and I was awake, and still pretty drunk myself, in a strange room in a strange house. I was in a single bed in room strewn with dirty clothing and unwashed plates. There were a few movie posters for films like *The Matrix* and *Terminator 3* on the walls, and a bullworker in a corner of the room. It was the bedroom of some young male adolescent. Up near the ceiling I could see a cloud of mould and fungus drifting across the room, slower than human eyes could perceive. Had I been anywhere else I would have turned over, pulled the duvet up and waited until it covered the walls, but something about the room made me uneasy. When I came out onto the landing I saw a handpainted sign nailed to the door that said 'Tomos', and I remembered about the Blethyn family. I descended the stairs, with their chocolate brown carpet, and stood not seven feet from the front door, slightly ajar, having probably been left open all night. Seven impossible feet. In two steps I walked past the doorway to the lounge, full of sleeping bodies, and some not sleeping, some red-eyed and rigid and still ploughing on, and in four I was outside the kitchen, and Gavin and James were in there sat round the table, spooning out instant coffee into Euro '96 mugs.

'Morning Magnum,' said Gavin, with reasonable cheerfulness. 'Come in. We want a word with you.'

I turned my back on the first rays of sunlight which were streaming in though the orange plastic glass of the aluminium front door, and stepped onto the sticky lino, into a cloud of tobacco and steam and coffee and old alcohol.

'You're off on your trip today,' he said. I looked over at James, sat opposite him.

'We told you about it last night,' said James, who would have sounded exasperated if he'd had the energy. 'But you don't fucking remember it, do you?'

I was fairly sure they hadn't told me anything like that at all, but fairly sure doesn't count for much, these days.

'What trip?' I said.

'Well we were going to go over it with you anyway,' James went on. 'You're on the ferry to Cork. We need you to sign for a collection of spirits; to take ownership before they ship out. It's for legal reasons, you know. Insurance.'

'Oh. Right,' I said, feeling fairly relieved.

'There'll be a driver and a lorry on there too. Don't worry, when you get near port he'll come and find you, tell you what to do. You just sit there and enjoy the ride and be a good boy.'

'Or fucking else,' said Gavin.

'Here's your passport.'

'My passport?'

It was brand new. The last one I'd had was black, leather, the real deal. This was a little red paper thing. I flipped it open to the back page and looked at the photo: me with eyes like a pair of cunts, leaning back against the metal door of the warehouse, my mouth wide open. Was that a strand of spittle hanging from the corner of my mouth?

'You can't use this. I look like I'm asleep.'

'You look pissed. It's how you look all the time. Anything else and they wouldn't recognise you. My lawyer processed it for you on the fast track.'

'Who took the photo?' I asked. 'I know passport photos are supposed to look bad but bloody hell. I look like I'm having a nightmare.'

'Perhaps you are,' said Gavin, grinning at some unpleasantness. 'Perhaps you're having one right now, hey? Now shut up a minute while we have breakfast.'

I stood there and gazed mournfully at the portrait in my passport while they drank some coffee. Could have been there for five minutes, could have been there for an hour. Eventually Gavin got up and said he'd get the car ready, and James disappeared upstairs.

I was waiting on my own in the kitchen when Tomos came in, looking even more violent than normal, what with being up all night drinking and probably one or two other things, and he lumbered towards me like one of those wrestlers you used to see on Saturday night telly years ago, and put his arms around my throat.

'You're going to see the Irish,' he said. I didn't realise at first that he was asking a question, I thought he was explaining why he was trying to kill me.

'Yeah,' I managed. His bulbous fat face, his big piggy bloodshot eyes, his red cheeks and his army of thick blackheads; up close, in the light of day, it looked like a face that had been pulled off and put on backwards. And if it had, he wouldn't have cared.

Even by my standards the man stank of vodka, and that probably made him a serious fire hazard.

'Fuck,' he said. I think he meant 'you fuck.' 'I want you to buy me a machine gun.'

It might have been my imagination but when he let go of my throat I swear I dropped, like I had been lifted off the floor a little. Then he staggered back out as abruptly as he'd come in. I looked out of the kitchen window and saw the purple Chrysler people-carrier appearing around the end of the street, but not quickly enough. Tomos came back in and thrust a bundle of notes into my hands so hard it felt like I had been punched in the guts.

'You fuck,' he managed, and out he went.

I did not want Tomos Blethyn's money at all. Not a penny. It was a death sentence with a watermark on it. I couldn't throw it away and I couldn't give it back and I wasn't sure I even wanted to admit it had happened. Mortified, I remained silent all the way down to the docks, sat in the back while Gavin and James swapped jokes up front, and said not a word while I waited for Gavin to come back from the terminal with my foot passenger ticket. The second before I had to push off I came clean:

'Your brother gave me this,' I said, scooping handfuls out of Scotty's jacket. 'He said he wanted me to get him a machine gun. You know how he is, I couldn't say no. He's not playing with a full deck, is he?'

Gavin, for the first time since I had met him, looked faintly surprised. James stayed blank.

'Take it,' I said, offering it up.

James got me on the right side of my jaw and I slammed back against the seat and then slid out, off the seat and through the open sliding door, onto the tarmac, breaking a good four feet drop with my shoulder. It was so sudden and unexpected I remember lying there on the ground wondering how I'd got there, if that had really happened.

'My brother tells you to do something you do it,' he said. 'Fucking tramp.'

And he slid the door shut with some force, and they turned around in the middle of the road and headed back off into town, and I joined the stragglers queuing to board, pedestrians who wanted to cross the Irish Sea on foot.

III

It was not an impressive start, considering I had not been out of the United Kingdom since I was a boy. It was nothing like Dover, not even the Dover I had known from the sixties, from our few self-improving family sojourns across England to the campsites of Normandy. Next to nothing could I remember about them now, save the big boats, and French toilets. There wasn't much traffic on foot or otherwise, and most of it was freight, and low-grade freight at that, small firms, little operators, hauliers you'd never heard of. Some of it was continental, some food processing firm from the Netherlands picking up spuds ('turning potatoes into profits', it said on the side of the units), although Christ knows, the way things were changing these days they could have been delivering. Being midsummer still there were a few families, although coming back or going out it was impossible to tell. They all looked equally dejected. Driving God knows how many miles in a European-sized car with multiple small children so you can spend your only fortnight off work under canvas is going to do that to you, and if they were going out, they'd have further to go yet. None of them were staying anywhere near Swansea, I was sure of it; their faces said as much but so did the terminal, its pools of mud and stagnant water, the ripped seats of the passenger area, its old, forlorn, untouched leaflets, a lonely activity board in a dark corner, advertising pony trekking centres and craft shops that had seen their last visitor years ago. There were beautiful places in Wales alright, although it was something that had to be taken on faith by some of us, and Swansea Terminal did nothing to help that feeing, promised nothing, was barely even an apology for its own existence. The glamour of travel was not in it. That's what Wales was to the world, I guess, if it thought of Wales at all, a place to pass through. But such is life.

'Purpose of visit?' said a lady constable wearing, like all the other officers, a fluorescent jacket, despite being indoors, on a bright summer's morning.

'Work,' I said. The worst thing was giving them too much.

Then I was up off the ramp with the rest of them, a dozen of us maybe at most, and a semi-circle of staff lined up at the top to welcome us in, of more or less the same number. At least I assumed that was what they were supposed to be doing, there was no actual welcoming being done, they were just talking to each other in some Slavic language, but the line was definitely a semi-circle and I think the sentiment was noble, or as noble as you'd get for work that was almost certainly under the minimum wage.

I milled about the main lobby, trying to orientate myself a bit, seeing how even the Swansea ferry was a lot bigger than anything I'd been used to, even if the paint was flaking. The Kilkenny Restaurant, the Acropolis Restaurant (I think the ship used to do the Greek islands, before it came over here to die), the Harbourside View Restaurant (although only for the next forty minutes), the TV lounge, a cinema, an Irish gift shop, a perfume shop, a pastry shop, something like a book shop, and Paddy Murphy's pub: it was all a load of rubbish. Naturally, as I'd just been given a couple of thousand pounds by a psychopath to buy a machine gun, I ended up in the pub.

The name of the place probably tells you as much you need to know, some wooden-walled drinking hole done up in the manner of your average Blarney boozer, whatever that was supposed to be, some bar covered in Guinness pennants, and a couple of Beamish and Murphys mirrors on the wall too, this boat being headed for the south of the south. There was a big photo of the 2004 Irish national football team, although someone had crossed out the face of that vicious shit that played for Man U, and had evidently tried to make a similar adjustment to the rest of the inevitable United imagery that was plastered around, before someone had got to him. There was a poster on the wall of Irish writers with about nine people on it, and I recognised two or three of them, which was more than I'd have done on a poster of Welsh writers, if anyone had ever thought to make one. In a rare outbreak of authenticity one of the bar staff had ventured to hang a red Polska scarf above the optics, a Polish eagle at either end. The optics were what it was all about for me. I couldn't complain, what with the oceans of long stuff back at the warehouse, but you could only run so far with them. You needed the shorts for a punch.

I had a double of Powers, with a little water from the jug, seeing how they had the spirits to match the decor. Paddy, Powers, Jamesons, Bushmills, I said hello to each of them, gave the time of day to Cork Dry Gin, and left the Baileys out of the picture. Very nice they were too. Suddenly I suffered the ignoble illusion that I was on a holiday. In no time at all I had forgotten all about the Blethyn family, about Swansea, about the lorry waiting for me in the hold, the unseen driver who would find me, and fancied myself on a little jaunt of my own choosing. Then two things happened. First, I became aware of the music they were playing: a Dubliners album, maybe, or something like it. The effect of this was not immediate, was simply an expectation met, but from that point on I never stopped hearing it, it was stuck on the sound system on repeat. Slowly, imperceptibly, the room began to get smaller until you could feel it around your skull. Secondly, the boat had started to hit deep water, had put shore out of sight and hit the Irish Sea proper, one of the roughest round these isles, and suddenly we were upon it. The ship started to pitch in a serious way, as if it was gearing up to really throw itself about once it had the draw.

A few minutes later I had left my stool and maybe even my drink to pace about the decks like it was some kind of cure, although all you could see was the grey fog of heavy, almost horizontal rain, and all you could smell was diesel, from one of the two belching funnels. If you stood in the right place you could get a faceful of water, but even that tasted more of diesel than of salt. I ambled about inside instead, stopped by the information desk, which was empty, now I guess everybody had been informed, and saw that from the sailing times I might have another eleven hours of this. I spent a couple of minutes getting my breath back, just out of habit, seeing all it ever did these days was creep further and further away. I stood still and looked at the photos of all the smiling staff on the noticeboard, a studio head-and-shoulders shot of each, just to see if my guts could somehow ease back into place on their own, which they did not, and then I just gave up and went back to the pub.

'What's the forecast?' I asked, once another Paddy was plonked down.

'Sorry?' said the barman, in a heavy foreign accent. There was a tankard for tips on the bar, right in front of the till, and somebody threw a handful of loose change in it. Automatically, the Slav turned around and squeezed an old car horn that was strapped to the wall behind him. When I repeated the question he nodded at a colleague just out of sight in a cubby round the corner.

'What's that?' said barman number two, who turned out to be from nowhere more exotic than Birmingham.

'The forecast? What is it?'

He gave me the once over, saw the state of me, took a gamble at my sort of character, and laughed. At about the same time the front of the ship reared up suddenly and then began to fall away, to fall without stopping, like we had sailed off the edge of the world.

'It's not good,' he said.

'Really?' I answered, after the hull had steadied, after those etched mirrors had stopped flapping around on the walls.

'Oh yeah. You know, one day last summer it came out of port and couldn't get back in, the weather was that bad. Everyone was stuck out here for two days. I think even the Captain was sick.'

I paused a moment to let the magnitude of all this sink in, and although the full of horror of it probably lay beyond my ken, the glimpses of hell I got were pretty vivid.

'But it was so calm,' I said, plaintively, thinking of the placid waters of the dockside.

'Doesn't matter, out here. Looks like a summer storm.'

Christ.

'What am I going to do?'

'If I were you,' he said, 'keep drinking. Just drink through it.'

'That works, does it?'

'Might,' he shrugged. 'You'll always be able to blame it on the drink, won't you? The tip jug is over there.'

It was how they talked to me, barmen, if they talked to me at all, either that over-easy informality which had you down as the sort of customer who didn't know what trouble was, or with the mealy-mouthed hostility that saw you as its prime originator. The middle-ground was a tightrope I seemed to hurtle over every time. Nevertheless, he seemed as familiar as he acted, that barman, so I went out to the lobby again, halfway down my whisky, to take a look at those staff photos again.

His was missing. There was a dark patch of backing marking the spot where it had been swiped. And then I realised where I had seen him before, or rather, where I had seen his photograph: I had thrown it into a bin on Swansea High Street after Rebecca Blethyn had given it to me. It was the same guy, the same size photo, the same blue backing curtain as all the other pics. Well I'll be. The name tag underneath was still in place, and read Neil Simms.

'I know who you are, Neil Simms,' I said, slouching over another medicinal.

'Oh yeah?' he said.

'Have you ever seen a big, fat, ugly, slightly crazy-looking, slightly cross-eyed woman, about forty years of age, stood around looking at you?' I ventured.

'Fucking hell,' he said. 'Not her.'

I felt my throat tightening involuntarily and found myself laughing. I must be in the holiday mood, I thought.

'Yeah, well, I believe she has something of a crush on you.'

'A crush? I thought she wanted to kill me. Do you know her?'

'Believe it or not, she hired me to do some surveillance work on you. She said you were engaged and that she was worried you might be having an affair.'

The man laughed again, but in a totally different way.

'Is that what you're doing now?' he said, freaked out.

'No,' I said. 'Woman's insane.'

'You're telling me.'

'She was on the boat, was she?'

'Yeah, she used to stand out there by the door and look in. She'd stand there for hours.'

I remembered the sight of her in her red plastic raincoat with her shopping trolley, peering through the big windows of the Wetherspoons. It hadn't exactly been a comfortable experience. If you didn't know her, and you couldn't leave the bar, because you worked there, say, I suppose that experience might graduate to unsettling.

'She belongs to this family,' I went on, not that I thought he would be happy to hear it, 'the Blethyn family, they're from Swansea: have you heard of them?'

He shook his head. He was lucky.

'I suppose she had one of them with her,' I said. 'She wouldn't have come out to Cork and back on her own.'

'Yeah,' he tilted his head to one side, picked a glass up and polished it intently. 'Huge bloke, looked like an old prop forward. I had some trouble with him too.'

'Yeah? Moi aussi. Anybody else?'

'Some other bloke,' he shrugged. 'Fairly normal-looking. I only saw her a couple of trips.'

'It must have been recent,' I said. The conversation had begun to take a vaguely interesting tangent.

'Yeah, once a week, last couple of weeks, why? What's it to you?'

'I work for them,' I said. 'I don't particularly want to work for them, but they've got me in a corner, you know. I'm going over to pick up a delivery of spirits with a driver of theirs. Stolen gear or something I expect. Tax dodge, maybe.'

'Yeah,' he said, 'well, there's a lot of it about.'

'Yeah,' I agreed. 'They're one of those families, you know. A lot of what? Smuggling?'

The man nodded in a disinterested way. I think he was getting bad Becca flashbacks.

'Yeah, well, I suppose. You don't always need your own boat.'

'No,' I agreed, thinking of wooden keels being dragged up pebble beaches in the light of the moon, secluded coves, Jamaica Inn, all that stuff. Now all you needed was a Ford Transit on the car deck. 'It's dodgy one way or the other, that's a cert. I'll find out, I guess. I've had things on my mind.'

'Tell you what,' he said, 'get off the boat, pick up the stuff, whatever, come and see me on the return leg. Maybe I'll be able to tell you something. Half these people use the same suppliers.'

'Alright,' I said, and then I asked for another whisky and bought him one, seeing the place was quiet, which he downed in a single surreptitious gulp, and then the two of us stood there not looking at each other, like you do, when a conversation has run its natural length.

'She's a piece of work,' he said, still looking off into the middle-distance, perhaps at the spot where she liked to stand, peering in.

'Oh yes.'

It just reeled off my tongue then, a whole list of anecdotes about the stuff she'd got up to and was said to have got up to back in town, surprised at my own fluency, at my ability to amuse another, and especially my ability to amuse myself. Some rare balance of forces, I suppose, of moods and needs, the booze doing what it was always supposed to do in the ads, a barman and a regular conversing happily like you see them do on the telly. Like a coin landing on its edge.

Sometime later I was curled up on the floor by the fruit machines, in the little arcade, when I got a foot in my shoulder.

'They said you wouldn't be hard to find,' said the lorry driver. 'Find the most pissed-up person on the boat, they said.'

Now without any great speed, I peeled myself off a suspiciously sticky floor. There was a crick in my neck from where it had rested against the base of the Mummy's Tomb gambler.

'We're there, are we?' I said.

'We're passing Cobh now. Won't be long.'

'I see.'

He gave me the once-over while I came to, and I did the same, out of the corner of my eye. Some local lad in old jeans, and a greasy barbour jacket, probably thought it gave him a touch of class.

'You from the Eastern bloc?' he said, meaning Cardiff. I hadn't heard that since I was a lad.

'No, other side. Llanelli.'

'Christ. You must think it's bloody Disneyland, Swansea and that.'

I made some kind of laughing sound and then kept my mouth shut, tuned myself off, which wasn't hard to do, once we were down in the hold, its steel walls reverberating with the drone of the ship's engine, in the cool, damp air of a different season. We sat wordlessly in the cab, waiting for the horn to sound, a couple of dozen idling motors slowly filling the place with fumes, and then the prow of the ship opened up like a jaw, and we rolled off down a long metal tongue, out of the belly of the whale, into the bright evening sunlight of County Cork, a westerly light, softer and clearer somehow. You could tell in an instant you were in another country, just from the lay of the land, fat, soft, and rolling, nothing like the dark hills of home. We breezed through customs, what with having an empty trailer, but they didn't seem to make too much of a show with anybody else either. Well, not the Caucasians.

We pulled out of the ferryport and straight into the car

park next door, if a car park was what it was; an empty and apparently ownerless patch of concrete. One of those vague urban spaces that accumulate on transient spots. Another lorry followed us in from a lay-by on the other side of the road, a rig with a crane carrying a big yellow container, and pulled up alongside. My driver turned off the engine and climbed out, and after a moment's hesitation, I followed suit.

Three men squeezed out of the other cab and assembled rather coolly around us, although I suppose if they had been all warm and friendly that would only have been more worrying.

'Alright, Brian,' said the one in the middle, some guy about my age in a three quarter-length leather coat. He nodded at me. 'This the new fella?'

Brian the lorry driver nodded back.

'He'll be coming with me from now on,' he said.

'Fair enough.'

'Want a quick look inside?' said another one of them, in a similar brogue. 'Check the merchandise, etcetera?'

I had a little of vision of Brian clambering into the back and pulling out a box of brandy for me to take a sip from, like the junky at a drug deal, checking the purity of the gear. Unfortunately not.

'No,' he said. 'You're good. Got the shipping documents?'

The man in the leather coat clambered up the side of the cab and reached for some papers behind the sun visor, held them out towards my driver.

'Give them to him,' he said, turning his nose up. 'He's the man for the paperwork now. Just show him where to put his cross.'

And there was some air of derision in his voice that the others caught, and matched, from here on in. The man with the leather coat flipped through them wordlessly, showed me all the right spots with the end of a biro. I signed on the dotted as requested, read a trade name across the top: Doran and Donnelly. They were a couple of official-looking forms with the harp at the top, something else maybe to do with insurance. Meanwhile, behind me, I heard the groan of straining chain as the unit's crane shifted the cargo, and when I turned around Brian and the third man were already angling the descending container into place. Five minutes and we were done.

'That it?' I said.

'Just about,' said the man with the leather coat.

'Excuse me, mate,' I imagined saying, 'but there isn't any chance I could buy a machine gun off you, is there?'

Then everybody turned and looked at me and a silence opened up as big as the Irish Sea, but there was no ferry to cross it with. Well, I thought, you were between a rock and a hard place. I flicked a glance at the guy with the Belfast accent, standing by the crane's control box. I knew they would take offence. Who wouldn't? The soft wind came in over the bay, and I felt an imminent kicking in the breeze. If I was really unlucky, I thought, they would actually sell me one.

'Ignore him,' said Brian. 'Pissed off his face.'

And lo, everyone did. It was not the first time.

'That it, now?' I said quietly to Brian, once the container was secured.

Brian looked at me in a way that was probably meant to express either yes or no, but just came over as a wave of utter contempt.

'Well if that's it,' I said, 'I thought I'd grab a Guinness or something, you know. Don't worry about me, I'll be on the boat when it next goes out.'

'You fucking better be,' he said, and then, as an afterthought, 'which pub are you going in?'

I looked down the road. There were only two pubs I that could see.

'That one,' I said, pointing indiscriminately at the space between them.

'Okay then,' he said grimly, turning back to that small huddle of men, in the middle of an expanse of empty tarmac, to finish the finer, private details of their little hustle.

The Lough Beg was the nearest, right next door to a mouldy little chapel with a massive painted statue of Jesus outside carrying a cross, a statue as big as the building itself. The pub didn't look much more inviting, and as it turned out, it wasn't. One long empty bar with an old man at the end and no one behind the counter. I went and stood at the bar, looked at the pumps, the same selection you got on the ferry, the same everywhere in Cork, as it turned out, and waited for service. A little while later the old man stubbed out his cigarette, climbed off his stool and disappeared. The next time I looked behind the bar I saw him standing there, his shoulders not four or five inches higher than the bar itself.

'What are you having, nipper?' he said, and I couldn't help but laugh. Not that he joined in.

I asked for a Guinness and he scratched his head and checked something around the back of the till, put some beer-mats into a tidy pile, and then reached down as slowly as he could, like he had a bad back, for my glass, and then flipped the pump and held it at an angle until it was three quarters full. Then he went off and fiddled with a few boxes of crisps and came back and held up the glass and finished off, flipped the pump back up, and then let it settle on the slop tray. He walked to the other end of the bar, fiddled with a bar towel, came back, and put the pint on the counter. I knew it took a long time to pour a proper pint of stout, but this seemed unnatural.

I looked at it sitting proudly there on the bartop, a perfect, unbroken white meniscus crowning a solid, jet-black mass, like the freshest double-cream on a block of ebony. I waited for him to ask for the money, to tell me how much it was. He looked at the upper right-hand corner of my head and felt some missing teeth at the back of his mouth with his tongue.

'Two forty,' he said, eventually, as if it was a proposition.

'Fine,' I said, relieved, and reached for my wallet, and before I could extract it, remembered I was in another country.

'I'm sorry,' I said, and explained my predicament, or rather, my stupidity, and the guy tutted at my arrogance and accepted a fiver in sterling instead. There was no change. I took a draught from my glass, which in fairness was a decent pint, and was pondering my options when a young woman, maybe about twenty years of age and slightly overweight but nice-looking, with some cheap gold on her, came in and looked at me and then stood next to the old man and looked at him.

'I think he's English,' he said, not quite quietly enough.

I said nothing. You cross the Severn and being English is an assumption you don't mind people making, although no one does. Cross the Irish Sea, it's the last thing you want, and of course they take it as read. We fool no one, really; well, not the way we want to.

The girl went behind the bar and poured herself a drink and came and sat down next to the man, and out of desperation I took a look out of the window and saw nothing but the road, the chapel, a couple of houses, and the other pub, which didn't look much better. Brian and the men from Doran and Donnelly were still talking with each other in the empty car park: he was getting down another box of phones from the bed in the top of his cab. You know, I could have sworn it was the same box every time: the fragile stickers were always in exactly the same place. Then I saw the guy in the coat sign for it and then hand it straight back over, and I realised that it really was the same box. And for a moment I thought, I'm too old for this. Bad lying and very sincere violence and people generally projecting way too much front for the little heaps of dirty money they were making, and all the other tediousness of the working crim. And my God, Christ knows what they really wanted me for, a security guard they had to lock in at night, a co-driver who couldn't drive, but there were plans afoot for me, you could be sure of it, unless I shafted them first, or died. For an instant I wanted to chuck it all in and go and sit under a cashpoint on the Kingsway with my hand out like everybody else.

It was about the only interesting thing I'd see around here, anyway.

'When's the next ferry out of here?' I asked.

The girl pretended not to have heard me and the old man did his usual trick and sat there looking all around me, and when he had finished that he sucked some air in through his teeth and said:

'They come and go every twelve hours,' he said. 'During the summer.'

You had to accept your lot, I suppose. You couldn't retire from being a bagman any earlier or easier than you could retire from being lazy, or unreliable. It was, I guess, a kind of a vocation, a calling of sorts, and oh my God yes, how they would call for you, at unexpected hours, from secret locations, alternately (if not simultaneously) threatening and cajoling. Maybe I only did it to feel wanted; it was never the money, that's certain. Always the bagman, but never any of the bag: the story of my life, or rather my life so far. The last chapter was still a blank, and we will see about this, I told myself.

'Well, it looks like a night in Cork for me,' I said, rallying. Brian had doubtless made his own arrangements.

Neither the old man or the young woman said a word. There was no clock, or you'd have heard it ticking. Perhaps if you'd strained hard enough you'd have been able to hear the mould growing in the grouting.

'Where is Cork, actually, then?' I asked. 'I mean this isn't it, is it?'

I waited. I considered putting the question in a letter and posting it to him, and then the man spoke.

'Six miles down the road,' he said.

'I see,' I said again, not feeling particularly buoyed by the likely prospect of further negotiations. Six miles is a long way to travel without valid currency. Just to keep me occupied while we had a little chat, I ordered another two pints of Murphy's (at the same time) and this time the girl served me, and turned out to be slightly quicker, but I still had my doubts. Eventually I changed fifty quid into euros at an exchange rate of one to one, and the old duffer said he would call a taxi for me; one of his friends, naturally.

'So you've stopped using the punts, then?' I asked. I don't know why.

'Yes,' he said, at about the same time my car arrived, which was not soon.

Cork City was nothing like the Lough Beg. The guy that came to pick me up was clean and polite and drove a brand new Toyota, and he drove me carefully but efficiently into town without any inanities, to me or some friend on his mobile. The city itself was bigger than I'd expected, bigger than Swansea, and far more beautiful, although it did not have the natural beauty of the landscape, did not have the wide sweep of bay or bleak hills at its back. But it had quays and river banks, narrow lanes and far better-looking buildings. The centre was on some sort of island between a river and a slightly smaller channel, and it was there he dropped me off, next to the bus station where he said I could catch a ride back to the ferry. The bus station itself was a work of art, bright and clean without a spot of graffiti or scrap of litter, although I spotted a few of the old stereotypes around the place, the grinning idiot, the aged queer in his tweed suit. Compared to the dank, piss-stained shit-hole back in Swansea, or most other British cities, for that matter, it was the Sydney fucking Opera House. Other countries, I thought to myself: you had to pinch yourself sometimes.

The pubs were a different kettle of fish too, even if the booze was all the same in each one. Tidy, warm, well-kept places where people talked and laughed, not a Wetherspoons or a jukebox or a Carling promotion in sight, nobody drinking out of the tin, no fruit machines, no karaoke, nothing. Smoke-free too, with even the bar staff nipping outside for a quick puff. I didn't miss the fags: I drink at too great a velocity these days. In thirty minutes I felt like Bach must have done when he bust out of Weimar.

It was a beautiful, friendly, sparkling place, alright, and the pubs rang with an eloquent buzz that sounded more and more like poetry as the night wore on. It could have been the beer, sure, but I've got drunker at home a million times and heard nothing like it, back home it's just a tapering stream of bitter and unthinking talk, like a coal vein running thin. The people there were well dressed and well spoken, still riding out the Celtic tiger, with lively minds and sharp tongues. They made being shit-faced look like one of the pinnacles of civilisation.

It got to you, though, sitting there like a foreigner all night in a country that thought where you were from really meant something. Being a stranger I could handle, being a stranger was what I usually was, on a good night, but it was something I was used to thinking of as a choice, that I saw some agency in. Being an outsider because of the way you sound when you open your mouth, that's a different thing. I did see a few happy visitors around the place, of course, a few loud and fawning Americans riding out that strange olde worlde identity trip that they like to do, or that they like to do in Ireland, anyway, and a troupe of Basque folk singers in national dress, all woolly waistcoats and big white socks. Basques, see. A tiny nation yearning to be free. And a bunch of Noraid Yanks that somehow managed to support the Contras and the IRA at the same time.

I heard a few Northern Irish accents about the place as the night wore on, and remembered that this was one of the places Republicans went to cool off, if they'd gotten into trouble with the law or each other. It made sense, this being the bottom of the country. Things weren't quite the same after that. I had this friend, maybe not a good friend, but a close one, a copper, who died in an IRA car bomb in Bristol in the eighties (that, at least, was the official story). I'm sure if you had the strength of character you wouldn't let it bother you, little histories like that, but I did not, and they did. The night was not the same afterwards, once the poison had set in. Difficult to live with that sort of latent difference. God knows what it must be like in Ulster, for everybody. A fucking nightmare, I expect.

The wee hours saw me sleeping without trying to look like it in the corner of a twenty-four-hour bowling alley, somewhere in the east of the city, lost, alone and confused, suffering for the first and last time from some mild form of what I understand is culture shock, and certainly, at the very least, pissed off my face. At some time in the night I got a boot in the shoulder that I thought I recognised. It was a lot a harder, but it was definitely the same boot.

'What the fuck do you think you're doing?' hissed Brian. 'Thought you'd do a runner, did you? Go AWOL?'

I got another boot in the shoulder, and put a hand up to feel it, to trace the ridges of my collarbone for cracks. It seemed to be in one piece, and I left my hand hanging off it, hoping to buffer another toecap, if I had to.

'The next crossing's not due till tomorrow morning,' I said. 'Fucking relax.'

'Wrong,' he said, and stamped on the fingers of my other hand. 'The next crossing was last night. Straight off, get the container, straight back on. They turn the whole thing around in ninety minutes. We were supposed to be on it. How long do you think it takes to put a container on a fucking lorry? I've already had to phone the boss. The buyers were supposed to be coming around in the morning to pick it up, they'll have to wait till tomorrow night, now.'

'Oh,' I said, 'right.'

I think he might have calmed down a bit once he knew I wasn't trying to pull some kind of fast one, and I think I lightened the trauma by offering to pay for a good hotel, for breakfast, for his trouble, anything. After that he only dragged me outside and gave me a few around the face, nothing serious, just cosmetic, for form's sake, I guess. It cooled him off a bit. Or, at least, he didn't hit me again, although he continued to insult me and generally shove me about a bit until we got back to Wales. He wanted to be going home, and instead he had been driving all around Cork city in his artic because he couldn't leave a container full of spirits lying about, and he was not happy.

We spent the night in a bed and breakfast on the outskirts, some place he knew from before, a little Georgian house with pink rooms and lots of frills. We had to buzz the doorbell for a good five minutes solid before we could rouse the landlady, it being the middle of the night, and she wasn't happy either. Brian took three hundred quid off me for the accommodation, which I knew was ridiculous, but it wasn't my money.

The next morning I was awake in good time, lying abed in no particular state of ease, waiting for another kick to the shoulder to get me up. If he kept going, I thought, he would definitely break something. Instead he burst in and grabbed me by the shoulders, flipped me onto the floor, did it that way. Once he knew there would be no comeback, I guess, he never stopped booting me about, should we be in the same place for any length of time. It may have been, I suppose, that he had some unresolved personal issues of his own.

At the docks we were queuing with the rest of the freight when the Gardaí appeared and singled us out, came up the driver's side with a few questions, and Brian pointed them in my direction and passed me the papers from the dash. They had a quick look through them, asked me if I was the person that had signed them, got my signature on another piece of paper and left us alone. Nothing out of the ordinary, it seemed like, nothing worth fussing about.

On board Brian shoved me out of the cab, told me that he'd come and find me when the time came, and left me to my own devices. Without having to think too much about it I found myself back in Paddy Murphy's magic shrinking pub, witnessing national identity condensed into some form of cultural psychosis, listening to the auld eye-diddly-oh music, drinking the black stuff with whisky on the side, hoping I'd catch sight of Neil again, and then drinking without hoping anything at all.

I caught a glimpse of him through the frosted window a couple of hours later, and managed to get out and catch up with him before he disappeared.

'I'm not doing the bar tonight,' he explained. 'I'm serving in the Acropolis.'

I took a hold of his arm so he couldn't move away.

'What's the forecast for the crossing?'

'Good.'

'Oh thank fucking Jesus Christ,' I said. 'Listen, I met up with those guys over in Cork,' I said, and passed on what little I had found out. I'd had stuff on my mind, I suppose, and the distractions too of a strange city just over the hill, waiting in the night. I was not the man I used to be. Years ago I would have eaten those details up without noticing it, would have hungered for them without feeling it. I was a private detective once. Perhaps I just didn't care anymore. It took work, certainly. It was a faith that needed sweat.

'Doran and Donnelly?' said Neil, rubbing his chin. 'They're bent as a nine-bob note. Just about everyone that gets done by the customs on this ferry has bought from them. They never seem to get burnt themselves, although they've been in trouble. I don't think they're allowed to export anymore.'

'Maybe that's why we had to go and pick it up ourselves,' I said. 'Does customs catch many, then?'

'They'll do a random check once in a blue moon, and they always find somebody then. Like raindrops in a storm, you know. Otherwise you won't see them unless they've done a little homework of their own, or somebody's tipped them off. What can they do? Do you know how much duty is in this country? If they taxed it any more it wouldn't be a tax, would it, it would be a fucking prohibition. It's no wonder there's so much of this stuff coming in.'

'Yeah,' I said, 'still, I can't see the firm I'm working for chancing their arm like that.'

'Oh no, they'll have a bonded warehouse; get a company to front it. A couple of directors who don't exist living out of a post office box somewhere. Import it under license, see, nothing declared, pay the duty in full every quarter, or what have you, straight to the Exchequer, at least that's the official line. They just won't write the cheque. The government might let it slide another quarter, maybe two, but that's enough. Dirt cheap booze for maybe three quarters of the year, as much as you can shell out for, as much as you physically bring over. You'd make some cash off of that.'

It was a familiar story. I had bought the stuff in a hundred cheap and not so cheap pubs across the country, can after can after whole shrink-wrapped slab, had smoked it too, rolled up kilo upon kilo of it, handed out my pound coins to diffident men with holdalls full of it in bus stations and bookies and launderettes and a dozen other such places. Now, for the first time, I was on the flipside, watching it come in, and I saw with a start that somewhere amongst all that spare change grimy cash fortunes were quietly amassing all over the country, even in cities like Swansea. J. P. Morgan said that when you finally understood how simple the basic principles of banking were you realised how obscene it was, and I had some similar revelation, stood there in the foyer outside Paddy Murphy's pub, thinking about the tidy sums that even the no-good do-nothings like me slowly and innocently accumulate in other people's pockets.

'There's nothing Customs can really do,' Neil concluded.

'No,' I agreed. 'Come out once in a while and scare the shit out of some daytrippers, impound a motorhome or two, that's your lot. There was one other thing.'

'Yeah?'

'Box of mobile phones. They've got it bouncing back and forth over the Irish Sea like a fucking ping pong ball. Never open it, never seem to send it on, just sign for it and boot it back.'

'Oh yeah,' he said, with some relish. 'That's the carousel.'

'The what?'

'The carousel. That's a good one. That's worth fucking billions, that is. It's simple. Two traders, right, both in the EU. Trader A registers his company, Potato Phones or whatever, exports a bundle off to Trader B, in a different EU country, who buys them. He registers his company in his own country too: Windsor Telecomms, or something. But every time you buy a phone from another EU country the importer, Trader B, is going to have to pay foreign VAT on the phones he buys in. Now he shouldn't have to do that, by law, goods sold between EU countries are VAT-free. The government of the destination country adds on the VAT themselves. So he puts a claim in, gets the money back for the foreign VAT he's paid from the Excise, seventeen and a half per cent or what have you on fifty grand, say, and HM Customs sticks on their own which Trader B writes down in his little ledger, ready for his first return.'

The barman paused for a flicker of thought.

'A little under nine grand,' he said. 'Cheque from the Bank of England, thank you very much. He does that every week, maybe every other day, whenever the consignment comes in. Nine grand or more week after week and all you pay for is the postage and shipping. Then, when your first quarter rolls around, and the knock is waiting for your first VAT return, low and behold: Windsor Telecomms is nowhere to be found, no business, no office, no trader, no little ledger, buggered off into thin air with as much money as he dared to make. Meanwhile, Trader A, over the sea, he's been doing the same thing with his own customs people. That's why they call it the carousel. Of course, that's a simple explanation. In practice, the more you spread it around the more cash you can haul in, so there might be half a dozen countries involved, Traders A, B, right up to Z, although they'll all disappear when the time comes.'

'The carousel,' he nodded. 'Money for old rope. I suppose they'll figure out a way to stop it in ten or twenty years.'

'Yeah,' I said. Dodgy money. It was seemingly a destiny of mine to be around it, like the way those little brown birds, the ones you see on the estuary, on the banks of a grubby river, were just destined to be around mud. Maybe it wasn't so much choice as a question of habitat, after all it was what they were supposed to do: skip around on the flats and hope the big oozing mass underneath might offer them a worm or some other morsel. They didn't worry about it too much, I guess. Some evolutionary ancestor of theirs found some muddy spot millennia ago and thought it was an easy life, and that was it. They were the same colour as mud now.

I had been a bagman all my life. Most people are, I think, in some form or another, without ever thinking about it, but it's different, down here; ironically, down here, in the land of the lawless, as guarded and dishonest as it is, there is a lot more nakedness in your relationships with those around you. Job titles, the question of a corner office, there are no such distractions down here. Sometimes, I guess, you can feel some wisdom in your disillusionment, some truth in your corruption, that others who do not suffer the same way are missing. You can tell yourself that society can only be seen properly from underneath, that whatever else, you were some kind of straight dealer and society was never anything but hypocrisy, you can trace some kind of dignity and meaning in your cheap lousy life. You can, but let me tell you, it takes a fuck of a lot of effort, and you just feel worse afterwards. In truth, down here, hate, fear and envy are the only real constants, and everything else is just justification after the act, a postscript that will do nothing to change the way you feel every evening, while the optic fills.

'I don't think I'll see any of it,' I said, and the barman laughed, easily, and looked at me and said he didn't think I would. He had my number. Then he asked me if I was going to come on up to the restaurant and have some crab claws in garlic butter, and I said I wasn't hungry, and went back to the bar, to make the most of those spirits before we came into dock. I got about four fingers of neat gin in a paper coffee cup and took it out on deck, into the sun and the diesel, and watched the slow creep up the Bristol Channel, till we pulled around Worm's Head. If my eyesight was better I might have been able to see my son's house, and I drank my gin and wondered if he was going to be able to keep it.

When the familiar shore of Swansea Bay pulled into view, with its wide sweep of yellow sand, those remembered hills, that omnipresent concrete, I clutched a hold of my empty cup and watched the dockers fussing about with the guide ropes down by the ramp, waiting for Brian.

If I was standing up, it stood to reason he wouldn't be able to kick me in the shoulder.

IV

'I tell you what we should fucking do,' said Tomos, 'fucking lock him in there, innit?'

Tomos had come down dockside with Gavin and James and had probably stood there with mounting excitement while the terminal staff had got the ramp in place and the first of the lorries started rolling out. Very probably he had been up half the night before too, like a child on Christmas Eve. My no-show this morning probably had him eating his own hands with impatience, and now, having somehow lasted until evening without spontaneously combusting, there was nothing under the tree. I told him they didn't carry that sort of thing around with them, but I'd given them the money and they were going to bring one with them for the next meeting, and he could have his machine gun then. It was perfectly plausible in the short-term, and the short-term was all I had now. He took out his frustrations by insisting I be locked in the container overnight.

James Blethyn stroked his chin. The container did present a bit of a predicament: it had over three hundred thousand pounds' worth of spirits in it at retail value, and it wouldn't fit in the warehouse, which was really just a small industrial unit, and already almost full. What was worse, it was still stuck on top of the lorry, and a sixteen-year-old kid from Port Tennant could have driven the whole thing away in an instant, if he felt like going for a joyride in a DAF.

'If you'd been on time,' he said, 'this wouldn't have been a problem. The customer wanted to come down here this morning and take delivery of the whole job lot, but you had to go sightseeing, didn't you? You had to miss the night crossing. Can't expect him to come down now, at nine in the evening, for fuck's sake. What are we going to do with this little lot all night? It's just as well Bri gave you a pasting or I'd have done it myself. Might still.'

'Sorry,' I said, for perhaps the seventh or eighth time. 'You'll find a buyer. I shouldn't imagine your overheads are that high: you can undercut anyone you want.'

'But I don't want to undercut anybody, do I, you cuntox? I could have the stuff flying off the shelves if I wanted. But I'd like to make a decent profit, if that's alright with you. Finding decent buyers takes time and effort and a bit of rep.'

'We should lock him in the fucking container, innit,' insisted Tomos, pig-eyed with enthusiasm.

'No,' said James. 'We'll wait for Craig to get here with the crane. He wouldn't fit inside anyway, it's floor to ceiling in there.'

'We could take a few boxes out.'

'Nah, what's he going to do in there all night? You open it up in the morning it'll stink of piss and maybe worse than that. Sides, someone wants to take it, how's he going to help, stuck in there? They won't fucking know he's in there till they get to where they want to take it, and it'll be too late then. And they might not open it up for days. He'd be fucking dead.'

'Yeah,' said Tomos, gurgling with pleasure at the thought. But his enthusiasm waned pretty quickly when he realised that no one else saw any pressing need to hurt or humiliate me, and after standing around for five or ten minutes waiting for the crane, waiting not ten feet from me, without feeling he could abuse me in some way, I think it got to him, and he said he was going down the Old Duke and fucked off. The lorry driver was down there already, had nipped off when he'd found out any kind of waiting was involved at all, when he'd sensed the possibility that somebody might ask him to do something.

'Next time I think we'll wait until the goods are here all safe and sound and then we'll ring the customer,' James said, turning to Gavin. 'I mean that'll only mean a day's delay at most.'

'Yeah,' I chipped in. 'You never know if there's going to be a bad turn of weather out there or something.'

'Shut up, bad turn of weather, fuck's sake,' said Gavin, who pulled a feint to my jaw, an obvious stupid jokey feint. I flinched anyway. People do. 'You're off again a week today. Just behave yourself, or there might be a little case of man overboard, alright?'

'There's that box of mobile phones in the cab,' I said to James, remembering about the carousel, wondering if I had this right.

He didn't open it, he didn't look at it, he didn't seem in any way annoyed at what was supposed to be a customer returning a box of phones off the bat without even looking at it. He just nodded.

'We'll send it out UPS tomorrow morning,' he said. 'You can sign for it then.'

The carousel was the only explanation that made any sense. The boxes of phones I'd been signing for all this time had really all been the same box, netting a seventeen and a half per cent return every time it crossed a border, and I was still thinking about this, about the awful, lucrative simplicity of it when Craig arrived with his flat-bed crane, a little wiry guy that could have been a jockey if he'd been brought up round horses, which I'd be prepared to bet he hadn't. According to the livery, he was with one of the big civil engineering teams that worked the roads, borrowing a bit of kit from site when no one was looking I shouldn't wonder, and earning a bit of the folding for himself in the process. According to the man himself he'd just come down from some three-month contract along the arse end of the M4, past Pontardulais.

Craig was nimble like a rigger, the sort of guy you could easily imagine jumping around foresails and topmasts in a different century. He had lifting chains attached to each of the four corner lug holes and was back at the control box on the side of his truck within two minutes of arriving. After some consultation with Gavin, he hauled up the container and landed it down with one end backed up against the warehouse wall.

'That's one door they won't be getting in through,' he said. After some consultation it was decided to 'borrow' a skip from elsewhere in the docks and drop it right up against the other end, so both doors were blocked.

'Put it back in the morning no one's gonna complain, are they?' said Gavin.

It had gone ten by the time all that had been sorted out. I had sat on an old tyre and watched the Cork ferry load up and sail away again, watched its lights disappearing slowly down the channel. Sometimes the world can seem a very small place indeed, and all of it the same. I didn't mean to, but I started thinking about what it would be like to get on that ferry again, and have a good few leisurely hours sat on the deck, out the back, and watch this fucking city slowly disappear, knowing I would never see it again, and enjoying it. It was an old dream, that. It wasn't always Swansea, and it wasn't always the Cork ferry, but it was a dream I'd had all my life. Fuck off somewhere else and never come back. It never worked out. Irony was, you didn't have to do anything and in time life would do that for you, for anyone; take you away, for good, and nobody waxed lyrical about that.

'That it?' said Craig, when the skip was in place.

'Yeah. You go on home, and not a word to anyone. Anything happens to this lot, you're the first person we come to. Alright?'

'Okay, Gav. How about some money? I'm out of pocket for the diesel.'

'Pop into the office next time you're in town. We'll sort you out with something.'

'Okay. Next lot's in Thursday afternoon, isn't it?'

'Yeah. But we'll have a rig with a crane on it by then.'

Gavin waited until the crane-man had left, taking his truck straight back to site before anybody found out it was gone. He had probably expected some money, I suppose, for the time and the risk, but he was fobbed off and vaguely threatened instead. Yet he hadn't looked surprised, and neither was I. I wondered what sort of hook they had in him. They must have had something, that seemed the basic condition of employment with the firm.

'The boss has the keys to the warehouse,' Gavin said to me. 'Can't lock you in for the night, can I?'

For the first time I realised that James had slipped off somewhere, probably after Tomos left, when we were still waiting for the crane to arrive.

'Where's he gone, then?' I asked.

He clicked his fingers and pointed at the Chrysler.

'In,' he said.

Gavin knew where James was, or if he didn't his first guess turned out to be pretty good. Having brazenly parked on the double yellows outside the front doors, Gavin limbered up the stairs to the main room of the Grosvenor Casino on the High Street, and at my own pace, I followed after him.

James was sat around the nearest blackjack table with a large pile of chips in front of him: his stake, I'd guess, considering he hadn't been here long. There were five stools around the table and four of them were full.

'Boss,' said Gavin.

James was about to speak but then caught me in the corner of his eye and looked up to Gavin for a suitable explanation. Gavin turned and saw me and a look of mild vexation, flecked with utter contempt, crossed his face when he realised I hadn't waited in the car.

'You've got the keys to the warehouse,' he said, haplessly.

'Yeah, well,' said James. 'Now you're here get some chips and stick your oar in for a few hands. Sit down next to me and I can bet on your cards and all, can't I, if your hand's any good.'

Although he might not have been there long, judging from his face he was already well locked in. The tension showed on his forehead. There had already been a few hands he should have passed by, or not passed by, at any rate his blood was up. Gambling with another hand: you lose twice as fast, you win twice as fast, but the feelings of intensity must be squared at least, maybe cubed or more. It wasn't an uncommon sight, by the looks of things. The other two stools were occupied by some sixty-year-old spiv in a patterned woolly jumper and a lot of gold and his tracksuited grandson, who were doing exactly the same thing. The kid couldn't have been more than twenty-one, and granddad had given him enough chips to stay on the table for an hour or two, as long as he laid down the minimum and never raised. The old guy chain-smoked Sovereign cigarettes, from a pile of cartons that were even higher than his chips. I stood there and watched for a couple of minutes and saw that stack of chips move up and down like a lift in an office building. The two of them must have been here for some time, and he was getting reckless, and tired, and his play got more and more volatile. He could have put his grandson through university with what he had on the table at one point, at other times he couldn't have bought him a set of encyclopaedias. How'd he get the money, I wondered? Bought his own council house maybe, get a few payments in, and then remortgage, take what you can get and bring it in here. That was my first thought. But he could have made it, it could have been used cars, or even savings, from some stall or workshop, but it was obvious he hadn't been born with it, and it looked pretty likely he wasn't going to die with it either. He would come in here while it lasted for the pep and vitality he could wring out of it, a retired man capable of betting a decent month's salary on a single hand, and then he would get hurt badly and he would go home and get bitter and die. But for now he had his hands on the reins of destiny, and a mystical wind blowing through the last of his hair.

James Blethyn must have had eight or ten thousand on the table when I came in. He played a slow and steady game, but his face was full of tics and his fingers couldn't stay still. Maybe he needed some fags, but I couldn't help feeling he wasn't really enjoying himself. He liked sitting at the table, behind a big pile of chips, that made him feel like a bigshot without looking too flamboyant or fake. Fair enough; but when he put the money down he grimaced like a man with a touch of the acid.

Some dentist, or accountant, or at any rate a guy in cufflinks with gold-rimmed glasses from the Gower, took up the last empty stool, and after twenty-odd minutes a small crowd of onlookers built up: this was the table for the highrollers. A couple of waitresses from eastern Europe came and went, delivering free drinks to the players. Pretty soon after that I sloped off to the bar myself, and reaching into my jacket pocket I peeled another tenner off Tomos's much diminished roll and got myself a Kronenbourg. Then I went and found an empty seat in front of a bank of electronic roulette machines, and looked around and drank it. It was a cheap casino, the Grosvenor, and a chain. The women that worked there wore a lot of make-up. If they weren't croupiers they were middle-aged or foreign, and if they were croupiers they were overweight and yawned, although they had nice haircuts. The men that worked there were gay. For the most part. The floor manager was an immaculate Persian in a black suit who looked like he'd walked off a film set. Behind a partly open door in the back wall I saw a room full of monitors feeding off the closed-circuit television, and a security guard who had actually shaved, who was watching them. Two more men with ear pieces walked the floor in black suits, both wearing black puffa jackets even though they were inside. They had bouncer stamped all over them, and I wondered if they were two of James Blethyn's boys. More than likely: I doubt he would grace the place with his patronage unless they were going to do something for him in return. And somewhere around the place there was probably a house dick in plainclothes, one eye on the punters and another on the staff.

The machines in front of me flashed and peeped. Each terminal had its own leatherette stool and digital screen, displaying a virtual roulette table randomised by some clever bit of programming to mimic the real thing as closely as possible. You slipped your notes into the slot and a little pile of virtual chips would appear on your monitor, and you could place them on the desired parts of the little digital table by tapping the glass.

A Malaysian girl, a prostitute, I think, from one of the town's brothels, sat next to me and fed twenties into the machine like she was working at a production line. Before each spin of the wheel she practically threw chips all over the table, outside bets, inside bets, corners, streets, rows, the lot. She couldn't get the money on that little baize screen fast enough, and she had a lot of it. She giggled when she won and betrayed absolutely no sign of anything whatsoever when she lost. Easy come, easy go. It's the only way the world makes any sense.

All in all I suppose it should have been a tired, desperate, washed-out sort of place, and maybe it sounds like it, but it wasn't. It still had an air of glamour to it. It might be tired and clichéd and stupid and unnecessary, but if you put your precious thousands on a number or a colour in there then you were staking a good bit of your life, and the quality of it, on nothing more than chance, and chance reduced by house odds, to boot. You sat there and watched some disinterested, sleep-deprived woman in a half-inch of cosmetics take the next card from the sock, or spin the wheel, and you looked on and took it. They say gambling is a mug's game, but it was no game in here. Played straight, a night in here could change as much of your life as you could afford to lay down, months, years, decades. I think that was the reason most people did it, just to know that such change existed, so they could feel its presence, and maybe tell themselves they could stand it, even master it. Certainly they did not come here out of hope.

I have been a gambling man for most of my life, whenever I have had something to gamble, but I always wanted to win, and I guess for a long time I could make myself believe that winning out was a possibility. Suffice to say, I never went to casinos. I spent all my time in bookies doing sports betting, on the horses mostly. You don't need high stakes or nerves of steel, just a little information and some long odds, a couple of quid on a yankee or heinz or perfecta. Some people knew what they were doing. Some didn't. All the bookies did was charge a fee for transferring the cash laid down by the many into the hands of the few: that's why they sometimes call themselves turf accountants, right? Bookies were different to casinos: no glamour, lots of hope, lots of time.

I got another couple of pints in and watched the girl next to me play. She looked happy enough. She would lose some and win some every time, and she liked it when she was up, and she didn't mind it when she was down, but it was the betting itself she seemed to like most, those long, glossy fingernails tap-dancing frenetically across the monitor until the call went out, thirty or forty quid a pop. I liked her a lot, actually. She let me look on without the slightest sign she knew I was there, in that demure way a lot of these Eastern women seem to have, although I think a few of the giggles and flourishes were there for my benefit. She liked me watching, all the punters in here liked somebody to see them (not so with the bookies, with that little folded slip handed shyly over; fifty pence on a six-way permutation).

At some point I realised that a number from the first third hadn't come up in six spins. Then seven. Then eight. Without any conscious thought behind it, my hand moved down towards the pocket of my jacket which had Tomos's gun money in it, and to my very moderate surprise, twenty quid found its way into the machine. Out of that I put a fiver on the first twelve, and when the clattering white ball came to a standstill it was under number five. I felt a flush of vindication and sat back, reminiscing idly about a cigarette, and waiting for another streak, a streak of anything that left something out.

Maybe halfway down another pint came seven odd numbers in a row, but by the time I'd double-checked the spin history the wheel had gone again, and sure enough, it came up even. Fine. It only proved the system worked. After half an hour or thereabouts it hasn't landed on the middle twelve once in the last seven. Cautiously, I put a tenner on. No ice. On goes a twenty. Likewise. This is impossible, I think, and I'm just starting to get worried, feeding in another forty off this violent idiot's roll just to stick it all straight on, but then I win off it, win off a nice big forty-quid stake. Like a genius, I decide that a long, nerve-wracking period of doubling is precisely what I want: the stake gets larger, the win gets bigger and more likely. The next time I see nothing in the first twelve for seven spins I put a fiver on it and find myself actually hoping that I lose, so I can ramp the stake. But I don't. I win.

A little later, having made four consecutive and successful bets, my winnings already total sixty-five quid. There have been over a dozen times in the last fortnight when I would have eaten my own shit for sixty quid. I would have boxed bare-knuckle to unconsciousness, if somebody found me an opponent in my own very particular class. Now, all of a sudden, sixty quid wasn't sixty quid anymore. In retrospect, I am not surprised. You can never really gamble without forgetting a part of yourself, without ignoring something you already knew. That's what gambling is. A search for a pattern and order where you know, rationally, there can be neither. It is, on that level, a kind of divination, just like that practised by the mystics and the holy men of old, and it too requires a certain kind of transcendence.

The girl next to me only became marginally less animated now that my attention was divided. I looked over and saw that she had almost two and a half thousand credits on her account, nearly five hundred quid. Whether this was more or less than she had put in was impossible to tell. She was still enjoying herself. I kept to my strategy with a cool patience and cold lager, brought out on a tray by a young Ukrainian, waiting for the right wave before I jumped into the sea. I had, of course, no way of telling the time in there, it wasn't something they wanted you to find out if they could help it, but I would say in about an hour I was up two hundred quid. In two hours I was up nine hundred. In two and a half I'd made I think something like two and a half grand, and in three I had nothing, except hair matted with sweat, the inability to taste anything, and mounting fear of a violent end. I left the Asian hooker giggling to herself and went into the toilets, where I used some of my loose change buying paracetamol from the machine, and then sat on the bog for half an hour. It was the only place where I could be alone. After half an hour in a pissy cubicle with nothing but the knowledge that I had knowingly and deliberately fucked myself up, I decided alone was something I didn't want to be, and went out to stand by the blackjack table. The same players were still there. Time had stopped for them, was still stopped.

I had lost all of my winnings and practically everything Tomos had given me, something like fifteen hundred quid, everything but loose change and maybe a hundred and fifty in crumpled notes in different pockets. I wasn't surprised at all. I am a bookies' man, and should never have gone in a casino. Gambling has probably been the only outlet for whatever hope I ever had; I play to win, and have always been too desperate to do anything else. That's okay in a bookies. You can stretch the odds and flutter away an afternoon for a tenner: there are rarely much more than thirty races in a day and it takes time to cover all that lot. In here there were so many chances flying about they could cut you to nothing in under an hour, and people laying down notes like wallpaper. I hadn't been ready for it.

Intuition, human emotion, tells you that if red comes up ten times in a row then one spin soon it will have to go black. It must go black. In the long run, everything evens out, right?

Not so, not the case, not here. That doesn't work in a closed system, where your previous selections are not discarded, but left in play. You can pick red seventeen if you like, but the next time the wheel rolls, red seventeen is still on the table. Memorylessness, the mathematicians call it: the last spin of the wheel does not influence the next. The past does not always matter as much as we think it does. But then we do not live in a closed system. People are born. And people die. And maybe in the long run everything does even out, but in the long run, as the economist said, we are all dead. So we cling to the mainsail, each of us, faces aft to shore, to our little histories blessed or cursed, and wait for the impossible, the inevitable run that breaks you and takes everything you have. Deep down, like most people, I suspect, I have known this for most of my life.

The five players around the table, the old gypsy and his chav grandson, the retired professional, and James Blethyn and Gavin, all had stacks that looked more or less the same size they started with. I don't think any of them had left the table since I came in, and it must have been the middle of the night by now. I got another lager with my spare change and poured it down, just for something to do. It still didn't taste of anything. I peeled another two pills from the foil wrap and finished it off.

My supposed boss still didn't seem to be enjoying himself. He winced with each chip he put down, and the only time he wasn't grimacing was when he was exchanging small talk with the guy with cufflinks and gold-rimmed glasses. I couldn't figure out what James Blethyn was really doing there; when he won he seemed more relieved than satisfied. He was so cautious it didn't seem like it was gambling at all, whereas everyone else was a bundle of nerves, which after all was what they wanted to be. That was how it worked in here for most people, whether they knew it or not. As long as they were sensible (unlike some) they could take a stool and put a pulse-quickening wedge of money onto the table and sit there all night, and when they left they would have more or less what they started with, probably a little less, maybe a little more; sometimes a lot less and very occasionally a lot more, but it would nearly balance out for most people if they weren't stupid. Over the course of a night they would lose and win, and their heart would be in their mouth and their stomach, but they would walk out close on with what they walked in with. They got their slice of excitement and the house got their percentage for providing it.

That was another reason why you couldn't play a system in here, even one as stupid as I'd played. Even if you had a very cautious, patient system you would see your money dwindle to nothing over time, as the house edge slowly bled you out. What you needed was decision, was one bold strike, like that guy from London, Ashley Revell. He sold everything he had, house, car, furniture, his bloody clothes, flew to the Plaza Hotel in Las Vegas and put it all on red, everything he had. I had seen a documentary on Sky One about it in the Heathfield earlier this year.

James Blethyn's face looked like cheap paper, and his eyes had turned into coin slots.

'I'm done,' he said, getting up from his stool.

Gavin nodded and we all went out to the car.

'I suppose we better take this idiot home first.'

Gavin suppressed a yawn, the night air, I guess, and nodded and shrugged at the same time, and we all got in, those two up front and me in the back. Inside the car smelt of soft leather and old cigar smoke and chemical pine. Nothing beeped, nothing flashed, nothing spun. It was lovely.

'How'd you get on?' I asked.

'Fine,' he said. 'Just fine. Mission accomplished.'

'Win much?' I pressed.

'Well, I didn't lose much, put it that way, and that's what it's about. I still have most of my money.'

I was a little incautious, I guess, what with having lost all that money, and the lack of sleep, and being made to wait for another two hours by the side of a blackjack table.

'Except it's all accountable now, isn't it?' I said. 'And tax free.'

All the money that comes off the table is won. Doesn't matter how long it was there for, or for what. You played it safe as you could and if you came out five or ten or fifteen per cent down then that wasn't too bad, for a laundry bill. Some nights I guess you even nudged ahead a little.

I saw Gavin's eyes shoot up in the rear-view. James spun around in his seat, the leather creaking as he did so, and put an arm over the back of it, looking at me straight in the eye. We crossed the New Cut Bridge, the obsidian Tawe oozing slowly below.

'Yeah,' he said, eventually, and smiled a phoney little smile. 'Yeah, it is.'

They didn't say anything else to me or each other on the way back to the warehouse, nor while they opened it, or locked me away, and not, I imagine, till they were a good way back over the river. I had probably given too much away, but still, I had received a confirmation, and was alone now, at last, and could sleep, or something like it.

He won, by the way, Ashley Revell.

THREE

DEFALCATION

I

By the Tuesday of next week Scotty had come round again in Chester's shitty little Nissan Bluebird, and I had pretty much decided what I was going to do. Not how, exactly, but what was settled. I'd had three nights inside the warehouse and three days spent outside in the yard, seventy-two or so hours spent doing nothing but thinking and drinking, and I'd had enough of both. Well, I'd made a decision, anyway.

'I'm going to fuck the Blethyns over,' I said. We were sitting on the concrete floor of the yard with our backs to the steel door, the sun beating down pretty much full on from the middle of the midday sky.

Scotty's hand scrabbled in the dust and came up with a small pebble, which he threw, squinting, at Chester's car, parked roadside at the other end of the yard. It dinged the front wing and Chester made some vague noises of protest but we had ordered him to stay in the vehicle unless told otherwise, so you couldn't really hear him.

'What?' said Scotty.

I repeated what I had said.

'I think I can take them for a couple of hundred grand,' I said.

'Are you serious?'

I said I was.

Scotty's opinions about James Blethyn had undergone

something of a volte-face in the last couple of days, since he'd been able to score again. The problem with the Neath boys had all been smoothed out, although neither of us knew how exactly, and the dealer I'd knocked out was up and about, and dealing to Scotty, even, without a single machete in sight. It turned out he was pretty cheap, too. Whatever Scotty felt towards me was forgotten, and as far as he was concerned, James Blethyn had become the sort of person you boasted about knowing when you were talking to certain people. That the two of them had never actually met didn't bother him.

'Fuck off,' he said. Another pebble arced invisibly in the blaring sun and was followed by the ping of metal and a distant murmur of dissent. 'You're talking funny money.'

I laughed. It seemed like funny money, that much, more than people ever saw, and I could only just believe it myself.

'Anyway, if they found out about it, which they will, if they found out you were even thinking about it, you'd be heading for an unmarked grave. James Blethyn is the man. Who'd miss you?'

'Nobody,' I agreed. 'But I'm serious, Scotty.'

Scotty's hand reached out for another stone.

'Fucking hell. I think you really must have cancer, coming up with that one. Cancer in the fucking brain.'

'You heard that story, then?'

'Yeah. That's one way to get out of a beating, I suppose.'

He picked up a tiny pebble, weighed it, and discarded it. Some things just don't fly, I thought. Some words just don't hang right in the air.

'But I have,' I said. 'In the lung. Really. I'm dying.'

I watched Scotty's hand scrabbling around, but it was not looking for anything now, just making pointless little sweeping motions on the ground, through the dirt and the dust.

'Sorry,' he said.

And the sun was shining so brightly high up there in the

sky you really had to squint, you had to close your eyes up tight.

'I don't know what to say'

'There isn't anything to say,' I said.

'Yeah, well,' Scotty said, meaninglessly, in a tone as flat as stale beer, as hollow as an empty can. 'Sorry.'

'It's not without its advantages, you know. Knowing you're going to die, in a small town, it gives you an angle,' I went on. I may not have sounded very believable. 'I won't implicate you. I'm going to need a little bit of help organising it, but I'll keep you out of the dirty stuff. And I'll bung you a couple of grand when it's done.'

'Alright,' he said, in the same voice.

'Fuck, I'd bung you a couple of grand anyway.'

Had we been the type, we'd have shaken hands on that, but instead we just sat there for a minute and listened to the gulls, out of sight somewhere in the distance.

'I'm going to need a run into town.'

'Now?'

I looked at my wrist but I had no watch, nor any idea what had happened to it, or when, only a vague certainty that I had looked at my bare wrist like that a dozen times before.

'No time like the present,' I said. 'I have to make a few phone calls to start with. As a matter of fact I was thinking of getting myself a mobile.'

'Really?' said Scotty, as we finished our cans.

Scotty seemed to know all about mobiles. Chester seemed to know all about mobiles too, and the suit-boy in the shop also seemed to know all about mobiles. But each one of them seemed to be describing a totally different invention. I didn't have time to hang about, and this character with a thumb-ring and spiky hair was trying to convince me I needed something called bluetooth, or blackberry, or whatever the fuck it was called. He had lost me from pretty much the moment he opened his mouth, and I was pretty sure Scotty and Chester had stopped following a while back.

'Even if you choose not to use it like that,' I remember him saying, 'the contract is so flexible it's not as if you'll be paying for the service.'

I had a brief moment of clarity, looking round at a mostly empty shop that sold nothing but mobile phones and the odd carry case, and watched another sales assistant give a similar treatment to a young couple on the other side of the room. They were all over the place, these shops, all over Britain, and they sold nothing but air. It was a scandal waiting to happen.

'I'll think about it,' I said. I wouldn't have passed the credit check anyway. Two minutes away in the market I got a seven-year-old Nokia on pay-as-you-go for twenty-five quid all in. I had joined the digital revolution.

Scotty and Chester were standing by the big cockles stall in the centre of the market with expressions of modest horror on their faces.

'I can't understand why anyone eats those things,' said Scotty.

'It's good for you, sand,' I said. 'Look at that. Twenty-five pound. A pony, as they say.'

And I held out my purchase.

'That's a fucking joke. My granny's TV control looks smarter than that. What's it got?'

'The numbers one to nine and a zero. It's a phone, Scotty.'

By all accounts the cockles stall had been in Swansea market since before the market had actually been built. Years ago you could get all kinds of seafood here. Fifty, sixty years ago there was fresh lobster from off the Welsh coast, cod as long as a man's leg, salmon from the Usk, trout from the Wye, elvers from the Severn. Now all it had was processed crabsticks made from God knows what, whatever they find on the ocean bed in the Sea of Japan, which were shaped to look like bits of crayfish (from a distance), and cockles. Swansea was still churning out the cockles. It couldn't stop. It would be nice to think somebody wanted them, somewhere.

'Aye, a phone. A phone for fucking losers,' pronounced Scotty.

'Well what about not having a phone? How sad is that?'

'I'd rather be without than have to carry around that piece of shite.'

I was going to say something but thought the better of it. There he was, a twenty-four-year-old man, homeless, unemployed, with no prospects and only what hope he could muster inside of himself, and he was embarrassed by my phone. He had told me that one bad night in Gloucester bus station two years ago he had sucked cock for twenty quid. That, presumably, was a necessary expediency. But my phone was not. I realised with a shudder that all those ignorant, cocky nineteen-year-olds in one-hundred-quid suits up and down the country, those salesmen with black shirts and ties with swirling tribal motifs on them, who put on sunglasses to go outside the shop for a fag, were probably making a very decent living. All they had to do was stand there, really, and people would eat out of their well-scrubbed, silver-ringed hands.

'Well,' I said. 'I need to have a look in the library.'

Neither of them moved an inch.

'I need a quick run to the library,' I said again.

'It's only up the fucking road,' said Scotty. 'What do you want in a fucking library anyway?'

'Why'd you care? It's not your car. Come on, Chester. Let's go to the library and then we'll have that pint.'

'You owe three pound sixty from last week,' he said. 'I gave it to you for the launderette.'

'The what?' said Scotty, laughing.

'Never mind,' I said, and paid up the princely sum, which had after all got me two pints in Wetherspoons, and more or less manhandled them out. 'Let's go.'

What I wanted in the library was a good look at the business directories for other parts of the country. I took some scrap paper from the box and a pen from one of the librarians and made a list of distributors who were far but not too far away: Liverpool, Reading, Swindon, places like that. While I was at it I grabbed the address of a tool hire company up in Cwmbwrla. When I had a dozen numbers I went out into the corridor and started to dial.

I needn't have worried. The first one took it, an outfit from outside Reading.

'I've got a full warehouse,' I told the boss there, 'and more coming in. Make sure you don't turn up with less than two hundred grand.'

Two hundred grand for every last drop of booze in the warehouse, and there'd be that new container coming in too, cash for the lot, all up front. I'd lay on the transport, but if they could turn up with their own lorries they'd be saving themselves some bother, as long as they had a crane on one of them.

'Lorries?' he said. 'Lorries plural? What's wrong with a couple of return trips?'

See, what it was, like, I was running the business myself, see, and going bankrupt, hence the quick and illicit removal of assets before the receivers got them. I gave them the date and the time and my new mobile phone number and told them it was now or never, and the main man down there said okay, and even gave me his home phone number.

'Three trucks be alright? Tell you what, I'll make it four. We'll be there.'

Fine, I said. Fine indeed. When I walked out I felt drunk again.

'This is a very nice library,' said Chester, when I found him, gazing at the metallurgy shelves in the reference room.

'Yeah,' I said, gazing up at the domed glass ceiling, the circular railed balcony, taking in the parquet and the reading desks and the bronze busts. It was. I take it back, they did leave us with some bits of quality building, the Victorians. Empty bits of quality building, mostly. There was hardly anybody here.

'How about that pint then?' I suggested, when we were on the steps. Scotty shot me a look of incredulity which I paid no mind.

'Really?' said Chester.

'Yeah, of course! There's just one other place I have to go first.'

You have to keep them sweet.

The tool hire company wasn't exactly what I'd imagined, to be honest. I suppose I was expecting something out of a *Two Ronnies* sketch, some dark musty room with old men in brown overcoats, smoking Woodbines under a naked bulb with oil-stained fingers. Not a bit of it. Instead there was a sparkling white office that could almost have been a dentist's, if it wasn't for the floor, which was still filthy. I was glad to see it. I was half-convinced I was in the wrong building.

'An angle-grinder?' said the clean-shaven young man behind the counter. 'For cutting steel? Absolutely no problem.'

Within seconds he produced what he called a Hitachi G23, a bit of kit as long as your forearm encased in green and black plastic. The blade looked like an old vinyl 45. It would cut through just about anything, he said. High voltage, see.

'It needs to be petrol,' I explained.

'Petrol?' he said. 'Petrol? There's not much call for those.'

Nor would there be, I suppose. Angle-grinders are serious tools, and if they're going to be used it would be on-site, most likely. Where there'd be a generator, at the very least. Who would need that kind of cutting power anywhere other than a building site? Criminals, most likely. People like me.

'Have you tried Russell's?' asked the man at last, with what might have been a very faint air of distaste, putting the Hitachi away. 'He sells all that kind of shit. Mansel Street.'

'I had no idea that was still a going concern,' I said. I'd walked past it a hundred times, and it looked like the sort of place that had stopped trading when they brought in decimalisation, its windows full of dust, crap and rust. No front, no sign outside to identify it at all, but I knew straight away that was the place he was talking about.

'It's a concern to us all,' was the young man's reply, and I left him to his tidy world of innocent, clean-living builders.

It wasn't too hard to convince Chester to swing by Mansel Street, considering it was on the way back into town, 'right by this great little pub I know.' I left the Bluebird idling in the street and after trying the door, gave it three sharp knocks.

'You don't have to effin' knock,' said a muffled voice. 'It's an effin' shop, innit?'

'It's locked.'

'It's not locked, you muffin, it just needs a spot of greasing.'

I tried again, then again, then gave it a bit of shoulder and found myself tumbling into a small room so full of machinery that its three walls were almost invisible. The shopfront was almost entirely glass, but there was no way of telling that from the inside. Just about discernable was a small wooden counter in the far corner with what you might call a typically Welsh-sized man behind it, bald on top but an awful lot of curly grey everywhere else. He was fiddling with some kind of chainsaw, probably the only thing in the whole place that wasn't broken or filthy, and in a setting like that its newness alone made it shine like the Star of India.

'What can I do you for?'

'Angle-grinder,' I said. 'Petrol.'

He looked up briefly from his gizmo and ran his tongue thoughtfully along his upper teeth.

'Yeah, I've got some of those. Chinese, they are. Let me nip into the storeroom.'

And somehow he extricated himself from behind the counter and disappeared through a tiny door into what was probably nothing more than a cupboard under some stairs. He came out with what looked like a soot-covered metal spider, with a tiny bulbous fuel tank where its body should be, and a semi-circle of rasping blade for a head.

'Twenty-two and a half cubic centimetres,' he said, brushing some of the black dirt off a small panel. 'Don't ask me how long it takes to do nought-to-sixty. The – the Yongkwang Singguang Corporation. Ah, pioneers in there field, hey?'

'So that would be a used angle-grinder,' I said.

'Yes,' he agreed, watching a small grey cloud lift and settle as he dropped it onto the counter-top. 'It has been used.'

It was about twice the size of the Hitachi, which it resembled not at all. It belonged to the props department of whatever studio made the *Mad Max* movies.

'Well, how much do you want for it? It doesn't even look like it works.'

'Oh,' he said, reaching under the counter, 'it'll work.'

He produced a jerry can that looked about half full and filled the tiny tank with fuel. After a couple of abortive yanks on the starter cord, which was no easy matter considering how cramped it was in there, she fired up alright. She was deafening too; so loud I could watch tides of dust jerk around the counter-top in time to the two-stroke.

'See? It'll work. Maybe it won't stand prolonged use,' he said, eyeing me in a strange way, 'maybe you wouldn't want it day-in day-out, but for a one-off job it'll be fine.'

I kept what I like to think is my poker face.

'What's that?' I said, pointing to the other, newer device on the counter. It looked like a chainsaw but it had a series of evil-looking barbs running down it, each one easily the size of a packet of fags.

'Masonry saw. Cuts though brickwork like butter. Some people,' he said, giving me that strange eye again, 'use it to get cash machines out of walls.'

'Not today, thanks. How much do you want for the grinder?'

Well, he more or less cleared me out of the last of Tomas's machine-gun money. Despite my best efforts he wouldn't go under a hundred, and that left me with a single twenty-pound note and some coins. If things didn't go to plan, this would be the last money I would ever have in the world.

'Finished, have you?' said Scotty petulantly after I'd dumped the grinder in Chester's boot. 'Or have you got some scaffolding you need put up or something?'

'I thought I'd buy you two a drink,' I said. 'I said I would.'

'And where's that?' said Scotty.

'The Tenby.'

'The fucking Tenby?'

'Oh yes,' I said, 'that's a lovely pub, the Tenby.'

But I had my reasons.

It was near two when we got there and there was the usual smattering of bikers and students on the tables outside.

'Sit wherever you like,' I said. 'I'll get the drinks.'

I think ideally they would have liked to sit in a different pub, but I left them to take their pick of the ripped polyester and went up to the bar. The bloke behind it was some tall, manky-looking guy all in black. He wasn't wearing any colours but on the patch of wall next to him there was a framed leather waistcoat hanging up with the Y-Rohirrin De

Cymru logo stitched on the back. Back in the early nineties some senior police officer said that motorcycle clubs were the biggest organised crime gang in Britain. Like if you were going to go about running a criminal empire you'd insist everybody did it in uniform. They were vaguely criminal, of course, and they probably weren't fantastically keen on road tax, insurance and speed limits, but they certainly weren't anything like organised. Round here I'd be surprised if they even had bikes.

I ordered two pints of lager for Scotty and Chester and a double rum and coke and a double Jack Daniels and coke for myself.

'Listen,' I said, when they were all served up. 'I need a driver for a day, cash in hand, just to run me about, no questions. Is there anybody round here?'

'Yeah,' he said, without having to think. 'There's the Baptist.'

'The fucking what?'

'This guy, John the Baptist. He's a car nut, he'll do it. I'll give him a ring, he can come round and er, show you his services.'

He reached for a cordless telephone off the shelf behind him.

'There's no need,' I said. 'I don't need to see him beforehand.'

'No,' he said sadly, his head to one side, fingering a thick silver earring. 'He'll want to show you.'

I went and took the drinks back to the table, which took two trips.

'He'll be here in a little while,' said the barman, the second time I came up. 'We've got a DJ on for the afternoon, you can have a listen to him. He's new.'

'Right,' I said. 'Good idea.'

And I took my last two drinks back to our awkward little circle, sat around a small round table in the far corner of the room, on the other side of a pock-marked pool table. There was a podgy guy in a brown leather jacket with a dappled greyhound at the far end of the bar and some thin-as-a-rake thirty-something with half his teeth missing at a table near the front, but other than that we had the place to ourselves, and Scotty and I sat back and waited for Chester to start talking. We understood that there was probably going to be some sort of conversation, but neither of us was going to help him start it.

On a small blackboard above the bar I read the words 'New!!! DJ!!!! DJ Tim Tuesday Afternoons DRUM AND BASE!'. DJ Tim was some fresh-faced student type in jeans and a T-shirt. He didn't look like trouble. I watched him set up his kit while Chester shuffled some beer mats and opened and closed his mouth silently like a fish. Scotty stared with a pained expression out of the nearest window, which seeing it was almost behind him, caused him to stretch awkwardly, but he wasn't going to make eye-contact with Chester unless it was absolutely unavoidable.

'Did your mobile phone come with a hands-free set?' said Chester, finally.

I shook my head. DJ Tim was plugging in two worryingly large stacks of speakers, each one about the size of a fridge-freezer, with a couple of smaller ones on stands behind him.

'Only if you want to use your phone and you don't have a hands-free set you won't be allowed to drive now. That's the law.'

'I don't think I should be allowed to drive at all,' I said, and then the loudest, heaviest, most absurd music I had ever heard burst out of the army of speakers like a series of controlled explosions, Napoleonic cannons set to fully automatic, accompanied by a high hat that sounded like it was being played by a small but vigorous child. I started another sentence and I couldn't even hear it in my own head. Chester was opening and closing his mouth again but I had no idea if words were supposed to be coming out of it.

Then everything stopped.

'Big up to Barman Bill, Tenby Jungle Afternoon,' said DJ Tim, in a nice middle-class English voice.

And then it started again.

'Fucking hell,' I said, 'what's all this, then?' But nobody was batting an eyelid. The podgy guy and the man with the dog and Barman Bill all carried on as if nothing had happened. Don't ask me how they were going to order any more drinks; point, I suppose. I looked at Scotty but he had already spotted the joke and was smiling wryly, and then I cottoned on, and the two of us sat there looking at Chester with attentive, interested faces while we couldn't hear a word he said.

After quarter of an hour some guy limped in, about average height and build, with long black hair and leather trousers, obviously a biker or more likely ex-biker, with that leg. Barman Bill nodded him in my general direction.

'Gentleman about a driver?' he said in a voice like a foghorn. I got up and made my excuses.

'I have to speak to this man,' I said, into the wind.

'Don't leave me here listening to this tripe, for fuck's sake!' shouted Scotty.

'Don't worry,' I said. 'I expect the police'll be here soon.'

'Aye, and then I'll have to listen to this gobshite.'

Nobody wanted to be alone with Chester for any length of time, even grown men. Whatever payment the Baptist asked for it would probably be well worth it, if my only alternative was spending a day in a car with him. I doubt if he knew how to keep a secret either, if push came to shove, and everybody loved shoving Chester.

The Baptist and I walked out of the side door onto

Humphrey Street, where he pointed proudly at a thirty-year-old blue hatchback that was parked on the pavement.

'Reliant Scimitar GTE,' he said.

'Aren't they the same people that made the Robin?'

'Well, yeah,' he said. 'Yeah. But that was for disabled people.'

He looked slightly hurt.

'It's good that you have a car,' I said.

'I've been restoring this ever since the accident. It helped pull me out, I think.'

I nodded.

'It goes then, does it?' I asked. I just wanted to know if it actually started: the thing looked like it had been sat on bricks for a couple of months. I shouldn't have said anything.

'Get in,' he said.

And instantly I was going back twenty years or more, into that hot summer fug that old cars always used to have, the fuzzy heat trapped in by all that heavy glass, that thick black plastic of the dash and the fittings, the shag-pile in the footwells. I leant back against the fake leather seat and I could already hear the peeling sound it would make when I got myself up from it.

He turned the ignition.

'That's a three-litre Ford V6. Just let me turn it around.'

The engine sounded alright. Turning around was definitely not the car's speciality: it came from an era of heavy metal, from the heyday of Dagenham and Longbridge, using British Steel, and lots of it. It probably weighed near-on two tonnes and had no power steering. I watched a thin film of sweat break out on the guy's forehead while he wrenched the thing around, mounting the pavement on both sides of a two-lane road, in a turning circle that would have shamed a small yacht.

'Constitution Hill,' he said, when he had it pointed in the right direction. 'You watch.'

The boy racers loved Constitution Hill, almost as much as they loved the Kingsway. Five hundred yards of steep albeit cobbled road that they bomb down in their little Novas, pulling a handbrake turn at the bottom to avoid an end-of-terrace.

'It's one-way,' I said, pointing at the sign.

'Yeah,' said the man, accelerating, and I began to get the picture and folded my arms and put up with it.

We were doing thirty or forty when we hit the bottom and halfway up we may have touched sixty. Then we were at the top. Is that good, for a car? I have no idea.

'What do you think?' he asked, pulling over.

He had proven that his car could drive uphill, and that he disobeyed road signs.

'Great,' I said.

He fished a box of Bensons out of his shirt pocket and offered me one, and I took it, and we lit up and looked out at the view, not quite as great as that from Townhill and Mayhill, but still pretty good. It was like we'd just gone up to the roof of a tall building in an elevator.

'How much are you paying, then?' he said.

I took a drag from my cigarette and found that I physically couldn't inhale. I couldn't get the suction on it. When I did try, I got a shooting pain across the inside of my ribs on the left side of my chest, and I had to bend forwards in my seat. So I could either leave the thing parked in my gob or dangle it out the window like hand-held incense until it went out. I picked the latter option and said,

'One hundred quid a day. Plus the fuel. How's that?'

'Fine,' he said, without a pause. It was a good deal.

'It won't be till the end of the week and I don't think I'll need you for more than a day. Then maybe another day a week or two weeks after that: I want you to pick me up and drive me somewhere a good way out of town and then leave me there for a bit, basically. Maybe you can run me round a bit when I come back. How's that?'

'Fine,' he said.

'Put your number into this phone here and then you can take me back to the pub.'

When we got there (yes, eighty-five on the way down, and he nearly broke his brake cable when he stopped) he came round to open my door and gave me a wink.

'Anytime you want a driver,' he said, 'you speak to the Baptist.'

I took a last look at him.

'Listen,' I said. 'I'm forty-six years of age and I'm not a well man and I don't have time for all this Baptist crap. What's your real name?'

'Jake,' he said eventually.

'And your surname?'

I watched him thinking quite transparently for half a minute.

'Midnight. Jake Midnight.'

It was all I could do not to laugh in his face.

'Right, okay, whatever you want,' I said. 'See you, Baptist.'

Back at the Tenby DJ Tim was hefting his gear out to an awaiting Volvo estate under the watchful eyes of two beat constables in yellow jackets, and Scotty looked like he was going to kill somebody, but other than that nothing had changed.

'Urine is sterile, but pooh is not,' Chester was saying.

'Can we go now?' asked Scotty.

'One minute.'

While I was up I got three shorts in, three vodkas, as a sort of goodwill gesture.

'There you go,' I said. 'One for the road.'

'I'm driving,' said Chester, shaking his head, pushing his drink into the middle of the table. I just about managed to beat Scotty to it.

'I wouldn't mind a bite to eat, seeing you're treating us,' he said.

I couldn't remember mentioning eating, but I didn't object. I hadn't eaten anything for days, didn't seem to want to, either. My stomach felt tight and empty and taut and I was getting used to it that way, but I wasn't sure it was natural, wasn't sure it was good for you at all.

'I fancied some food the other day,' I said, as we all slid back into the Nissan Bluebird. 'I fancied some fish and chips. But could I find any? Could I fuck. They're all kebab shops now.'

'What are you talking about?' said Scotty. 'Did you go into any of them?'

Well, no.

'They sell fish and chips as well as the rest of the stuff, fuck's sake.'

'Bollocks,' I said, elegantly.

'Christ, it's hardly fucking rocket science, fish and chips. You don't need a three-year apprenticeship.'

We stopped on a place in the Kingsway near Jumpin' Jaks. It was mid-afternoon, and the place was dead, a couple of listless stubbly Turks lolling about in the back moving boxes of frozen chips, finishing the defences before the onslaught of evening, the Alamo hours before the assault. They had all the usual kebab shop guff but they had a hot counter as well, just like you'd get in a normal chippie, with all the usual stuff in it, the battered sausage and saveloy and meat pie. It took up half the shop.

I bought three fish and chips and we sat down around one of the little formica tables and dished out the salt and the vinegar and went to work with our little wooden forks. They looked and smelled alright but I couldn't muster up much enthusiasm for some reason, and my dry mouth had been slowly and mechanically chewing for four or five minutes when the attack began. Even now part of me blames the chips.

It was the stabbing pain in the left side of my chest again, and a tightness I could feel all across my ribcage, right up my sternum, to my throat, even, it felt, to my mouth itself. I wanted to spit out the sodden potato mass that was blocking my airway but I couldn't. I didn't have the wind. I could only open my mouth and hope it would fall out, my breath rasping like a blunt saw, totally immobile with the pain. One day, one day soon, I remember thinking, this will not pass. This will come and stay and simply get worse, and it could be now.

It was maybe a minute or two before anybody noticed.

'What the fuck is wrong with you?' said Scotty.

I couldn't say anything. I was dimly aware that both of them were looking at me, and that one of the Turks had come up with a glass of water.

'You should take him outside,' he said. I don't think I could have looked too appetising. But I couldn't move.

'Doctor's,' I managed to say. 'High Street.'

Scotty got as much of his meal down as he could and then the two of them had to lift me up like I was a mannequin, and carry me round the side-alley to the car park at the back. They pushed me into the back seat like policemen taking in a criminal.

When we got to the surgery Chester parked up outside on the double yellows, which must have caused him no end of concern, and they brought me into that little waiting room which was supposed to be closed, except for the addicts, sitting on those little cushioned seats clutching their arms a little more nervously now.

'Is he registered here?' was the first thing the receptionist said, in an alarmed voice.

I was nodding, or I thought I was, but she wasn't going to look at me.

'Yeah,' said Scotty.

'What's his name?'

'Robin,' said Scotty. 'That's all I know. That's what I call him, anyway.'

'Is there a surname?'

A desperate pause.

'Well, some people call him Magnum, like, as a nickname.'

'That's no good,' said the woman, who continued to stand there doing nothing, an alarmed expression on her face. Some other woman came out from the back somewhere, an older woman, sterner-looking, matron to the rescue.

'We're closed,' said the older woman, firmly. A brief look of hope crossed the younger woman's face.

'If you don't leave we'll have to call the police,' she went on. I daresay the police got called out to the High Street Surgery pretty frequently, what with the private practice clientele. Calling the police was something they were happy to do, and even more happy to threaten, but Scotty, God bless him, had nothing more to lose than I did, and stood his ground, although Chester was tugging nervously at his elbow.

'He's fucking dying here,' he said, maybe, and then the woman said about calling the police again, and the two of them stood there like that until I motioned for a pen and paper and wrote down three words:

'Doctor. Waiting. Medication.'

It was all I could write. It was enough for them to put a sock in it for a spell, while they scratched their heads and wondered what I meant. Chester excused himself to move the car, but also I imagine to avoid any trouble with policemen, what with his reputation. The older woman said she was going to call the police but I don't know if she really did. Shortly after she left the younger one asked me if I could remember the doctor's name.

I shook my head.

'I'll ask around,' she said, and went through the surgery door to the right of the counter.

Two minutes later and a man came through the same door, a man my age, in corduroys and a fleece jacket with a doctor's face, worn, but smooth and solid, like rocks a long time in rushing water. I had seen him before.

'Come through,' he said, sounding a little impatient, and we went into his little room, with the desk and the examination table and the cack-handed portraits by small children.

'We found your x-rays from the Singleton,' he said, 'they were never sent down. They confirm what you said. So I can give you a prescription for something to take the edge off. You're clearly in a lot of pain already, breakthrough pain, as it's called. So I can prescribe some liquid morphine, which is the most direct way of taking you out of the pain zone. However, I have to tell you, you should hold off from taking it as long as possible. Once you have begun to use liquid morphine as a painkiller you have committed yourself to the terminal stages of your illness. In time, the morphine itself will kill you, or any healthy person. You'll feel no physical side-effects but there will be damage to your liver and kidneys, and you will start to experience some loss of your mental faculties. However, the pain will go. We may have to increase the dosage, but the pain should go. I have to tell you, that if you intend to fight your illness, or even if you think you might, you shouldn't take it until you've seen a specialist.'

He reached across to his desk to a tidy full of free pens and paperweights and padded stationary with the logos of drug companies emblazoned across them, and took out a business card.

'This is the name of a private clinic. They're very good. If your financial situation allows it, or can be made to allow it, you might want to see them first. Before you take the drug.'

I nodded and took the card; some place in the Mumbles. Then he gave me the liquid morphine there and then, in his room, having made me sign the prescription slip. Because this stuff was so dangerous I had to come to him to get it, he said, and not the chemists; although the chemists could provide it he wanted to keep an eye on me, he said. I appreciated it but all I was able to do was nod again. I took the drug, in some little black plastic canister like camera film used to come in, and held it tight in my fist.

'Are you ready to go?' he asked. I wondered whether he meant to go out of the room or to go for good.

'It may be that you will want to think about getting care in a hospice, for the final stages,' he said, while he waited for me to be able to speak.

He talked a little more but I wasn't listening. I was gripping the little black canister with both my hands, until I couldn't feel either of them anymore, waiting for the pain and the terror to abate. Now that the answer to all this was here, in my hands, I felt in control again; although I hadn't taken any, I knew I could, and I suppose that was some kind of psychological advantage.

'…your nearest pharmacy,' the doctor was saying, when I resurfaced, when my sensory apparatus started reporting back something other than pain.

Pharmacy, I thought. From the Greek, pharmakon, which meant cure. And also, poison. I looked down at the tiny canister in my bone-white hands, its persistent outline carved into my pressed flesh, the imprint of its lethal benevolence.

'Thank you,' I said, partly out of gratitude and partly just to end the show. The doctor took me by the arm and walked me as briskly as he could to the front and then went back to his room. He was on his lunchbreak again, I suppose.

'You alright?' said Scotty, who broke off from talking to one of the addicts on the seats around the walls, some young blonde with bad acne who he knew or wanted to.

'Yeah. Where's Chester?

'In the car.'

'I'll see you,' I said. 'I better head back. Come round Thursday morning, if you want, you can watch it all happening.'

Chester took me back to the warehouse, too awkward about the whole incident to say anything, and I got my Chinese petrol-powered angle grinder out of the boot and patted the car's roof in thanks and watched him drive off. I dumped it in the skip, rolled up in a bit of old carpet, and then sat back down against the steel door, still in the beat of the sun, and breathed shallowly and evenly, with one hand in Scotty's jacket gripping the morphine. There was something else in there too, and I reached in and took it out. It was a brand new asthma inhaler. The doctor must have given it to me while I was still hurting, I must have sort of blacked out. I had no memory of being given it at all. Christ, I thought, not your mind as well, not that, the body you could cope with but there was still so much to do. I wondered what it would be like to use, but I would wait until I felt normal again until I tried it, in case it made me feel worse. If I ever felt normal again. I put it back in my pocket.

I waited until my breathing got properly even again, and the dizziness went, or at least evened out, and then took my new, old mobile out. I had one last call to make.

'Her Majesty's Customs and Excise,' the voice sang, from a reception desk on the sixth or seventh floor of Tŷ Nant on Swansea High Street. I looked over to my right and I could see the building, could imagine them in there.

'I need to talk to an inspector,' I said. 'I have information.'

'One moment please.'

A deep voice came on the line, some gruff ambitious go-getter who introduced himself as Inspector Cramer.

'I have information relating to an ongoing VAT fraud in the Swansea area,' I said. 'Small-scale carousel fraud with mobile phones and duty evasion on alcohol. I can give you names and addresses, but what I want to know is how long you're going to sit on them for.'

'As long as it takes.'

'That's not what I want to hear. You should be able to get them on the carousel stuff just by checking your own records. The alcohol might need a few witnesses, but you'll have to chase them up after you've pulled them in. It shouldn't be hard. I can give you names, dates, descriptions, a few license plates, some addresses, but you have to move on it. As fast you can.'

'You're concerned for your own safety,' said the voice.

'You could say that.'

'We can protect you...'

'That's not going to work. This is my only condition: I give you the information, you pull in the central figures as soon as you can. How long will that take? Honestly?'

'Two or three days,' the man said, 'if your information is correct.'

'That's fine.'

I was prepared to give them two or three weeks, God knows, that was how long it probably would take them, even if they were going at it full pelt, bureaucracy being what it is. But I was glad they weren't going to wait. The wait-and-see policy wasn't something I had time for.

'So what have you got?' said the man from the knock.

'Tell you in two days, Cramer,' I said. 'Just make sure you're ready to move.'

As I was putting the phone back into my pocket a purple people-carrier came around the corner on two wheels, or rather as near to two wheels as it was ever going to get: Gavin pretending a Chrysler Voyager was a Gran Turismo. Half a second earlier he would have seen me on the mobile, which would have been enough to arouse suspicion. Half a minute and he would have caught me close to informing. Had I not had the attack, maybe Scotty and Chester and I would be down a pub somewhere still, and I'd be just as fucked. I was taking some risks, I thought to myself, heart going over the hundred, as I watched him walking towards me across the weed-cracked concrete.

'Had a nice day?'

I spent the entire day scheming how to fuck you up, I thought, nodding.

'Oh good,' he said, 'I'm so very glad. Bedtime, Magnum. Better get your beauty sleep for tomorrow.'

It was an hour or two earlier than usual, but I didn't mind. It had been a nerve-wracking day. I watched the door descend, the light diminish, eager for the clang of steel against concrete and darkness and security.

It wasn't the same, though.

I drank slowly, can after can, a little nervous, a little scared. Would the attacks come tonight? Would my chest tighten and warp some more? I had my inhaler and my anaesthetic in my jacket, my lucky charms, but I was too scared to even touch them. Touching them might jinx it. So I left them in my pockets and pretended I was well.

When the next day came around I had already been awake for half an hour or so, was standing in the middle of the floor, squaring up to the low chink of light from which the dawn would suddenly rise, and suddenly release the blinking glare of another morning on Swansea docks, thinking about dying, thinking about the deal. Braced. It's not rocket science, I could remember Scotty saying, the day before.

Gavin was stood there, staring in, over his left shoulder the Cork ferry waiting six or seven hundred yards away at the end of its pier.

'Ready for your little trip?' he said.

II

I spent both legs of the crossing with my lips stuck to a litre of Paddy whisky, like a baby with a bottle, fearfully waiting for another summer storm to appear, black clouds and lightning and fierce waves out of nowhere, but there was nothing, a flat glass ocean and a clear blue sky. A couple of hours' delay on the return journey would have been enough to skewer the whole set-up. Fuck it, an hour's storm either way would probably have killed me: I was not well, not well at all. If you threw in nausea on top of it, well, let me tell you, I spent a long time looking out at the Irish Sea and thinking it would be a nice way to go: off over the side when no one was looking, with everything over in minutes. Once your feet left the rail there was nothing more to worry about. And it looked so big and clean and peaceful.

It wasn't of course. It was the most polluted, roughest stretch of water around these isles. Some seasonal trick of the light, some fluke of good weather, and maybe some dark personal pit of dread contrived to make it look otherwise. But even so, there was no storm. The crossing was smooth, and I didn't go on deck once. Didn't move from my armchair if I could help it, lodged in a corner of Paddy Murphy's, a customer in a pub that lets you bring your own booze. I should have worked this out on my last trip: into the onboard shop for a bottle of something strong and then sit in the bar like you're a paying customer, which you are, really. I saw that truck driver around but he kept his distance, or sometimes he stared me out for a bit of a laugh. For some reason or other I was in his bad books.

When we docked I was still able to walk and talk, although I couldn't always remember how I'd started a sentence by the time I'd got to the end of one. Brian found me waiting at the exit of the passenger terminal and manhandled me into the necessary places at the appropriate times, and I nodded my hellos to the same small bunch of people.

'Still no machine gun, sorry,' I remember the blonde one sneering.

'It's alright,' I'd said. 'I've lost all the fucking money.'

Once the container was on the truck we pulled into the customs lane and showed our documents to the relevant official. I had to sign something again and gave it a good go but whenever I got to the end of my surname I ran out of space on the page. It just kept slipping off. Once I'd done it three times the man said three mostly finished signatures were probably just as good, if not better, than a single completed one, and gave us the usual wink and nod, and then we were back in the bowels of the Superferry, as the ship, without any irony, I'm sure, had been named; in that warm fug of diesel and carbon-monoxide, ready for the return leg. Trip over. Another short break in the Emerald Isle.

Brian kicked me out of the cab and I fell about five feet, but hit the car deck solidly on both feet. It was the reverberations that got to me, some imaginary recoil, maybe even the shock of not having fallen over in the first place, that made me slither slowly to the ground. Getting to the stairwell took time, and drew a lot of evil looks, but thankfully most of the travellers had already boarded and were upstairs. Getting up all four flights of the stairwell itself turned out to be an even more Herculean achievement. Sometime after reaching the next flight up from the car deck, another storm began. The tempest broke. The ship was thrashing about so much I couldn't get up more than two or three steps before being thrown into one of the walls. After a while I worked out a strategy, took it a step at a time, sat down whenever I got out of sorts and gathered strength. It took me hours to make it to the top, to the bars and the shops and the people and the windows, from the empty and lifeless lower reaches, with their steel walls and electric light. The rough weather bounced me up and down that steep, narrow corridor like a tarnished pinball, until half the day had gone, or so it felt. When I got to the passenger deck I saw that we were still moored, and the sea was so calm it looked like it had given up and decided to become a reservoir. I put a palm up to the cool plate glass of the window, saw my own face in it, then pressed that against it too, my hot flushed face against the cool glass, until I could see nothing but two shades of blue and a tiny green peep, in the corner, of County Cork. I wasn't used to it, the spirits, going straight back onto them.

I went and sat down in one those blue felt armchairs and minded my own business. My bottle had gone, I had finished it or dropped it or had it taken away from me. Maybe I'd thrown it away. Maybe I'd hit someone with it. The possibilities made me dizzy. Sitting down made me dizzy. Closing my eyes made it worse. I kept them open, closed down everything else but kept them open, and fixed on a patch of wall, like I heard they trained the auld boys in the 'RA to do when they were being interrogated. Fucking murderers. The patch kept moving, though, and the wall wobbled and shifted, and in time the only thing I found I could cling to was the quiet buzzsaw of my own breathing, the broken bellows in my chest, barely moving now at all, though it took a lot of effort. Nobody paid me any mind. In time I must have slept.

When I woke up the sun had gone down and outside the window there was nothing but darkness. The ship had the gentle swell that I associated with being at mid-sea. Most people that didn't have cabins seemed to be settling into their Pullmans, but I didn't need to see that to know that we were in or around closing time. My own body clock told me that.

The bar was mostly empty, and the customers were dozing now, around the barroom tables. On the high stools there were a couple of drinkists still working, but they looked more tired than drunk, and they were only getting tireder. I plonked myself down next to them and thought I could probably manage a lager, just to top up the tank, and see me through to midnight. Three or four or five or six of them and I could bed down again, come up the other side of night more or less as sober and rested as I could ever hope to be. I had one, a Carlsberg. The guy behind the bar was another Pole.

'No more,' he said sternly to me once he'd put down my glass.

'What's the trouble?' I said.

'Trouble? You sick all over the fucking stairs to car deck,' he said.

Those stairs had given me a lot of trouble, I remembered.

'Shit,' I said. 'Sorry. I was seasick.'

'We were in port still, fucking dickhead. You holding empty bottle of whisky like this.'

He grimaced and made a tight fist.

'Fucking dickhead,' he said. 'You fucking sat there and we hoover it up around you.'

'Sorry,' I said, and threw some change into the tankard. Without making it look like anything but another part of his job, he turned and squeezed the car horn, without the scowl leaving his face. I put a note down.

'Have one for yourself.'

Wearily, cautiously, he leant over to the empty glasses.

'Get another one for me if there's enough,' I said.

I didn't catch what he said to that but I remember sitting there with an empty glass waiting for a long time. Funny thing was, I didn't seem to mind. I'd had enough to be getting on with, I reckoned, so it wasn't the end of the world. I was drinking for tomorrow now. Building up a surplus, just in case. Getting the quota in ahead of schedule. You can't be too careful. But when you try and look out for yourself, there's always people who want to pull you down. Who want to stop you from getting ahead. I was dwelling philosophically on such injustices when Neil turned up, on my side of the bar, although still in uniform, and then I sort of pulled out of it.

'Alright,' he said. 'Back again?'

'Yeah. Supposed to be a regular thing, you know. How are you?'

'Alright, yeah. I'm coming off shift. You look fucking wrecked.'

'Oh, I'm tired. This travelling.'

The Pole came over.

'He is fucking wreck, mate. I'm not giving him any more.'

'This guy? Come on, man.'

But the barman just picked at his blue waistcoat and shook his head.

'He is fucking wreck,' he said.

Neil nodded towards where he had come from.

'Want to come hang out in the staff cabin?' he said.

I looked down at my legs, dangling from the stool. I wanted them to be still and they were still. It should stand to reason, I thought, that if I wanted them to walk they would walk.

'Is it far?' I asked.

'Is it far? You're on a fucking boat!' he said. 'No, it's not far.'

'Okay,' I said, and we gave it a go. Actually it wasn't more than thirty yards away, and on the same floor, and I managed very well.

The staff cabin wasn't anything special. There were a couple of fairly standard-looking seats that had been pushed together to make a sofa and a couple of blue armchairs that had been dragged in from the passenger lounge. Blu-tacked to the walls were a dozen or so centre-spreads, women from the television that'd had tit jobs done, and a few that hadn't needed tit jobs in the first place. On the opposite wall somebody was mounting a counter-offensive with Peter Andre and David Beckham. It was pretty harmless stuff. In the middle of the floor was a large coffee table covered in the sort of magazines the pictures came from and a lot of very full ashtrays. It looked like a busy room but it wasn't at the moment: Neil and I were the only two in there. It fairly stank of weed.

He caught me sniffing the air, clocked me checking the ashtrays, and gave a roguish smile that was a little bit more wicked than it needed to be.

'I've smoked a couple myself, like,' he said. 'I'm pretty high, actually.'

I smiled back, haplessly, partly to let him know that he wasn't going to get any shit from me about it, partly from some sense of awkward obligation. It was something that druggies did, I guess, even some drinkers: boast about being incapacitated, like they wanted a fucking medal.

'Can you get away with that?' I said. 'Shitting on your own doorstep, isn't it?'

'I don't care,' he said. 'Three days and I'm out of here. Got a job in the Caribbean, on one of the cruise ships out there. Working behind the bar. Again. Still.'

Neil's smile turned into a big happy beam and he shrugged, holding his palms upwards, and then neatly collapsed onto the armchair behind him. I nodded.

'Fair play,' I said. 'The Caribbean.'

He might as well have been talking about outer space.

I sat myself down on another one of those stolen armchairs and breathed in the smoke hanging in the air.

'Want one?' he said, taking a bundle out of his shirt pocket and kneeling forward towards the coffee table, reaching for a bag of Old Holborn and some papers.

I shook my head.

'Wouldn't mind a normal one,' I said, and after he'd finished his little Cheech and Chong routine he handed the pouch over to me. My fingers weren't doing the job to their usual high standard, but I was making progress, and then I thought about getting some duty free rolling while I was onboard, and then I remembered about the duty free in the lorry downstairs, and then I remembered what I was supposed to be doing.

'What time is it?' I asked.

'Dunno. Past midnight.'

'By much?'

'Don't think so.'

I took out my mobile phone, clinging to the last fading bar on its battery meter, and dialled the home phone number of the man that ran a drink distribution firm in Reading. Nothing happened.

'I don't think I've got a signal,' I said.

Neil delved into the space between the arm of his chair and the cushion underneath him, and pulled out some tiny silver sparkling thing.

'Here,' he said. 'Have mine. But don't be long.'

I got up and went over to it but the keypad was tiny, and to make matters worse the numbers were swapping places.

'I think I'd like a cup of coffee first,' I said. I wasn't going to make much of an impression, with my slurred words, my random pauses, assuming the guy could understand me at all. It was a miracle that Neil could. He pointed in the direction of a nearby worktop, which had a kettle on it and a couple of packs of those stacked plastic cups with powdered drinks at the bottom of each one. The first one was chocolate, although I was halfway through before I had realised. The second was tea (ditto). I struck gold with the third, made a couple of them, and knocked them back, soon as they were poured. I knew I had badly scalded myself but I wouldn't feel it till the morning, and right now I needed all the zing I could get.

The first time I dialled I got an old man with a Yorkshire accent, badly panicked and about as nonsensical as I was: wrong number. I checked, and rang two more times. No one answered. I kept going. Eventually he picked up and almost as soon as I'd said who I was he said:

'Have you been drinking?'

'Sorry,' I said. 'It's the stress. I haven't gone under before. And there's the family to think of.'

I told him to be at Junction 41 of the M4 by half nine tomorrow, and I would give him a ring about the pick-up.

'That's short notice. Why all this cloak and dagger stuff?'

'I don't want the receivers to get wind of it,' I said. 'And I need the money now. You know how it is.'

I myself was stunned by how plausible the whole thing sounded, even if I could barely speak. The man said something about how everyone was entitled to a proper night's sleep and then hung up.

'Sure you won't have one?' said Neil.

'I'm sure,' I said. I had a feeling I might be able to sleep now. My chair was becoming increasingly comfortable, more comfortable, I thought, than I would soon be able to consciously stand.

'When I'm in the Caribbean I'm going to bring back a big bag of this,' he said, holding his joint aloft. 'Couple of big bags three or four times a year. That,' he said pointedly, 'will be a nice little supplement.'

'Yeah,' I said. It was as much I was prepared to contribute.

I watched a rather shaky smoke circle drift across the room and dissipate.

'An extra five or six grand easy,' he said.

'For what?' I said.

'What do you mean, for what?'

'The cash,' I said deliberately keeping syllables to a minimum.

'I don't know. I thought maybe I'd save up and go out to Australia, you know, for good. Emigrate.'

Without lifting my head from the back of the chair I looked down my nose and saw him lift and sink in the space of a single utterance.

'But I don't think that's me,' he went on, sadly. 'That's fantasy stuff. Maybe I'll go to London and blow it.'

I could understand him. At one time I had thought that kind of money could turn my life around; five, six, ten grand. I had stretched a long way to get it, and it had got me nowhere, or Swansea, any rate, and homelessness.

'The thing is,' he said rallying, animated again, 'I'm not one for the land. The sea, that's my life. What can I say? I'm a mariner. This is in my blood.'

This bore closer investigation. I pulled my head upright; almost grunted as I did it.

'A life on the ocean wave?' I said.

'Just that,' he said, laughing. 'Just that. It's our tradition, innit?'

'The nautical tradition, you mean?'

'Yeah.'

'Treading in the footsteps of Nelson and all that?'

'Yeah,' he said. 'Yeah. I'm the only British guy on the bloody crew now. Half of them are from countries that don't have coastlines, you know? It's fucking ridiculous.'

I didn't have anything to say to that. He leant forward, with the air of a man about to make a point, and fixed his eyes on mine.

'My granddad went down on the Royal Oak,' he added, meaningfully.

I nodded.

'You don't think it's a bit camp?' I said. 'The waistcoat and the customer service and all that? For a man your age?'

'Fucking John Prescott was a ship's steward,' he shrugged. I reflected that whatever else John Prescott might be described as, camp was not on the list.

'When I get to the Caribbean…' he said, falling back into his armchair. 'When I get there…'

When he got there he was going to smuggle back some weed, that's what I reckoned. But I didn't know for sure, because he never finished his sentence. As soon as he sat back the bastard was gone, drifting off rapidly into REM.

I watched him go, through half-closed lids, engaged on some smoother, trickier descent of my own, unaided by bedtime dreams of tradition and primacy, by the notion that the dark perpetual waves beneath the keel were something we still had some claim too. There were millions like him all over the country, all head down in the sleeping draught of history. Maybe twenty minutes later I was asleep myself, two Jolly Jack Tars catching forty winks before the sun came over the mizzen, or whatever the fuck it was they used to say.

I don't remember anyone else coming in or going out, but when I woke up things had been moved.

'Ahoy there, matey,' I said, once I had satisfactorily fulfilled the onerous responsibility of getting up, and circumnavigated the room.

No response. I waved a hand slowly over his eyes and nothing flickered. Perhaps he had woken up in the night and smoked some more.

'Good luck in the tropics,' I said, and headed out. We were docking already. That bloody truck driver would be wondering where I was, and anyway, I had a plan to stick to now, a timetable to keep, so I went down to the car deck to seek him out, which, given that he was driving an articulated lorry, was not that arduous.

'Fucking twat,' he said, as I climbed in.

'What's the matter? What do you care? Everybody's on time.'

'You're stinking my fucking cab out,' said Brian the lorry driver, and for the second time I got shoved out of the passenger seat and took the five feet fall on my shoulder and side. When I hit the riveted steel floor I coughed up a spray of blood and phlegm, felt the usual blend of terror, embarrassment and pain, but I was so low to the ground that nobody saw. I watched my expectorate drip slowly down the front tyre of an Alfa with Tipperary plates. Then I got up, clutching my sides, but not too tightly, because they were tighter than a drum already, and moved off back towards the agony of the stairwell, to the passenger deck and the gangway, the ramp back to hell.

Gavin and James were waiting for me when I finally reached the warehouse, after I had crossed the vast concrete graveyard that was Swansea Docks, after I had stumbled through its oily earth. They were stood there leaning against their cars, fifty grand's worth of Merc, twenty maybe twenty-five grand's worth of Chrysler, shooting the breeze, watching from the corner of their eyes the slow approach of their servile tramp. Beside them, by the side of the building, was the drinks container. Now that he had a lorry with a crane on it Brian had dumped it and fucked off.

'Made it, then,' said James, when I got within earshot. I said nothing. I couldn't. I was still winded.

'We'll be back around midday. The buyer won't be here till late afternoon at the earliest. Sit here and keep an eye out,' he said, and the two of them drove off. Once they'd turned the corner I got my phone out and rang the Baptist; told him to get round here, and just for the sake of completeness, to bring a heavy chain, and a padlock with him.

'That may take some time,' he said.

'You haven't got much more than twenty minutes,' I said. 'There's an extra hundred in it for you if you can make it.'

If the guy from Reading was on time he wasn't more than quarter of an hour away already, and the screen on my mobile told me it was nine thirty-five already. I was in no shape to, but I clambered into the skip and dug out my angle-grinder. After a while, I managed to get out, and a little while after that, I even managed to get the thing started. The blade was as dull as other people's dreams, but it turned, albeit in its own sweet time. Inset into the steel shutters was a small door which had always been padlocked shut, but I began to work away in a small circle around the bolt, and just before the little smoking engine was about to burn out I'd completed the loop, and the whole lock fell to the concrete floor. I pushed the little door open with my foot, just to check I was in, and then I saw to the chain around the container next door to the warehouse. I was through that in seconds, and then the angle-grinder was back in the skip again, where it would stay this time. It was soon followed by all the paperwork I could find in the warehouse (except for the stock list), and then covered by the same old stretch of old carpet. Then I went back once more into the warehouse and hit the electric switch to raise the shutters, and watched the lid on my own tomb roll up, and almost laughed, although not for long.

In five or ten minutes at most this businessman from Reading would be on his mobile asking for directions into town, and I wouldn't be able to stall him for long. I sat down on the ground with my back against the wall of the warehouse, for what was almost certainly going to be the last time, however this panned out. I closed my eyes, and watched the sun filter through the veins of my eyelids, watched them pulse, watched the bright dots on my sun-stained iris move and disappear. I felt the furnace in my chest, heard its steam, witnessed the wakening twinges of my bruised and battered side, took the time to experience the full diversity of pain my body was in, and the pain it would be in, later, soon, the pain waiting in my body in its folds and organs, in its invisible coded imperfections, as it waits in yours too. Five or ten minutes and I would know. They were very long minutes.

My phone did not ring. My eyes remained closed, and were closed when I heard the engine of a single car bumping its way towards on me on the empty, ruined road. Gavin or James: I was fucked. The Baptist: I was not fucked. I opened them and saw a familiar blue Nissan, and that things were still undecided.

Scotty got out of the passenger side and came over.

'What are you doing here?' I said, when he drew near.

'Came out to help, didn't we, you ungrateful fuck.'

I opened one of my eyes. Smelt money, more like, I thought. But it was an ignoble sentiment.

'How'd you know when to come?'

'Bumped into that biker guy. The Baptist.'

'He's supposed to be here now,' I said.

'He's on his way.'

I closed my single open eye and tried to concentrate on the warmth of the sun and nothing else. In the distance I could hear the oddly solicitous burr of Ken Bruce on Radio Two. Scotty sat down next to me.

'You'd better hang back,' I said. 'You know, go and sit in the car a little way off. Near enough to see but far away enough to pretend you might have nothing to do with it.'

He made some vague murmurs of dissent.

'Please,' I said. 'Go on.'

And he went. I heard the engine start and roll a little further down the road, and held my pose, motionless and blind, a pebble at the bed of a dry stream, waiting for a change of season.

Another car. Unmistakably, the engine of an old but not underpowered car. The Baptist. When I looked up he was walking towards me swinging a heavy chain over his head, like he was out hunting mods.

'Go and put the chain and padlock on that container,' I told him, 'and give me the key.'

The Baptist went to wait in the car and I dialled the guy from Reading, who had just pulled into the lay-by out by the main road into town, and guided him in. Then I went and sat on the front wing of the Scimitar, and folded my arms, and felt a bit like an extra in *The Sweeney*. The nerves were kicking in mightily, though. Apparently, some guy was coming here to give me two hundred grand, and I have lived long enough for it be rational to believe there was something fundamentally wrong with that picture, and I knew too I was going to find out what, but I hoped it would be sometime later, some revelation retrospective and gradual, not sudden and violent. I particularly hoped it wasn't going to happen in the next half hour. When I saw a small convoy of four lorries pulling in off the A-road I knew it was them, knew there would be no other traffic coming down here unless it was to pick up the drink: it was either the Reading firm or God save us, James Blethyn's buyer, a few hours early.

Standing out there in open ground, in the broiling sun, I felt a rapid and rising coolness spread over me, felt ice in the base of my spine, my temples, the brow of my head. The dry bed is flush with water again, cold water, from a high and far-off place. My pulse has pulled closer, drawn into itself, become a single humming throb. These people are supposed to shake my hand and give me more money than I've ever seen in my life and then just walk away again; thanks mate, cheers, nice doing business with you. God, this is naive. I turned around at what was probably the last possible moment, and whispered over my shoulder into the rolled-down window:

'Have you got anything on you?'

'I thought you said this wasn't going to be any bother,' he hissed.

'It isn't,' I said, getting a grip on myself, 'don't worry. I was just asking.'

And I turned to face forward, to put on some entrepreneurial front while they were still approaching, but before I turned I saw the Baptist lean forward in his seat, saw his face tighten as he reached for something from the footwell, and I found myself hoping that he didn't have anything down there but a gammy knee, but it was too late now.

There were two of them in the first cab, one guy well over six foot, and heavy with it, who I assumed was the clobberer, should anything go wrong, or maybe if everything went right, and some guy maybe a foot shorter with a wiry frame who I took to be the businessman. But I had it the wrong way round. The big one introduced himself as the owner, and the little one said nothing, just stood a little way off with his hands in his pockets and didn't blink. It was scarier, that way round, I thought. Everything was scarier, and getting scarier all the time.

I opened up the container and let him have a look around it, gave him some bullshit, took him around the warehouse and answered a few questions about my failed business as noncommittally as I could, tried to look like this was just another day at the office. I don't think I did very well. The owner was intent on going through as many boxes and palettes as he could, just to make sure I wasn't selling him milk, I suppose, and all the time this little guy, built like a flyweight, keeps his hands in his pockets and his eyes on me, and I can't help but stare back, and in doing so I think give too much of myself away. All the other drivers are still waiting in their cabs. I flick some perspiration from an eyebrow and realise I am sweating profusely.

'Shame there isn't time for a proper stock-take,' says the man who is the owner.

'Just what you see, mate,' I say.

The man who is the owner has finished looking through the boxes. He has gone over to the man who isn't the owner, and they are standing on the concrete twenty yards away talking quietly by the side of their cab. Behind them are three other HGVs in a line, and eighty yards in the opposite direction I can see Chester's Nissan Bluebird, but it is too far away to see either of its passengers. Off to the left, in a lay-by on the A483, not far from the docks' gates, there is a black Saab with people in it: are those his men? Is that his back-up squad? I had a cripple, a junky and a probable paedophile in mine. Christ. I looked back over my shoulder, as casually as possible, at the Baptist, a man with a steel rod in his leg whom I had not known for longer than twenty minutes, who I had been introduced to by a barman I hadn't known at all, but his face was inscrutable. By which I do not mean that it showed signs of collectedness and cool, but only that it was glazed, like the whited-out window of a closed-down shop. This could go any way at all, I remember thinking.

The two guys from Reading came over and the owner started speaking and I began to pay attention but I wasn't really able to tune in until the final sentence.

'A hundred and twenty grand,' he was saying, and I was shaking my head. I couldn't even remember how we'd got here.

'I can go up to one forty-five, maybe one fifty,' he said, 'but I'll need more time.'

I had three hours at most.

'You didn't drive down here eighty grand short,' I said. 'Not all the way from Berkshire.'

The owner shrugged.

'One twenty,' he said.

'Bollocks.'

'One twenty.'

'Let me see it.'

'It's in the cab.'

He wasn't going to bring it out, so I went over and stood on the uppermost step on the passenger side, while the flyweight sat on the driver's seat, and the owner stood behind me. It was in two carrier bags, one full of used notes bound in elastic bands and the other full of crisp fresh stuff straight from the bank, with the paper seals still stapled around them. I tried to count it but it was like counting water. I just dipped my hands into it and let it flow through, thousands upon thousands of pounds. I couldn't count it: it was impossible. I tried to make a show of it, after feeling a bit self-conscious, although I never got further than thirty or forty grand. Nobody said anything.

Maybe they exchanged glances, rolled their eyes, I don't know. I couldn't look up. After a while it started to suffocate me and I had to climb down and get myself some space.

Outside, with my feet on terra firma, and the money out of sight, it was possible to tell myself that they were finessing me out of eighty thousand, and all you could do with it, all you could change. It was a cast-iron certainty they had at least another thirty with them, and odds on the full two hundred, but they had taken their time, considered their options, sniffed the air and caught the scent of desperation. So they thought they could haggle me down, bluff me out, go back on their word, and exploit me. This was my only chance at turning things around, my expectations had not been unreasonable; my price inflated; my take implausible, but now they wanted to bite off almost half of that again.

'Fine,' I said. 'One twenty is fine.'

What else are we for, we the desperate, if not to exploit, to lean against and chivvy down?

The bossman gave the nod to the guys in the other cabs, and they began to get themselves into motion. One of them tugged the peak of his baseball cap in my direction.

'Ain't you got no forklift?'

'Receivers,' I shrugged.

'Fuckin' 'ell.'

They did have a crane jig on of the trucks, thank God, so they could lift the container and the shrink-wrapped pallets without too much trouble. Clearly, though, it would still take them an hour or two at least. Things were going to be very tight indeed. I looked out towards the A483, saw the Saab still sat there in the lay-by, grown men in the front and back seats. It wasn't something you often saw, that, grown men in the front and back, not in the middle of the day. 'I have to be off.'

Nobody moved. Nobody said a word.

'Alright?' I said.

The bossman and his little sidekick looked at each other, the quickest, the briefest of looks. Maybe the flyweight looked over at the Saab, maybe he just looked in its general direction, maybe he didn't look anywhere.

'Alright,' said the owner, after what felt like a couple of years. The other guy went back to the cab and gave me the carrier bags.

'Thanks, mate,' I said. 'Cheers. Nice doing business with you.'

I watched a little movie then, of me walking back to the Baptist's car, and getting in, and him starting the engine and shifting into first and then second as we drove away, stopping at the turning to tell Scotty that should the Blethyns just happen to be arrested in the near future, he should give me a ring when the two of them were safely in custody, and then we pulled out onto the main road and turned right, away from town, and drove past that Saab full of men which stayed in the lay-by and did not move, although I told the Baptist to put his foot down anyway, but it already was down, and then I watched the movie play on, this strange, personal film footage, where we reached the end of the road and he picked a direction at random, and kept his foot down until we were just a mile or two short of the ton, running down the Vale at ninety-nine miles an hour, with no one following and no one who could follow, because not even we knew where we were going, and in this movie I looked down, and there was a hundred and twenty grand in my lap.

III

'I have,' said the Baptist, 'prepared a special audio cassette compilation for this very occasion.'

'Hold on,' I said. 'Pull over.'

We were eight or ten miles down the Vale of Neath, coming up to Blaengwrach, past Resolven Mountain. At the roundabout we came off the A-road and parked on the outskirts of the village, and I took my mobile phone out and rang Inspector Cramer at the knock, and told him every single thing I could remember. He thanked me and told me to stay in touch, and I said I would, I even said, carried away by this unusual sensation of success, that I would testify, if needed, if I was still around. By the time I had my phone back in my jacket we were back on the road.

'What very occasion?' I said.

'Well, I think I can figure it out now,' said the Baptist.

'Now, yes, possibly, but not before. So what did you think this was about?'

'Well, I knew you had money, or you were going to get some, because of what you'd said you'd pay me. And I knew, of course, that you wanted to get away, you said that much. So the gig had all the signs of being a kind of getaway. So I made this.'

Out of the front pocket of his lumberjack shirt, underneath

his leather Rhyderrin waistcoat, he pulled out an old music cassette and slid it into the tapedeck.

'Mind, I didn't know it was going to be an actual getaway,' he said.

I braced myself for the worst, but it didn't turn out to be that bad. You can probably guess: The Spencer Davis Group (wonder which track), Canned Heat (ditto), The Animals (no prizes there either), that sort of stuff. It made a change from the noises that had been booming out of every teenager's hatchback for the last ten years, music I couldn't understand at all, didn't think you could understand it, not in the same way you could understand the old stuff. Kids probably only listened to that new stuff just because they wanted to break away, and have their own thing, at least it was the only reason I could think of, that and maybe new and more interesting drugs, that would probably compensate. It wasn't as good though, what they had now, couldn't be. Then again, being suddenly given two carrier bags full of money is going to put you in a receptive mood, and I had not listened to music in years, any kind of music at all. It was something like frankincense and myrrh.

'This is a pretty good sound system for an old car.'

My driver gave a happy, vindicated grin and nodded his head.

'Friend, there are woofers on the back shelf which are bigger than the wheels. Of course, that fucks up the original interior a little, messes with the lines, but you know, sometimes you have to compromise. And the interior design, if you pardon me for saying so, was never one of the Scimitar's real accomplishments.'

'I'm surprised you haven't got a CD player in here.'

'No way, man,' he said. 'No way. They just don't feel real. I'm a tape man, you know?'

I knew, I told him, and sat back, into the thick vinyl, warm as boiler-plate in the summer sun, felt the gentle tarmac undulate with lightning quickness beneath my seat, and thought myself a man arrived, a traveller in a mobile jukebox, passing through the biggest pub in the world. Except there were no drinks, no drinks and it was almost midday. I held my open hands out in front of me and watched them stay more or less steady, especially considering I was in a car. Maybe the motion of the car counter-balanced the shakes, maybe if you stood someone with the dt's on a table that vibrated at the correct frequency, he would look perfectly normal, it all depended where you stood. Or maybe it was the massive, life-changing amount of money between my legs, the rare thrill of it, proving intoxication enough: midday and I felt only the faintest pangs, the ghost of a thirst. But you had to celebrate.

We stopped off in Hirwaun and I sent him in for a four-pack. I wasn't going to leave him in the car with it, and I wasn't going to take it into the shop, so I gave him a tenner and told him to get something for himself too, if he liked, but he said he was driving. If there was a glimmer of displeasure at being treated like this, it showed on him only for a second, but money will do that to you. It will breed hostility and mistrust and more, but for me the worst of it was over: back in the docks I thought I was going die. He came back with some relatively cold Ultra, one of the brands you only ever see in the little shops.

We ran into the A470 outside Merthyr, the humble two-lane blacktop (for the most part) that is the spine of Wales, running right up the North–South divide; the Millennium Stadium at one end and Llandudno Pier the other, and not much in between but big hills and reservoirs, maybe the odd lonely market town, and a few low, gaunt villages clinging to T-junctions as if the wind might blow them away. We followed it as it curved through the Brecon Beacons, watched as the valleys closed and opened up around us. I saw a couple of kestrels circling above the firebreak in a mountainside of Forestry Commission coniferous. I gazed with envy at the isolated farmsteads, the mystery cottages, stuck out there in the middle of all this bleakness and beauty, with people living in them, presumably, hacking it, getting on, tending to their lives and minding their own business. Maybe I could have clung to the straight and narrow if I'd fled up here, instead of to some English city; worked the land, or made something in a toolshed somehow, married the mother of my child, raised a family. But it was illusory. They weren't living on nuts and berries, these people, they are not self-sustained: behind each of those rustic doors there was independent wealth or government subsidy or both. You see a home like that these days and it's an ivory tower, a gated community of one, that's all: the real yokels, the uneducated poor, the truly isolated, live back in town, in the estates, in the tower blocks. I bet they all cost a small fortune, those little, run-down retreats in the middle of nowhere.

We passed Pen-y-fan and the Brecon Beacons parted, revealing the low hills that lay around Builth, and before them, Brecon itself.

'Is this where you're taking me?' I said, becoming aware that I hadn't made a decision since getting in the car, unless stopping for booze counted.

'Yeah, well, it's a nice town, Brecon, isn't it?'

Brecon was where half of Swansea went for the weekend, if they had a caravan and didn't fancy the beach. It seemed a little obvious to me. I had the feeling that in my passivity I was being led somewhere, and then came the rest of it: I didn't know this guy at all, I was carrying a lot of money, the money belonged to somebody else and they would be looking for it, rewards would be offered, punishments threatened.

'Take a right,' I said, when we had come down from the hills. 'I don't fancy it.'

'Alright. Where do you fancy?'

'We'll see.'

'I guess we will,' he said, and sounded only vaguely put out about it. Perhaps Brecon was where he put his caravan, on the bank holidays.

Next thing we were putting the Beacons into the rear view mirror, and then it was the Black Mountains that were rising now on our left, a dark, solid mass even in the early afternoon, a high, jagged plateau of bracken and open pasture. Whole patrols of Norman cavalry had disappeared up there in the days of the settlement, after the Marcher Lords had crossed the Severn, about nine hundred years ago. Nine hundred years ago: I was pretty sure I knew what nine hundred years felt like, nine hundred years and more, I had waited longer than that in a single morning, in a single Swansea afternoon.

'They used to say,' said the Baptist, with the raised eyebrows of somebody who is trying to sound interesting, as we pulled a long sweeping right before the northern edge of Table Mountain, 'that once a Welshman crossed the pass of Bwlch he would never return.'

'Who's they?' I said. 'And when did they say it? A bunch of farmers on the other side of Carmarthen, a hundred years ago. They may have said it, but stay here and help the old man get the fucking hay in, that's what they meant.'

'Live in your country and praise it,' he said, slipping effortlessly from the sociable to the sententious. They were pretty much the same thing, round here. 'That's the proverb.'

Live in your country and praise it. Sit still and hold your hand out, more like. Yet where and what had it got me, ducking out, the way I had? I'd stopped off in the first city after the bridge, and stayed there, party to the same Welsh small-mindedness, prostrate to it and perpetuating it, with not much more than a hundred miles between us, me and my erstwhile, abandoned family. Enough rope to hang myself with.

From what I gather it happens a lot, with us missing male progenitors; we step outside the circle and the world closes in around us. People moaned about single mothers all the time, but the men that helped make them, well they were almost invisible. They had chosen absence, and absence enveloped them. Sure, I suppose some pulled out, turned up five or ten years later with decent jobs and new starts, spilled their seed in some other place, and pretended the past didn't matter. For the rest of us there was nothing but failure, our choice and our destiny, the sour legacy we cannot help but create, all on our own. Take it from me: you do not see us or want to. We had chosen absence, and absence, I thought, as the steep silhouette of Gader ridge loomed up in the North, as we continued another one of my kneejerk getaways, was what we deserved. I watched the shadow of a single cloud move slowly across the bracken, and was filled with sadness.

We did not speak at Bwlch, or Crickhowell, or Abergavenny, or Raglan, not for the next thirty miles. Then we went through a tunnel and came out the other side at a town called Monmouth, not far from the border with Gloucestershire, and I said this would do. I had run out of beer.

'This is that town with the schools,' the Baptist said. 'Posh kids.'

We came off the A40 on the slip road after the tunnels, crossed a little river and cruised up the high street.

'Doesn't look that posh to me,' I said.

'No. Well, it's in Wales, isn't it.'

'Not by much.'

The high street had the same kebab places and carpet warehouses and poundshops you'd get anywhere else.

'There's a Waitrose,' said the Baptist.

'The supermarket?'

'Yeah, but the bread costs two quid a loaf. And there's a Marks and Spencers food hall, look.'

'Yeah. Little differences,' I shrugged. They were all you ever got. 'Do you fancy a pint?'

'A pint?' he said. 'I'm driving.'

'Just the one,' I said. One. A word in the English language used to denote a single thing, but with it always the implication, no, the knowledge, that it is in essence the first of a sequence: one, two, three; ten, twenty, fifty; pints, days, weeks, years: they come and go of their own accord. I don't think one exists. I think it's a human fallacy to keep things manageable, at least that's what it looks like, from the dark, narrow end of my own particular angle.

'No,' he said, 'I don't suppose one will hurt.'

'Course not. Never know, you might pull a schoolgirl.'

He gave me a grin. That's the only reason half of them got motorbikes in the first place, that lot, although I suspect things have moved on now, in that pleasant, alien little world of female adolescence. After all, I thought, as I looked at my driver, the bikers are all balding now, and overweight, and still as poor. Plus, the dawn of male grooming has not left them in a good light, cosmetically. Whereas in contrast, apart from some superficial differences, the teenage schoolgirls are still young, still fresh and beautiful and all that jazz. From a distance it looked like a phenomenon of nature, like a tide that never recedes, a shaft of sunlight that never dims. Of course, if you got in close, if you got to know one personally for any length of time, the illusion would kind of fall apart. Lots of things would.

We parked in a pay and display opposite the boys' school, and I gave the Baptist a twenty and told him to get me a decent bag to carry this cash around in. He was seven minutes exactly: I timed him on the dashboard clock. After the first two I was already having visions of him making phone calls, to the Blethyns or some biker friends of his own; breaking into a cold sweat that infused rather interestingly with the hot sweat I had been having since sun-up. But if he had made a call, it would be at least an hour and a half before anybody from Swansea got here; enough time to get a few rounds in and then send him off home, whilst I fucked off somewhere else in a taxi.

He came back with my first ever briefcase, black leatherette and a combination lock on each of the clasps.

'Just like in the movies,' he said.

I got him to stand outside the car and keep an eye out while I transferred the money, not because I was especially worried, but because it felt somehow obscene, this amount of money, like bodies in a train wreck. You knew full well they were going to be there, lots of them, but every time you looked it seemed like there were too many. Some people might be used to seeing what that kind of money looked like, but I wasn't. Most people aren't, I guess, what with the popularity of plastic and credit and all that. Naked money: it didn't look quite decent. The fetish of us all, I suppose. I checked that his back was turned, and then I took the time to stack it all neatly inside the briefcase. Just like in the movies.

The two of us made our way towards the middle of town, exchanging the odd glance as the odd imaginary nymphet walked by, just for the show of it, really. I was long out of the game and I shouldn't have thought the Baptist was going to impress anybody, not unless he was carrying a lot of free drugs. Some of those kids looked like they'd be able to buy a better car than his with their own pocket money. And so could you, said a devilish voice in my own head, you could buy a fucking Ferrari if you wanted, and run the fuckers over in it, and I cast my face to the ground while I walked, so as to permit myself a crazy smile.

We ended up in the Wetherspoons. This one had been a hotel (and still was), so it wasn't as bad as some of the warehouses you usually got. I bought the Baptist and myself a lager and we sat down near the beer garden, close enough to see the light, but not near enough to it to start sweating again.

'Cheers,' he said.

'Why do they call you that?' I said, after a silence. 'The Baptist?'

'It was where they found me, wasn't it? Penmaen Church. Of St John The Baptist. Out on the Gower.'

'Found you?'

'Yeah, I was left there.' He gave me a look of incredulous patience that would have sat quite well on any of the faces of the teenagers we had passed on the way to the pub. 'It was in the paper.'

'What paper?'

'The *Evening Post*. And the *Western Mail*.'

'Oh, yeah,' I said, with no memory of it whatsoever. 'St John the Baptist. So what's wrong with being called John, then?'

'What fucking sort of name's that?'

'John? What sort of name is John? Well, never mind. If you don't like it you don't like it, I suppose. So you were abandoned?'

That's a harsh word, I thought, the moment I said it. But fuck it.

'Well, yeah. Foster family brought me up, most of the time, anyway, me and seven other reprobates,' he said, chuckling.

'What was it like?' I said, when I came back from the bar with the second round.

'What?'

'Did you ever wonder about your real parents?' I said, a little sordid lump of self-pity forming in my own throat.

'Well, yeah. When I was younger. A lot. You find yourself hoping they might turn out to be great people, loaded, you know, and that the whole thing had been some sort of terrible accident, some thing that had been forced upon them, and that there was a whole different life waiting to open up for you somewhere.'

'Yeah,' I nodded, with a little sympathy. The only sudden corner life takes is the one into the fucking ground, and even that will not be sudden enough for many. Ah, the wrong kind of hope. It is a kind of slow death all on its own.

'After a while of that, you get to thinking that the people that left you, or the person, I suppose, couldn't have amounted to much anyway. Probably some daft, young, hopeless woman, with no better idea than the church steps, and a father that probably wasn't even around, or at least I hope he wasn't, because if the pair of them were really trying and that was the best they could do then fucking hell. What chance is there for me? But no, you get to wondering. Then you realise they probably didn't amount to much.'

'Yeah,' I thought. That was me he was talking about right there.

Then I realised that we were both, somehow, on our third pint. We had been there an hour easy, and for a man with a long drive ahead of him he didn't seem to mind knocking them back. I had the feeling that maybe I was being strung along, played out: was that why he'd gotten all personal about his life? Then I was aware of a tautness around my eyes, and felt some steel dust in the back of the throat that with me was always the first taste of paranoia. But that briefcase wasn't full of spare change.

I looked around again but saw nothing, just the usual

bunch of pensioners and alcoholics. There was nobody waiting by the exit. I finished my drink more or less in a single go, and pulled a couple of notes out of my jacket and put them in the Baptist's hand, I don't know how much, a couple of hundred tops.

'Here you go,' I said. 'You better go now.'

He was in no hurry. He unfolded them and counted them out, maybe he even licked a thumb first.

'Is this all of it?' he said.

'It's just a tip. You'll get the rest of it when you pick me up and take me back.'

'And when will that be, then?'

'A couple of days. I'll ring the Tenby and leave a number.'

'Alright,' he said, taking a sip of lager, and smacking his lips. 'You staying here then?'

'Yeah,' I said, it being one of those Wetherspoons that had rooms.

'Okay.'

I had one eye on him and the other on the door.

'Mind if I finish my lager?' he said, after a while.

'Sure.'

I had seen people drink quicker, I have to admit, I have seen dredgers clear sand banks faster, or so it seemed. Finally he put the glass down and looked at it the way a big game hunter might gaze upon his stuffed lion.

'Hot out there,' he said. 'I'll be off, then.'

And I watched him go, counting the seconds, surveying the street from one of the pub windows for shady characters. After a couple of minutes I went to check his car had gone, and it had. He was just an easy-going guy, maybe, going home after earning a little easy money, to get on with whatever he had to get on with. Maybe. Probably. If there was any criminality in him at all I was in a lot of trouble, with what I was carrying around it wouldn't even take malice. Over a hundred grand, there for the taking. It was not the sort of worry I was used to at all.

I wasn't going back to the Wetherspoons. I wasn't even staying in town. Once I got out of the car park I headed back to the high street and the nearest off-license and stocked up on provisions, then went in search of a taxi. I found one in a little rank by the market square, a silver Peugeot estate with a chubby little grey-haired man inside, a big shiny bald spot almost glowing in the middle of his head.

'Got your pop, I see,' he said, in a Hereford accent, eyeing my shopping. 'Where to?'

'Out of town, please,' I said, politely. 'Get on that big road outside town, the dual-carriageway, and let's see where that takes us.'

He didn't move.

'I can't take you somewhere if you don't know where it is you want to go,' he said, incredulous, offended at the impropriety of it all. It took me a while to register this was a serious complaint.

'I don't know where it is I want to go yet,' I said.

He repeated exactly what he had just said.

'I have money,' I said, limply.

A little more slowly, and a little bit more enraged, he proclaimed his first commandment of cab driving for the third time. Noticing that the car still wasn't moving, I fished out a few notes and put them on the dash in front of him, and without missing a beat he took them and put them down in his money bag in the driver's door. His face stayed fixed towards mine the whole time, fixed in some stern expression of expectancy, as if for an apology.

'Well?' he barked, finally.

'Like I said, just down the dual-carriageway.'

'How far?' he yelled, before I had finished my sentence.

'Thirty-eight miles,' I said, at random.

'Fucking people,' he said, turning the ignition at long last. 'Come in here want to go places think I haven't got anything better do than go off on some magical mystery tour like I was born to do their beck and call.'

I would like to say that he said all this under his breath, that he was mumbling to himself absent-mindedly, but no. A little later we were back on the A40, although we were going the wrong way, back the way I had come. I didn't say anything, I just kept hold of my briefcase and my carrier bags, felt the reassuring weight of nine litres of cider, and reflected that if you got in any taxi in this country and really did say 'follow that car' each and every one of them would probably tell you to fuck off, although not always in as many words.

I got him to pull over at the first hotel I saw, which was a service station with a Motor Lodge just outside Raglan, maybe eight miles down the road. He didn't seem to mind any more than he would have if I'd asked him to wax my back.

'Thank you,' I said, through the window, once I had disembarked. 'It's been an absolute delight.'

I watched him reverse out of the bay in the service station car park.

'Have you ever been a bus driver?' I shouted.

He leant out.

'No. But let me tell you: I'm the only driver with an MPV license in the valley tonight.'

And with that he sped off, or at least he moved as fast as he was ever prepared to, with all of my forty quid. It had been a self-advertisement for his services, presumably, or at a stretch some sort of professional boast, but it had sounded strangely like a warning.

I walked across a mostly empty car park and booked

myself into the Motor Lodge, which was even more lifeless than the car park. It was nearly quarter of an hour before I found anybody inside, and when I did, some sad, empty-eyed queer working out a self-imposed exile from society, he seemed unsure of the procedure for actual guests. In the end it worked out at something like twenty-two quid a night, which seemed reasonable.

The room was nothing much, just what you'd expect. A double bed, a wardrobe, a bathroom, a window with patterned curtains looking out onto the lorry park, a portable television, a travel kettle and some free tea and coffee, a little fridge under the desk with some alcoholic miniatures inside which definitely would not be free at all, and the smell of a lot of stale cigarette smoke. It felt like unbridled luxury. I kicked off my shoes, closed the curtains, turned on the television (I don't think I ever switched it off), grabbed a big bottle of cider and lay back on the bed, then got back up and took my socks off and put them in the bin, laid back on the bed, then got up again and took the bin together with my shoes into the bathroom, put the fan on, and closed the bathroom door tight. The room began to smell a bit better. I unscrewed the bottle, flicked the cap absently into the corner of the room, put it to my lips, and stared meaningfully at the neat, new briefcase full of cash that I had placed with some reverence on a chair at the foot of the bed. Other than I did not move for the next six hours. I amounted to something now.

Sometime that first night my mobile phone rang, and I answered it with real reluctance, I had settled in so well. Part of me wanted to stay there for ever. Considering the amount of time I had left to live, I probably could have done.

'They can't have been nabbed already,' I said.

'Nah,' said Scotty. 'I just wanted to check your phone was working.'

Awkward pause.

'Yeah?' I said. 'And?'

'I could do with some of that money you said you'd give me,' he said.

'I'll put a few thousand your way when I get back. I said I would, didn't I?'

'What if you don't come back?'

'I'll come back,' I said. 'Stay put for a couple of days and keep your eyes out for me. It'll be worth it.'

'Yeah,' he said, resignedly. 'When that happens, fuck, am I going to get high.'

I nodded, although it was a wasted gesture, of course, seeing how we were in different counties. I was at the tail end of the second bottle already.

'You seen my son about?' I said.

'A bit,' he said, was definitely what he said, but it sounded like not at all, in that part of my brain that was actually listening.

'How's he doing?'

'How the fuck would I know?'

'Is he doing well? Is he on the way up, do you think?'

Another pause.

'This is Swansea, isn't it,' he said, quietly, bluntly, by way of an explanation.

'Yeah,' I said, eventually.

'You know what I've been thinking,' he said, with a change of tone, 'what you did this morning was a drug deal, really, wasn't it? A big deal of your own, from the man who hates dealers.'

'Booze is nothing like drugs,' I said, for this was old and familiar ground, as much for me as for anybody, whatever side of the argument you were on.

'No,' he said, 'maybe not usually. But that booze this morning might as well have been drugs.'

'How so?'

'It was illegal, wasn't it? I mean it was stolen, for starters, sure, but it was hooky, wasn't it? There was no tax on it. Big money shifting hands, down in the docks, for a shipment of stuff that will get you fucked up. Sounds like dealing to me.'

'It's nothing like dealing,' I said.

'Looked like it to me. No tax, no duty, all that money that should have gone on hospitals for wee little bairns and schools and that.'

'The fuck you care. They'd only spend it on killing Arabs, anyway,' I said.

'Yeah, well.'

A little while after we hung up. And a little while after that, right in the middle of the night, the chest pains started again, just as bad as before. Breakthrough pain. Without trying to think about it too much I reached over to my jacket, on the floor below my bed, and got the liquid morphine out of it, and held it in my hand tightly, just like before, and the pain might have lessened a little. I kept on drinking the cider, and put the little black vial on top of the briefcase, and stared at that instead. I knew I could take it any time I wanted, and that helped, knowing the pain would drift away, with my mind following slowly after it. I didn't particularly want to take it. I figured if I kept getting the prescription and saved it all up, well, if things got really bad I could drink it all at once and buy the farm in an evening. It would be like the death pint. It was a strange kind of solace, but solace nonetheless.

People sometimes say of the dying that they died fighting, bravely, struggling on with the lamp of humanity raised in their wavering hand. But people don't really die like that. They die afraid, untidily, damaged and incomplete, they can die grotesquely, deranged, or unconscious, they can wheeze on for months as invalids, and we say all these nice things about them simply because deep down we have no nice feelings about any of it at all. We call them courageous because they terrify us, and we call them noble because secretly we pity them, and think them losers. It is why you like to keep us in separate rooms, in separate buildings, in separate worlds, we the dying. You will find out. You have been born in an age where death is an obscenity.

I made it to morning, and by then the cider was gone and I'd hit the minibar, which helped me pass out for a couple of hours. The chest pains eased off a little, or the rest of me felt so rough I didn't notice them, and by mid-morning I felt I could get up and move around. I knew I had to, or I wouldn't be able to score any more booze, and then I would start to sober up, which was a far scarier prospect than it had been this time last year. I found somebody behind reception and told them I was staying another night and that I needed the minibar filled.

'Do you have a slip, sir?' she asked. 'What was it you drunk?'

'All of it,' I said. 'And you'd better change the sheets.'

Outside the lorry park was empty but the car park was half full at least, what with the holiday traffic. Lots of people heading for Pembrokeshire and Tenby, I guessed, and maybe a few going the other way for the Cotswolds, or the upper Severn and the Vale of Evesham. Inside, the service station was as near to capacity as it was going to get. Lots of young families and a few teenage groups in the Burger King, your older couples and sales reps in the Little Chef, a few pasty-faced guys, always guys, smoking at the fruit machines. I went into the Little Chef and ordered a plate of chips and drank four or five small bottles of Becks, watching them all go by. None of them looked like they were dying.

When the lunchtime rush had tailed off I asked for the manager and paid over the odds for half a dozen bottles of wine to take out, which took a bit of diplomacy even then. I hardly ever drank wine, but it was the strongest stuff they had, and I thought the change might do me good. I could hardly taste anything anymore anyway. In the little shop by the petrol forecourt I asked the man for a corkscrew but they didn't sell them.

'We've got screwdrivers,' he said.

'How does that work? I'm, ah, I'm not a wine connoisseur, you know.'

The man looked at my six bottles of Little Chef house red but passed no comment.

'You stick the end into the cork and push it down into the bottle.'

I couldn't believe I hadn't thought of that, or ever seen it, but like I said, not my drink. Still, I thought, pressing one open on the small stretch of not very neat lawn round the side of the lodge, you learn something everyday. I drank a bottle out in the sun, watching the dual-carriageway, listening to the roar of the traffic, just to make sure they had time to fix up my room.

When I got in I was so hot I ran a cool bath, popped open two bottles of wine, put them by the tub, and opened the bedroom window so I could still hear the traffic. I'd decided I liked the sound of it. Sitting there in the cool water, in a dim room, with a clean bed waiting on the other side of the door and no one in the world who knew where I was: now that the bastard in my chest had called a ceasefire, it was bliss. Just for the hell of it, I even washed my hair. Knackered from a fairly sleepless night, I drifted off for an hour or two in the afternoon, and woke up in a bath full of blood red water. I thought I'd started haemorrhaging until I saw the bottle bobbing about in the suds.

The stabbing pains did not come back that night. I

expected them to, I drank myself to the verge of passing out, but there was no need. I actually feel asleep, for once, for the first time in ages, I lay with my clean head on a clean pillow and listened in the warm, night air to the sounds of solitary drivers on nocturnal journeys, the slow sounds of their engines approaching from some place beyond the curve of the road, over the fields. I watched the faint glow of the headlights send long, dark shadows moving quickly and silently across the wall, and listened again to the sound of that same unseen stranger riding inexorably away, on some unknown trip of their own, work or pleasure, outward bound or coming home. It was so beautiful I almost cried. Maybe I did. And then I felt the exotic pull of the body's natural, unprescribed senselessness, its own in-built intoxicant. My dreams were bad, but it was still sleep.

The next day, the luxury of staying at the Motor Lodge had worn off a little. I did pretty much the same things; made a cup of coffee and put some Johnny Walker in it, opened another bottle of wine, went to the Little Chef and poked a plate of plaice and chips around, drank some Becks, bought some more wine, just to build up a cellar, sat on the grass around the side of the hotel and watched a lot of television. My chest was in pain but I wasn't incapacitated. The day after that it began to get boring. The day after the day after that it was purgatory, and purgatory I could not do, I did not have the time. I began to get worried, and then I got the call. All of man's unhappiness stems from his inability to stay quietly in his room alone. That's what the man wrote.

'They've been nabbed,' said Scotty. 'That's the word on the street. Not that I've been out on the fucking street.'

'I was beginning to wonder,' I said. 'Should be safe now, anyway.'

I told him I'd meet him round the back of the council

offices down by the beach at five, and began to get my things together, which as you might surmise, did not take long. I was going through my pockets when I found the card for the private clinic I'd been given in the High Street Surgery. I had forgotten all about it, and now it caught me unawares. But why not, I thought? Everything else has been going too well to make any sense, why not this? Five minutes later I was in the lobby area, good to go, under some impression that I was taking on the world and winning. It wasn't something I was used to. Maybe that was why, when I reached into my jacket, and pulled out the card for the taxi firm, which was not for the taxi firm but the private clinic, I rang that instead. They said they could fit me in that same afternoon, if I wanted, and yes, it transpired, I did want. An unguarded moment of weakness, was what it was. All of man's unhappiness stems from his inability to stay in his room alone. Sure. Thing is, if you don't walk out they carry you out in a box.

Then I rang the taxi cab and asked, specifically, for someone who was not a cunt, and if you thought that request was treated as being in any way unusual you are sorely mistaken. I would have tried to get the Baptist, but I didn't trust him now, hardly trusted anyone, now that I had the money. He would have taken longer to get here, anyway.

Barely two hours later I was walking the Kingsway, me and my briefcase, and thinking about a quick pint. It was almost as if nothing had changed.

Oh, almost.

IV

'May I just take your name?' the woman in reception said, sparkling, polite, respectful even. They didn't smile like that in the High Street Surgery. I cast another glance over to the wide, wooden-framed mirror on the wall opposite, and stole another look at myself.

I was wearing a dark navy double-breasted suit and a crisp white shirt with a Llanelli Scarlets club tie. I had on a pair of black brogues shiny new out of the box that morning, so new the stiff leather was cutting into my ankles, and in Bunnies, a knocking shop on Mansel Street, I had paid some blonde Butetown refugee to do no more than wash me down in the shower. I found a place where you could still get a shave down by the mosque on St Helen's Road, some sort of male grooming salon run by a couple of optimistic gays waiting for the day when Dai Tredegar would decide to get his nails done, and after they'd finished with the cut-throat razor I got a haircut too, a tidy one, and a lot of free advice about moisturiser. I smelt of sandalwood and talc, I had clean nails and tied laces and people were giving me the time of day like life had never been any different.

'Llywelyn,' I said, staring at the reflection, to myself as much as her. 'Robin.'

'I think you'll be able to go straight through,' she said,

while she tapped away at some keyboard, shooting me another smile. 'Just bear with me.'

I was in a grand Edwardian terraced house, at the end of a long striped lawn dotted with shady trees, set back from the upmarket end of Walter Road, not far from where my son's aunt lived, in fact, same side of the street. It was nicer in every conceivable way than any NHS building I had ever been in. It even smelt better. It smelt of apples.

'Dr Hill will see you now,' she said, smiling, closing some leather-bound book.

'I didn't think they called surgeons doctor,' I said, 'on account of them all being barbers, or what have you, back in the long ago.'

'Oh, Dr Hill isn't a surgeon,' she said. 'He's a specialist doctor. He'll be able to refer you to the right surgeon, if a surgeon is what you need.'

She led me into his room and it had the usual desk and examining table but it had a sofa and a coffee table too, a couple of potted plants, a few framed pictures. Fairly banal stuff, but nothing I'd ever seen in a doctor's room before.

'I'm Dr Hill,' said Dr Hill. 'Please, take a seat.'

I stayed away from the sofa, paid the soft furnishing as little attention as possible, truth be told. Some sort of psychology was at work here that I did not understand. Then I realised where I'd seen him before.

'So,' he said, screwing the cap off a silver, or at least metal, pen. Even his voice seemed more soothing, a notch or two lower. 'You're new to the clinic. How did you hear about us? Are you a referral?'

'Yes,' I said.

'From whom?' he asked. He was sitting slightly forward in his seat with a pen in one hand and the other loosely clenched along the pleat of his corduroy trousers. His eyebrows were arched in professional inquisition, but his face stayed gently neutral. At the corners of his mouth maybe there were some traces of friendliness, suitably subdued. The professional in his field. He was a real picture.

'You,' I said.

'Oh, I see.' He remained perfectly composed. Nothing flickered up there, across the eyes. 'From the High Street surgery? I work there part-time. And part-time here, also.'

I'd tried not to, but now I made a show of looking round the room.

'Pays the bills, I suppose,' I said. It drew no response that I could see.

'It's lung cancer, isn't it?' he said. 'I have your papers here.'

'No problem finding my records in this joint,' I noted.

'No,' he agreed, and even smiled. Then he settled down to his usual seriousness, and took out a sheaf of x-rays and papers from a concertina file on the floor by his desk.

'Although it's fairly advanced, it appears to be localised. A single tumour, by the looks of things. There is, of course, the constant risk it will spread throughout the body, appearing in other organs, or that a second cancer will develop in the lungs. There is a type of cancer that grows all over the lungs, and that's very hard to deal with indeed. Fortunately, this isn't it. There are no guarantees, of course, but at this point I have absolutely no hesitation in putting you forward for surgery.'

'A single tumour,' I said. I hadn't been in there a minute and already I couldn't think straight.

'Yes,' he said, taking out the x-ray, and making some noises about it which I didn't listen to. I didn't even look. I had seen it once before, in the Singleton Hospital. Once the girl operating the machine had gone all po-faced I had pushed in front of her to see it myself. You didn't need any medical training to see I was fucked. It had been late winter, I remember, not long after I'd come back. I saw the shape of my coming death, the doom my body was host to, all in black and white, and turned round to the girl who I had just shouldered out of the way and said sorry. Sorry I pushed in. Your GP's supposed to show it to you, like. It was as if I was concussed. Then I went out for a drink, and then it was summer. My last spring, come and gone, and I couldn't remember a fucking thing about it. I caused some trouble. I got in some fights. I lost whatever I had, which truth be told, was next to nothing anyway. I remember once, in an off-license, being refused service, although I was being perfectly polite. I realised afterwards that I was being refused nothing, I was simply so drunk I couldn't talk. As a general plan it might have worked, if I hadn't run out of money, hadn't woken up in the Heathfield, realised it was summer, and that I was still alive. A dead cat bounce, the economists would call it: an illusory upsurge in a steady, certain decline. One last shimmering summer on Swansea beach.

'Anyway,' he was saying, once I'd tuned back in, 'the first thing we should do is take you off the liquid morphine. That stuff will kill you all on its own, given enough time. Once we've ascertained precisely how far into the pain zone you are we can get you on some slow-release tablets like Fentanyl or Buprenorphine which are far less harmful. If the cancer gets worse you will end up on diamorphine eventually, of course. They'll pump it continuously into the bloodstream.'

The man had finished talking, had been doing a lot of it, and was putting the papers back into their foolscap folder, thank Christ.

'I see,' I said.

'Do you have any questions?' he asked.

'What are my odds?'

'I can't answer that,' he said. 'At the least, treatment should give you more time, perhaps a couple of years. There is a chance the results may be better than that, but let us not dwell on that at this juncture. Nevertheless, there is a chance. Without treatment, there is no chance at all. Your condition is terminal.'

I was used to odds that were quantifiable, five to one, three to one on, a mathematical ratio, something solid. This guy was saying nothing.

'How much will it cost?' I asked. I had to draw him out on something real or I felt I was going to fucking faint. I got the same kind of learned evasion, the same shuffle, but he never said 'I couldn't answer that.' I pressed it, maybe more than I should have done, or so he made me feel, and kept pressing, reaching out from the mire, from the hope, for some kind of handhold. I grasped something eventually: eighty thousand pounds, I think he said, give or take, for a three-year package. Obviously they won't bill you up front; it's not like selling a car he said, with an air of disdain.

'If you want to be realistic,' he added, 'the treatment will probably be ongoing for the rest of your life, and from what you tell me about your personal life, you will need professional care during periods of debilitation, and recuperation, if any, as well as the terminal stages. You might also want to avail yourself of all the necessary medical aids, when it becomes advanced, such as electric wheelchairs and oxygen tanks and so on. If you want to seek the services of this clinic, I can assure you we will be able to provide everything you might want. Or that you might not even know you want. That's the package.'

'From here to eternity,' I said.

He nodded, indulged me in a slight smile.

Eighty grand. That made it easy. I had a hundred and twenty in the case at my feet, less what I had promised Scotty, my getaway expenses, a few little treats, any outstanding debts and drinking money. What did that leave, after that package? Thirty, thirty-five maybe? What sort of a legacy was that? Then there was the money I'd need to live on, for my last few miserable ailing years, never mind the treatment. Where would that come from? Eighty grand made it easy.

'Fuck you,' I said. I had it in my mind to abuse him until he threw me out, or got someone else to do it, but it took him aback a bit. Down in the High Street I daresay he was used to it, here it threw him. He had been working off an intricate script and now it had been cast rudely aside he looked almost frightened for a second, as if somebody in the audience had just figured out the whole thing was a show. And then I lost the stomach for it.

'Goodbye, Dr Hill,' I said. It was the way of things, I guess. Now that the acutal ideology behind free health care had been abandoned, what was there to keep it going? People only cared about free health care these days the way they cared about not paying over the odds for a car, or making sure the hotel matched the one in the brochure. You could argue the toss for privatisation as much as you liked, but the health service was already withering of its own accord. I was brought up to think doctors were saints, called to vocation like priests, to help and heal. Throw away free health, and the Hippocratic oath with it, and half of them reverted to what they had always been: hucksters, quacks, sharks, businessmen. Old barbers and butchers the lot of them. At the door to his study I gave him a parting shot:

'I can see you have a real incentive to cut down on waiting lists,' I said.

'If you think I have acted in any way improperly,' he said, 'there are several regulatory bodies you should refer the matter to.'

'Fuck you and your bodies,' I said, and I walked out, as

evenly and as straight-backed as I could manage, down past the striped lawn into the sedate traffic leaking in and out of well-to-do West Swansea, in mild discomfort, clutching the black unopened vial of my fatal medicine like a talisman, feeling the high sun beating down on my wet forehead, and feeling a faint but exotic sensation of heroism. Maybe secretly I had gone in there with that scene in mind all along, like it was something I needed to do. Certainly I felt lighter now, now it was over, my one brief flirtation with the notion of not dying. It was all a con.

After thirty minutes of laboured walking I was outside the Tenby again. The jukebox was off, and DJ Tim was nowhere in sight, so I popped in and snarfed two lagers before I knew I was even there. At the bottom of the second one someone came up behind me, said hello, and I turned and it was the Baptist. I suppose the barman must have phoned him when I walked through the door.

He looked me up and down and gave me a bit of a comic eyeball about my new image.

'Money burning a hole in your pocket?' he said.

Of course, I had to pass the time of day, listen to a few jokes that neither of us thought were funny, make a few of my own that were just as bad, show some interest at the sad news his Scimitar had been impounded because he'd been unable to produce a road tax disc, or an MOT, or any insurance, or a driving license, or any kind of documentation at all, apart from a membership certificate for the Scimitar Owners' Club.

'So,' he said, once we were in a corner, once the agonising preliminaries were over, 'I thought you were going to give me a ring when you wanted to get back?'

'Yeah,' I said, and explained how things had all been so sudden, how I wasn't the most organised person in the world.

I didn't mention the creeping, monstrous mistrust that had fallen upon me, that was gnawing at me that instant.

'Sorry you're out of pocket,' I said. 'How much do I owe you?'

He stroked his beard, pretended not to find anything in it.

'Five hundred quid,' he said. I knew I had never mentioned a sum anywhere near that amount, that I had paid him more than I'd said I would already, but there was the money right at my feet: both of us were looking at it. I almost expected him to make a grab for it there and then. I had no muscle to call on, and how much of a crime was it, to rob from a robber?

'Fine,' I said, trying not to seem nervous. 'Just let me go to the gents a minute.'

'You're not trying to run out on me are you?' he said, half-laughing, half-serious. It was the bit that was half-serious that scared me, half-serious was worse than being full-on threatening, if you had something to lose. It was the uncertainty.

I laughed and did my best to sound like I meant it, although I was no more convincing than he was, went into the urinals and pulled out half a grand. Back in the pub I passed it to him under the table, and sold him a line about how I had more deals lined up, how I would need his services again. Anything to keep him sweet.

'What you doing this afternoon?' he asked. 'Want to run down to the Gower with me? I could introduce you to a few people.'

'No,' I said. 'I said I'd see a friend of mine.'

'That Scottish lad? The junky? How'd you end up friends with someone like him?'

I shrugged.

'I gave him a pound once, when he was sitting on the pavement outside the post office.'

'Yeah?'

'Yeah. And the next day I had to ask for it back.'

Then I bought us another round and passed the time of day, although I can't remember another word of what we said, just the vaguely predatory expression on his face, and then I made my excuses and fled, and at a brisk pace, feeling almost too unlucky to look back. But no one was following me. There were going to be no sudden moves from the Baptist camp, although given time he would pull one eventually. However much money I had nabbed, this town would not let me keep it for long, but then that did not matter now. I had my own plans, which were soon to be acted out, and the internal deadline of my own body.

The battery on my phone had finally run out of juice, so outside a Chinese takeaway called the Goldfinch I made a call in a phone box to Merlin Auto Parts. I didn't need any scrap of paper: I knew the number by now. A million other everyday things had escaped my recollection, but those six digits had stayed firmly lodged.

'Is Owain Griffiths there?' I asked.

'He is around this afternoon,' said the uninterested voice of your average employed man, 'but he isn't here right now.'

If he was in at all today I was in luck. I didn't want to wait much longer.

'Tell him to be at the Tesco's car park over the road at five o'clock this afternoon, as soon as work finishes. There's a man that wants to give him some money.'

'Right you are,' said the voice, without a hint of curiosity.

Then I hung up, and got out of the phone box, with its smell of piss and stale smoke, and out into the sunlight, and walked down the road into town, walking tall, and straight, like a man of purpose and competence. I walked straight past a dozen pubs, a hundred handpumps, an army of optics on a myriad of walls. It all meant the same thing in the end, the same night, the same morning. For a little while I pretended it wouldn't happen. It made me early, which was something that didn't happen everyday, and I was at the council offices with ten minutes to spare.

Ten minutes early, of course, wasn't early enough for a skint junky.

'I thought you weren't going to show, man,' he said, coming up unseen behind me. There was another guy and a girl with him and I did not like the look of that at all. It put me on edge, and it couldn't have boded well for him. 'What's with the suit and everything?'

'I've got to see someone,' I said. 'When did they get pulled in?'

'The Blethyns? They were pulled yesterday morning, two of them, the guy from the docks and his brother. His brother: they kicked the door in and he came at them with a Samurai sword. He'll do time for that alright.'

'That's why they call them the knock, you know, Customs and Excise. They don't need a warrant. If this was down to the police I'd still be sleeping in a Motor Lodge.'

'I guess the Customs are the boys, then,' he said. 'They're harder than the police, are they?'

'Well, it's tax, isn't it. Moolah. The coppers are just there for law and order. For the schmucks.'

'Cool. Speaking of money...'

'Of course,' I went on, 'that doesn't mean they don't miss a good few billion every year, what with times as they are. They sold their own fucking offices to an offshore property company, would you believe? So when they do something they like to make a big bang: it's a deterrent, and deterrence is the only thing they've got.'

'Right on,' he said.

I looked past him at his two pierced friends, but neither of them spoke, although they were looking straight at me, and not in any friendly way. I waited for an introduction but none came. I couldn't blame them for the hostility. They were down there at the bottom, and they had nothing, even if it was because they had some compulsion to piss it all away, or whatever they did with it, and suddenly they're confronted with the friend of a friend who has a briefcase with over a hundred grand in it. You didn't have to be anywhere near as fucked up as they were to see me walking around with one hundred and twenty big ones as an affront to the way life should be.

'Let me sort you out,' I said, trying not to look at them. Whatever I gave him, the two of them would be all over it like flies on shit, them and more besides, but that was no excuse to be stingy.

'Come over here,' I said, and went around the back of the bench, by the big shrubs, and he came with me, and with a flourish I opened up my little fake leather case like it held the glowing manna from Jesus himself. I couldn't help myself. It very nearly did.

'Fucking hell,' said Scotty, 'have you ever seen so much money?'

'Yeah,' I said. Well, something not far off it, anyway: over the bridge I had been the bagman for a bent policeman for a while, although it wasn't something I'd planned.

'But I couldn't call it mine.'

On the top, on the left-hand side, there were some crisp twenties banded by the bank into sheaves of five thousand. It felt cheap to break one up, or count out a few of the crumpled ones. It felt cheap just to look at it. It felt like an affront to myself too, that much paper, sitting there, with so much power behind it, the potential to change so much. I physically couldn't handle the stuff, never could. Maybe that's really what it means, to be good with money, just to be able to hold the fucking stuff in your hands.

I picked up a banded five and handed it to him.

'Cheers, mate,' he said, trying to stuff it into the pocket of his jeans.

'Here,' I said, 'have your jacket back.'

After he had buttoned the money down in one of the jacket's numerous pockets we got up off our knees and brushed ourselves down and did our best to pretend that the money had never been there at all. His two friends, on the other hand, looked as if they could happily club me to death. God knows how long Scotty's five would last him. Not for the first time I was thankful I had plans for the stuff, was putting it to imminent use, because there was definitely some strong natural force at work which would stop me keeping hold of it for long.

'Want to come out with us for a couple of drinks?' said Scotty. 'We're going to Crowley's.'

'That heavy metal place?'

'Yeah. You should see the red-head behind the bar, she's a fucking stunner. Want to come?'

'No,' I said, 'I've got stuff to do.'

'Well, suit yourself. You're looking well. See you around.'

'Yeah. Cheers. See you, mate.'

I watched him walking down the prom with his friends, heading off into town with a small fortune in his jacket, a guaranteed good time for a couple of months, at most. Still, it was as much as he ever asked from life. Twenty-four and he had less of an outlook than I did.

'See you, mate,' I found myself saying again, as he turned the corner to cross the sea-front road, watching him go, waiting to feel good, which I guess I did, a little bit, in a short while. It was kind of like getting into a pool of warm water.

I never saw him again.

After that little exchange I figured I had something like an hour before I had to be in Tesco's car park, before the big event that was supposed to be the high point of my entire life. That may sound conceited, or a bit premature, but when the rest of your life can be doled out in months it's easy to be certain about these things. One thing was for sure, I wasn't going straight into it from this. I wasn't going to say hello to my son for the first time in our entire lives, wasn't going to hand over his inheritance, straight from handing over some pocket money to a Scottish addict. Not that I didn't mind it, not that I was ashamed, not in the least, but if you were going to pull off the summation of your mortal coil you wanted to punctuate it with something that put it apart from the other stuff. You owed it to yourself.

I asked somebody the time, something I could do now that I looked normal, and found out it was still a couple of drinks well short of five o'clock. Of course, it's never just a couple, and I had to be very careful now, but what with the big occasion and the new threads, I thought maybe, just for the hell out of it, seeing I've got the suit on, why not have a few cocktails. It was the best I could come up with. I went in the bar of the Dragon Hotel, which was probably the only decent hotel in town, and picked a tall stool in the softly-lit bar and drank a long gimlet, and then another, looking out through the darkened glass at the people outside. If I had been here three or four weeks ago I would have seen myself walking by looking for change in phone boxes, grizzled, bedraggled, worn by the dross of the street. Sometimes you have to have stood in some fairly unusual places to see how funny money really is. Funny and terrible.

I drank my pair of cocktails, listened to something like a Harry Connick Jnr record playing in the background, looked at all the empty seats and pretended I had the place to myself, pretended I wasn't really getting pissed at all. The gimlets made the world seem smooth and civilised in the way that good cocktails normally do if you don't drink too many of them. I thought about a third but let it go, realised maybe I was drinking out of nerves, that maybe the hotel and the clothes and the shave were all just attempts to put off the inevitable, and if so, they partially succeeded. I was ten minutes late, when I got there.

He was sitting on the bonnet of his BMW watching me approach with his arms folded and an expression on his face that I was too far away to read. I would always be too far away to read it. Even when we were standing face to face he made no sound, no move. Out with it, I thought.

'I'm your father,' I said, or somebody that sounded like me, a ghost talking. It took a strange kind of strength to say it, to overthrow the shadow I had darkened my whole life with, to take that single step nearer to some kind of reconciliation. I'm not saying, and I didn't think, that reconciliation was possible, but it is an extremely unusual direction to feel yourself travelling in if you've never gone that way before.

Again, he did not speak, he did not move. Perhaps he doesn't believe me, I thought. He was doing alright for himself, or he had been, had taken on the responsibilities of family that had always terrified me, he probably wasn't the type to suffer fools gladly. Perhaps I needed to prove my credentials.

'I'm Robin Llywelyn,' I said.

'I know who you are,' he said. That, I suppose, was where things started to go wrong. Right at the start, or more accurately, before then. I should not have been surprised. He had probably seen me about town, I was a high visibility character, seeing I had nowhere to go but outside. Maybe he knew about Bristol too, maybe he had looked into it, done some investigation of his own. I don't suppose it would have been difficult.

'I know who you are,' he said again, and everything I was going to say became pointless. The bell tolled at the masquerade of all my hopes and dreams, and they removed their visors to reveal the old, familiar assembly of lies and fantasy, indulgence dressed up as altruism, selfishness as selflessness, wrongs as rights. Part of me had wanted to be a mystery, a question, an answer wanted, and instead I was just an embarrassment.

Maybe it would have different if somebody had given me a hundred grand when I was his age. Money can do things for you that we are probably ashamed of admitting, it can give you courage, it can give you confidence, principles, a whole bunch of noble qualities that are not supposed have anything to do with something so base. In any case, irony of ironies, it had flowed around me, pooled, bundle after bundle of other people's cash, and now I had finally sluiced some off for myself. I didn't think it would change anything, between him and me, but I wanted him to have it.

'I have something for you,' I said, and passed him the briefcase. He put it down on the bonnet of his car and flipped it open.

'I don't want your fucking money,' he said, and closed it back up. 'Fuck knows where it came from.'

And he held it out, for me to take back.

'You must think I'm a fucking idiot,' he said.

How I wanted to tell him that the money was legit, that he should take it, that he should think of his wife, his beautiful wife, and his little children. I had no right to tell him such lies. I had a lifetime to make up for, and all I had was a hundred and something grand. Stolen. Hospitals for wee little bairns, was what Scotty said. I hadn't even taken the money from criminals, not really, I had taken it from customs, from the government. It was our money in the first place, I guess, all of us. Fuck knows what I thought I was doing. I managed a hollow little smile, and told him anyway.

'What about your family?' I asked.

'My family,' he said. 'Not yours. You walked out on it, because you're a cunt. Is that all you wanted to see me about?' he said.

I thought of his mother, raven-haired and hazel-eyed, six foot under now, in some well-to-do cemetery in Cardiff.

I nodded.

Then I watched him get back in his car, reverse out of the slot, and drive off, off onto Oystermouth Road, and then the Mumbles Road I guess, and then over Clyne Common, and back onto those little awkward lanes that led to his house on the tip of the peninsula, my son, the stranger I had made. He had a lovely home, and he was going to sell it. My money made no difference. It was probably for the best, I thought, you cannot live in a house that was paid for by the sins of others; it was not something that had occurred to me, but I began to understand it. Honesty, integrity, a family, a home: you would lose, sure, but it was a better way of losing. I was proud of him, and then I realised I had no business being proud of him, no business being anything but sorry.

Beyond the streetlights sat the brick and orange façade of the Singleton Hotel, looking about as welcoming as it ever did.

'Off you fuck,' said John the barman, 'right this instant.'

I felt the unfamiliar weight in my right hand of a hundred and twenty grand in a cheap briefcase, shifted once on my feet, looked around at the peeling paintwork, the soggy beer mats, the dog-eared dayglo stars with low, low prices on them, house singles, house doubles, house trebles, house odds: 'look!' with eyes drawn in the o's, and in the dark corners of the pub, an emptiness, a darkness, rising like a tide.

Look!

'Yeah,' I said. 'Maybe you're right.'

Over on Wind Street I checked the briefcase into a security box, in an old, dusty family pawnbrokers, the last extant business in a sea of bars and restaurants and novelty drinking holes, and tucked the key into my sock. I was the last customer to leave, and they locked the door behind me. It was half five.

I walked into the nearest den, a place called the So! Bar, I think, and ordered a house brandy, the cheapest stuff they had, and drank it neat, without ice, glass after glass, beating myself to death with it, knocking myself about the head, again and again, watching the place fill up with happy, smiling amateurs, innocents who didn't know about the battle waiting in the bottle, who maybe didn't even know why they were here, hitting a club bar straight after work on a weeknight. I watched their dancing and listened to their music. By the time things got ugly I would be too gone to notice.

The wrong kind of hope. It should be a sin.

Over the road was a pub called the Adelphi, and Rocky Marciano had been minding his own business in there one night during the war when Wind Street had a pop at him, a pop at the Rock from Brockton, one of the best boxers in the world. Some people said it was the Coliseum, but everyone agreed some guy jumped him, and everyone could believe it was Wind Street. Wind Street will do that to you. It doesn't care who you are.

I was ambling down Trawler Road the following morning, with the sun in my eyes and the sand in my hair, when the car picked me up.

FOUR

DEAMBULATORY

It was a Jaguar S-Type if I'm not mistaken. I wouldn't know what it was like to drive, and it wasn't that much to look at, but I recognised it from the adverts. The adverts cost millions, and the adverts said it the sort of no-nonsense car you wanted to drive if you were a man who knew what was what and had little time for baubles, for the mere trimmings of success. Who was I to disagree with that much money? It was a Jag, and I suppose it was very nice car, and when I got in it I thought I was going to die.

There were two men in it, and I recognised neither of them, at first. There had been no badges, no warrant cards, but even so, I thought initially they might be the cops, or the knock, acting moody. After five minutes I realised this couldn't be the case: even moody cops have to read you your rights, and even the knock, I guess, have to say something. The next logical conclusion was they had something to do with the Blethyns, and they would take their money back and then they would kill me, painfully, probably, and hide the body somewhere it would never be found, underneath the bracken in the Beacons, or flipped off the side of some pleasure boat in the bay one night, weighted down, to sink unseen in the dark shifting sands of the channel.

I was surprised by how calmly I took it. I was scared, of

course, terrified, but it made little difference to the overall balance of terror I had been feeling anyway. I had been scared of lots of things before I got in the car; of my creeping tumour, my shortening breath, my lonely end. At least this had some drama. Think Doc Holliday, I told myself, and was not unpleased. Then, as the car rolled on, as we waited at a couple of lights, as the adrenalin wore off, I had time to see more clearly, and my intuition was that these two had nothing to do with the Blethyns. Nice suits, clean cut, nothing overstated, the absence of a certain neediness: they were nowhere near pathetic enough to be running boys for that bunch. Their silence was not the silence of killers, but of mannered, middle-class awkwardness. I even remembered where I'd seen one of them before: the guy with cufflinks and gold-rimmed glasses had sat next to James Blethyn in the casino. With something like a sense of disappointment, but also great relief, I sat back in my seat, put my arms out across the back shelf like a local celebrity, and waited for them to play their card.

We ended up in a small semi-detached in Pontardawe, some leafy suburban street parallel to the Gelligron Road, some dark pre-war place shaded by a massive privet, set into the hill, slightly lower than the street before it. There was a For Sale sign up by the roadside for a firm called Davis and Sons, and there was a garden gate which the other man opened, and I followed him down a short and narrow garden path, bisecting a little lawn that had been well looked after not long ago. At the front door he took out a big bunch of shiny new keys with a Davis and Sons fob on it and flicked through them until he could let us all in.

Inside it was clear the place hadn't been inhabited for a good few weeks. The surfaces looked clean but the sunlight caught the dust, and its sparse furniture was covered in white sheets. I was led into a front room where two other men were waiting already, and I recognised both of them straight away: the People's Champion, that lawyer from the offices in the middle of town; and my son. The hostility was palpable, but none of them were going to do me any damage: an estate agent, most likely, a solicitor, some other nobody in fancy spectacles and my own son. All that courage for nothing, I thought.

It was the lawyer who led the chat. I supposed he was used to it.

'Mr Griffiths here says you approached him yesterday afternoon with a sum of money,' he said, nodding in the direction of my son.

'Yesss,' I said after a beat, wondering if there was some trap here, but the four of them looked like they were all together. I wasn't dropping anyone in it but myself, and I was fucked anyway.

'The day before yesterday,' he went on, 'James Blethyn and his brother were both arrested by Customs and Excise on suspicion of duty evasion.'

'Yes,' I said again, in the heavy pause he left between sentences.

'The Customs and Excise were acting on information that was supplied by an informant.'

I let that one hang.

'The information was supplied shortly after a very valuable container full of spirits, which belonged to the company James Blethyn managed, disappeared from Swansea Docks. You came in with it. In fact, not only did you come in with it, you also disappeared at roughly the same time.'

'Oh, give it a break,' I said. He had the professional regard for his own voice that all lawyers had, that desire to flex it in front of others, like they were some kind of mirror. 'This isn't a courtroom.'

'So you're not going to fuck us about with a load of

bullshit?' said the man who had let me in, the guy I thought was an estate agent. He had a strong West Wales accent and one of those long Pembrokeshire noses.

The four of them seemed quite calm. Villains would be strutting about the place by now, brandishing something, reeling off the threats, while I dangled from some hook or groaned on my knees, all that pantomime. None of it was necessary for these boys, was probably not necessary at all, most of the time. There is crime and then there is criminality, I guess, and they are two different things: one is breaking the law and the other is just a kind of flavour, a mood, a personality, an obvious fucked-up uselessness that was self-distancing and from which society distanced itself, frightened and judgemental, thinking somehow the two things were one and the same. These were all well-adjusted boys.

'I was worried about my son, you know,' I explained, trying hard not to look at him. Even in the circumstances, with the strong, mounting suspicion that I had badly messed something up, it was still hard: I had stood face to face with him for the first time only yesterday. Even so, I took a couple of steps closer to him, and if I didn't quite face him, I did something not far off.

'Your house was on the market,' I went on, 'and you'd left the car parts business, and you had a family. I thought you could use the money.'

'Use it?' he said. He was livid. 'It was my money! That's why the house is on the market. That's why I sold my stake in the business: to raise the capital for this!'

I couldn't understand, or I just couldn't accept it.

'Why wouldn't you take my money?' I asked. 'It's not like you're a puritan. I mean, look, I can see you take an advantage of an opportunity like anybody else. Why didn't you let me help you?'

'Because you've never helped me,' he said. 'You've never helped anyone. The biggest favour you ever did anyone was to stay away from them. Now I'm not some sort of fucking Boy Scout, I admit, but I stayed by my family, and I can look after my family on my own, thank you very much. You're a fucking liability anyway.'

'I thought you could do with the money,' I repeated helplessly. 'I didn't think it would matter.'

'I was one of the fucking backers!' he said.

It was a very quiet house, in a decent part of town, not actually in Swansea at all, really. Very quiet and still. I remember standing there in the silence waiting without knowing what for and hearing nothing, the bark of a dog, somewhere in the next street down, something big, like an Alsatian or a Staffie, a single angry bark, and then nothing.

'We are the investors that provided the bulk of the money for the venture,' said the lawyer, again. 'And we need that money back. It is our money.'

'You're not going to play funny buggers, are you now?' said the estate agent, trying to sound hard, I daresay, but more nervous than anything.

'He wants to help his son,' said the lawyer, with some kind of smirk.

I looked at my son's feet.

'You can have the money,' I said. 'I didn't know.'

Maybe there just weren't any honest people anymore. Maybe there was just looking after people, and that was the best you could aspire to. You spend your whole life thinking you're some sort of pariah and meanwhile all these innocuous people you never even see on your side of the tracks have been working their own angles all along, and much better than you could, probably.

'How much did you get for it?' he asked.

I told him. A sharp intake of air ran round the room, four men set their teeth and quietly swore.

'It was worth more than that,' said my son. 'You fucking idiot. And you think I need your help.'

'How much of it is left?' asked the lawyer.

'Pretty much all of it,' I said. I looked at my son, had to look at him, had a question I wanted to ask him alone, a nuance I wanted only him to get.

'It's perfectly safe. What do you want to do? Do you want me to give it to you now?'

I thought maybe that if I had lost him cash he could pull a number and keep the money for himself, shaft his colleagues and take the lot: he would have to end up making a profit then. It was the only thing I could think of, and I was desperate, in the way you can only be if you are desperate for somebody else. It was not a feeling I was used to.

'Yeah,' he said. 'Of course I fucking want you to. Give us our money and fuck off, you twat.'

I knelt down and reached into my sock, took out the small key for the security box in the Wind Street pawnbrokers, told them what it was, and where they could use it.

'I'm sorry,' I said again, without looking at him. 'You'll get your outlay back though, right?'

'It's not that,' said the estate agent. 'It's the sacrifices we made to get in the game in the first place. It's all been wasted now that customs know about it. And what's more, now that customs know about it, we're all in the firing line, aren't we?'

'The Blethyns have decided to dispense with my services in their defence,' said the lawyer. 'I can't blame them. They will be hoping for some kind of plea bargain, I expect, if they can name enough people. After all, James was only an overseer, a manager, practically an employee, if the financing of the project is considered. All four of us can expect to end up in court ourselves.'

'Fucking twat,' said my son, without looking at me, and without me looking at him. But I did glance, and he had his face to the window, to the sloping, uneven lawn that led up to the pavement and the privet hedge, and his eyes were red. He had a young family, after all.

'Give them me,' said a voice. 'Pin it on me.'

It was not a voice I thought I recognised. I looked around the room, but there was no one who looked like they were offering themselves up. They were just looking at each other.

'Give them me,' said the voice again, and this time I felt it in my throat.

'You fucking twat,' said my red-eyed son, looking at me now at last, like a man who was squaring up for a punch. 'Who's going to believe a fuckwit like you could be behind anything like this?'

He had a point. I was about to get a little red-eyed myself, when the People's Champion took the floor again

'That was why he was there, Owain. That was the only reason he was involved. James and I made sure he signed the correct documents to ensure he was the authorised warehousekeeper. In the case of a bonded warehouse, the law is quite specific. He's the fall guy. He always was. Why'd you think he was there?'

'I'm sorry,' said the estate agent. 'You always said you never cared about him. We didn't think it would be a bother.'

'It isn't,' said my son, in between heartbeats. 'Give them him.'

In the next street down I heard that dog bark again, twice now. That still made him a quiet dog. Maybe he was only after a passing car, something he could never catch, something he didn't even understand, just a sound he thought he should make, seeing how this was his little patch, how he had his own people he thought he had to look after.

'He'll have to be adequately briefed,' said the lawyer, leaning against a wall, crossing his legs at the ankles, all easy now. He put his hands together and made a roof with his fingers, just under his chin.

'It will take time. We will need to cover some ground, make sure you are fully informed, and then you will have to confess. Sign a statement. It won't be too hard. Orginally, of course, we thought we could put him in the frame posthumously.'

'How long will it take?' said the estate agent.

'Not long. Not long at all. All we have to do first is contact James and his brother, so we can ensure everyone's testimony meshes. Then we brief Magnum here, we brief your father.'

'You know where to find me,' a voice cut in, a voice that sounded a lot more like mine.

Then I turned and walked out down the short empty hall to the front door, up the little path into the quiet Pontardawe street, into the sun and the heat, took my bearings from the lay of the valley, pointed myself in the direction of the Tawe, and walked. Nobody stopped me. Down on James Street I found a bus stop that would take me into town and waited for the bus. They had the key for the briefcase, but I had whatever was left from last night, a good few notes, a lot of change, and whatever hours were left to me. You have no choice but to spend them. You have no choice.

I got off the bus outside the railway station, crossed over the road into the boarded-up picture of doom that was Swansea High Street, and stopped off in the nearest off-license. I got a two-litre bottle of strong cider, a bottle of sherry, four cans of Special Brew and a ten-pack of Marlboro reds. On a shelf behind the counter was a row of porcelain shepherdesses in pastel colours for a tenner each, and I bought one of those too.

They were only up the road, the little flats of Tom Williams Court, and the doorbell that played God Save The Queen.

'What?' she said, when she came to the door. 'What do you want this time?'

She was wearing a red tartan miniskirt and black tights: it was not a pretty sight. I don't think it would have been a miniskirt if somebody else was wearing it. She was also wearing fluffy powder-blue slippers and a T-shirt with a guy on it who looked like a welder and the slogan 'don't break my achy breaky heart.' I smiled despite myself.

'You hired me, madam,' I said. 'Remember?'

The woman's stance became a little less defensive, and she stood there in the doorway with some vague reluctance, some pouting disinterest, and waited. She reminded me of a little girl who was getting ready to be lectured.

'It's about the man you asked me to observe, your fiancé. Mr Neil Simms.'

She snapped out of it a little bit.

'I have some news,' I said.

She raised her bulbous nose an inch into the air.

'It is with deepest regret,' I began, 'that I have to inform you...'

I stopped. It was what they said on military telegrams.

'I've spoken to Mr Simms,' I said. 'He assured me that you hold the highest place in his affections, and you always have, but he has been called away, Miss Blethyn. He's getting a foreign posting. The sea is in his veins, Miss Blethyn, and you knew that from the moment you laid eyes on him. He's on the other side of the world now.'

For a moment I wondered if I was pushing it, if she

would turn up outside the cocktail lounge of the SS Queen of Trinidad or whatever in her red mac, staring in.

'He said he would think of you always, whenever the west wind blew. He wanted you to have this.'

And I gave her the porcelain shepherdess. It occurred to me I should have ended every case like this. We would all have been better off.

She took it and held it and looked at me with some vague sense of trouble behind her wet, dull porcine eyes, some minor confusion in her insentient head. She put the shepherdess down on a hallway dresser and pulled out a slip of paper that had been tucked into the corner of a hanging mirror.

She shook her head.

'This is my boyfriend now,' she said, and I took the slip she offered and looked down at it. It was a television chef, if I'm not mistaken, clipped from a copy of the *Radio Times*. From bad to worse, I thought. Then, before I could say anything, the clipping was snatched from my hand and the door was shut in my face. She couldn't very well ask me to tail him, I suppose.

'Good luck to the happy couple,' I said, through the letterbox, and that was where I left her. Becca Blethyn: our Cathleen ni Houlihan.

Eighty or ninety yards down the road I passed the Grosvenor Casino, and found myself wandering up its mirrored staircase, catching half a dozen different reflections of myself from different angles, and not really caring for any of them. I took out the remaining notes I had in my pocket, sixty quid, the last sixty quid I would ever see, and folded them open and closed in my hands. The casino was pretty quiet at this time of the day, although there was the usual scattering of Far Eastern visitors, and a local poker school quipping away to itself in a corner.

I walked over to the far roulette table and put my cheap

striped carrier bags full of booze down by my feet. It was near enough to hear the poker players nearby working their little one-liners, stuff that they'd seen on telly or in the movies.

'Don't change your horses in mid-stream, buddy.'

'Read 'em and weep, fat boy!'

It was sad. You cannot really beat the house, but there was always some dignity, I thought, in trying. Once in a thousand years people did. There are more than a few people in this country who could tell you the name of the man who broke the bank at Monte Carlo, and that was over two hundred years ago. These guys, the poker players, they came in here and let the house take a set cut off each of them and then they sat around trying to break each other instead, sat there trying to look like a film star, spouting hack dialogue and feeling big.

'Read 'em and weep, fat boy,' said a bloke who was fairly fat himself, for the second time, in case anybody had failed to appreciate it first time round, and scooped up thirty quid's worth of chips from the middle of the table.

Read 'em and weep, I thought. No, we are not the people of whom a nation is made. But then who is, these days?

I put everything I had on black, or red, I don't remember which, and sat there waiting for the lift, for the suspense, as the dealer called and span the wheel. Nothing happened. I waited until I heard the staccato click of the ball skipping the cradles, waited until it slowed, and you could read the individual numbers. Still, nothing happened. While I still had the time I got up and walked out. It didn't matter anymore, whether I won or lost. I didn't want either, I suppose, I wanted to believe things were still undecided, so I left. Perhaps the best that can be said of any of us is that we took a gamble somewhere that might have paid off.

'You're going down, bluffer,' I heard some bald guy say, as I crossed over that sticky blue carpet towards the door.

Down by the Marriott I saw Chester fiddling with the settings of his metal detector, and so bore a hard right, turned about, and walked west along the beach, down from the prom. When I got out further I might find a nice spot in the dunes and sit down, or maybe I would just keep walking, up and down, until they came to get me. Five or ten minutes later, I turned around, saw how far I was from town, was further, it felt like, than I had been in a long time. I had not been this way before. I could see my footsteps arcing downwards from the council buildings, like a big sagging rope, laid in the sand.

A man walks some kind of line, I suppose.

And then I turned, treading on, away from the sun, under the tideline, on that dark strip of sand that would never be land or sea, clutching my carrier bags, my cider and my sherry, my Marlboros and my morphine, my potions and elixirs.